Keeping Score

Keeping Score

A Willow Creek Romance

Shannon Stults

TULE
PUBLISHING

Dedication

To Momma and Daddy. I told y'all I'd use
that English degree for something.

Acknowledgments

I can't tell you how many times I've rehearsed this, the big "thank you" speech we all secretly practice in the shower or while folding the laundry. Now the day has finally come, and suddenly writing a three-hundred-page novel seems like a piece of cake.

First and foremost, thank you to God who had a plan for me far beyond what I could ever have imagined for myself.

To Mom, Dad, Laura, and Manda. You guys have been my first readers and my biggest supporters since the very beginning. There's no way I could have gotten this far without your advice and encouragement. Not to mention all the hilarious stories I get to use in future books. You know the ones (she said before taking a sip out of her new, GI-NORMOUS, pink coffee mug).

To my PBFF, Codie Dickerson. You knew I'd get here long before I ever did. Whenever I doubted, I pulled out the small Superman notebook you bought me with the hand-written note inside reminding me to have faith and never give up my dream. You are the most inspiring and kindhearted friend a girl could ask for. I never would have had the gets to take this first step to "thirty-five bestsellers" without you.

To everyone at Tule Publishing. I've been truly spoiled to get to work with Tule on my first book ever. To Meghan

Farrell, Jenny Silver, and Nikki Babri for all your hard work and enthusiasm. To all those who took a hand in editing: Julie Sturgeon, Shannon Cave, and Beth Atwood. It was truly a team effort, and you three made Cole and Logan's story a million times better than I could have hoped for. And of course, to Lee Hyat and Michelle Catalano for the beautiful cover.

To the amazing Amy Brewer, Patty Carothers, Stephanie Hansen, and the rest of the team at Metamorphosis Lit. You guys took a huge chance on me, and I hope I can prove that faith was well-placed in the years to come.

And finally, to every one of you reading this (and those who closed the book the second they saw The End). You took a shot on me and my story, for whatever reason, and it's because of you this shower "thank you" speech finally gets an audience. Thank you. With all the love in my heart.

Prologue

August—The Farewell Bonfire

COLE WATCHED THE flames flutter in the pyre as they danced along to the music, surrounded by friends and classmates he'd graduated with almost three months ago. At least twenty trucks, cars, and SUVs were parked in a wide circle around the fire, creating a ring of tailgates and car hoods for available seating. Some, like Cole, sat in folding lawn chairs while nursing a Solo cup. Music blasted from the speakers hooked up to Roy Finnick's Jeep, and a dozen or so girls danced together by the fire. He could hear cheers from a nearby game of beer pong being played on one of the truck beds.

The field was about five acres in size, surrounded by trees on three sides—which was perfect since, technically, they were all trespassing. They'd been meeting up regularly in this very field since their freshman year, lighting a fire and having a few beers, courtesy of whoever had convinced their older siblings to buy for them that week.

Fortunately for everyone involved, they'd never once gotten caught in the four years since the tradition started. The field was hidden away among hundreds of acres owned by Harrold Carithers. Old Man Carithers was a cranky bastard, and everyone in town—especially Cole, who'd worked for the man for the last three years—knew better than to get on his bad side. So no one ever suspected that a bunch of kids would be partying in a random field mere miles from his farm.

This was the last bonfire of the season, the big send-off before half of them headed out to start college classes or careers in new cities and states. It was supposed to be a celebration, only Cole wasn't in much of a party mood tonight.

He drained the last of his beer. Maybe he'd duck out early and call it a night.

"It's not fair." Cole turned his head slightly at the feminine voice coming from behind him somewhere. "After tomorrow, you're going to be off living the dream life at school in Texas, and I'm going to be stuck here without my best friend and without any sort of college-life experience."

His heart beat as fast as a heavy metal drum solo. He'd known Carly Malcolm's voice since elementary school, and if Carly was here, that meant *she* was, too.

"At least you're not getting married and shoving out babies right after school like half the girls in this town do," Logan responded.

"Not for lack of trying."

Cole refused to look over his shoulder in case he got

caught eavesdropping.

The voices grew louder behind him. "My point is that you're going to OFTC, and that's a lot better than what you could be doing."

"It's called Oconee Fall Line *Technical* College for a reason. As in, it technically doesn't really count. It just means that I couldn't get into a four-year school like you."

"You didn't get into a four-year school because you didn't apply to any. And you didn't apply to any because you've known you wanted to be a hairstylist since you were seven, and those fancy four-year schools can't give you the degree you need."

Carly was quiet a moment. "I guess. God, I'm sorry. I'm over here being all Debbie Downer, and we're supposed to be celebrating you leaving for school tomorrow. You've got to be thrilled."

"Yeah, so excited." Logan's voice dropped on the last word, a tell he'd picked up over the years that meant she was lying.

"I'm really going to miss you," Carly said.

"I know. I'll miss you, too. And I promise I'll fly home every holiday and break."

"You bet your ass you will." Carly sniffed and let out a small laugh. "Okay, that's enough of that. Now, let's get this party started."

Two figures moved out of the corner of his eye. His gaze followed them as Carly Malcolm and Logan Kase sat on one of the empty tailgates across the circle.

Carly pulled out a mirror, checking her makeup and fixing her long, blond curls. She offered the mirror to Logan, who just shook her head.

The corner of Cole's mouth hitched. He'd learned a long time ago that Lo wasn't like most girls. Where they were concerned with their makeup or clothes, she was more worried about showing him up with whatever bet or prank they'd gotten caught up in. Like when she put something on his church pew that left a dark brown smear across the butt of his pants. Or in seventh grade when he bet her she couldn't catch one of Mr. Hudson's small pigs. She'd been covered head to toe in mud, yet she was beaming when she took that twenty from him.

She'd always stood out against the others. Even now, just sitting on a tailgate in boots, jean shorts, and a loose Lynyrd Skynyrd tank top, he struggled to tear his eyes away. The warm glow on her tan skin cast by the light of the blazing fire. The way she tucked her chin-length, dark hair behind her ear as her mouth moved to the lyrics of "Tennessee Whiskey." How she bit her lip when Carly whispered something in her ear.

She sat up straight as Darren Whitehead approached them, offering each a red cup. She grinned and tipped the cup back for a healthy sip. She and Darren exchanged a few words before his full attention turned to Carly.

Good for him. It was no secret that Darren had a crush

on Carly. He was tall, fit, and, in Cole's objective opinion, one of the better-looking guys in their class, even with the bright orange hair and face full of freckles. And he was a genuinely good person. Ironically, with all those good looks also came a serious lack of confidence. And Carly usually went for the ones with game.

Cole's attention shifted back to Logan. She sat watching the movement of bright flames between them. Despite the fire, her eyes were dark and focused on something far away as she scowled.

What he wouldn't give to know what she was thinking.

"Hey, stranger." Sarah Newnan fell into Cole's lap, yanking him out of his daze. She swayed, and he put a hand around her waist to steady her. "I haven't seen you around much."

"Been busy." Between working for Old Man Carithers and training at the fire station, he'd barely had a minute of free time this summer. "You havin' a good time?"

"It'd be better if you'd come dance with me." She pointed over her shoulder to the group of girls grinding their hips against each other, their heads and arms swinging all over the place. It would be hot if they weren't all completely wasted.

"I don't think I'm drunk enough for that."

She leaned closer, ran her fingers through his hair, and licked her lips. "I heard you and Cowboy started renting a house together," she purred in a low, sultry voice. "Why don't we go there right now?"

He shook his head. "Maybe some other time," he said.

He looked across the fire and found a pair of blue eyes shooting daggers at him. Whatever thoughts occupied Logan earlier were gone. She turned away and downed the last of her cup.

Sarah grabbed Cole's jaw in her hand and pulled his face toward hers. Her bottom lip stuck out in a pout. "You're no fun, Cole Tucker." She planted a quick kiss on his lips before ambling away.

Cole rubbed the rough shadow on his jaw. When he glanced up again, Lo was gone. He stood and navigated around the circle until he spotted the short-haired brunette over by Levi Rossetti's truck.

Standing in the bed of the truck was Cole's best friend, Cowboy, in jeans and a red and black Willow Creek High football T-shirt. He wore his favorite black UGA baseball cap over his blond, shaggy hair. He gestured at Logan with the keg tap in his hand.

"Can I interest you in a celebratory drink?" Cole heard him ask her over the music and the roar of the beer-pong spectators.

"Depends. What are we celebrating?"

Cowboy grinned. "Aside from everyone heading off to the real world this week and me and Cole getting our own place? There's the fact that my boy is almost done with his training. A couple more weeks and he's gonna be a working firefighter."

Logan crossed her arms in front of her. "In that case, I think I'll pass."

"Ah, come on. Have a heart. The guy's been wanting this since he was a kid. And now he'll be out there every day, risking his life. He could die heroically in the line of duty."

"Yeah," Cole said, coming up behind her. "I could die, and then you'd have to deal with the unsettling realization that you'll never see my handsome face again."

She spun around. "Never see you again?" she mused. "I guess I can celebrate that at least."

"Harsh. But I like where this is going." Cowboy leaned down and took Logan's cup, filling it up and giving it back before he grabbed his own. He raised it high in the air and shouted, "To Cole!"

There was a joyful echo all around as red cups found people's lips. Logan sipped, her attention shifting to the game of beer-pong in the bed of the next truck over. She snickered when Katie Samuels tossed the ball and missed the cup by a foot.

"You think you can do better?"

She turned back to Cole, pointing at Katie. "Than that? Easily. I bet I could even take you."

"Is that a challenge, Logan Kase? You lookin' for a wager?"

She shrugged, eyeing the game. "Why not? Ain't gonna hurt me none."

A fire ignited in Cole's chest, burning away any remnants

of his sour mood. "Good thing I love a challenge." He downed the contents of his cup and tossed it to Cowboy, who hadn't been paying attention. "Start filling 'em up, buddy. And we're going to need you to officiate."

"Officiate?"

He grinned at Logan. This night was finally looking up. "Lo here just challenged me to the next game of beer-pong. Can't blame her for wanting one last bit of fun before she goes off to Austin tomorrow."

Cowboy sighed. "What are the terms this time?"

Cole let his eyes trail down over her. "I'm sure we can come up with something."

Chapter One

LOGAN STOOD WAITING on the curb in front of Wade's Bar, a pitiful-looking wooden building on the outskirts of Willow Creek, Georgia, almost ten miles from the center of town. To outsiders, it looked like a heap of old, rotted wood, but all the locals knew just how sturdy this bar was. It had withstood the test of time, along with fires, tornados, and the recession. Wade's was solid, never coming down.

"Are you sure you want to eat here?" Jacob asked, finally pulling himself from the car. He looked as though he feared getting tetanus just walking through the door.

"Trust me. It doesn't look like much, but Wade's is the best restaurant in the nearest five counties. And if you give her the right look, I bet Lilly will get you a drink on the house."

"And what look is that?"

Logan shrugged. "Any look, really. She's not picky when it comes to men," she said, nudging him forward.

Jacob finally relented and followed Logan as she led them inside to a small table along the wall opposite the bar. Several tables were already filled, and every stool at the bar was taken. Not surprising for a Saturday night.

Only a moment after they sat down, an older woman with straight, red-dyed hair down to her shoulders and rough skin like tanned leather sauntered up to their table. She had on tight black pants and a leopard-print top so low it looked like her ladies were preparing to say hello. She smiled at Logan. "Heard from yer daddy you was coming into town. Couldn't get the chief to shut up about it when he came in for his weekly lunch with the mayor earlier today."

She snickered. "Good to see you, too, Lilly. We actually just drove in a few hours ago."

"You back for good or just visitin'?"

"For good," she lied. "I wanted to be around to help Carly with the wedding in two months."

She looked Jacob up and down. "And this one?"

"Right, sorry. Lilly, this is my fiancé, Jacob. I'm showing him around town for a few days."

Lilly gave him a slow once-over, taking in every detail with the look of a lioness ready to pounce. "A few days, you say? What do you say you ditch the little girl here and let a real woman make those the best days of your life?"

Jacob's eyes went wide, and Logan patted his hand across the table. "Careful, Lilly. Jacob won't know you're teasing."

Lilly gave her a pout before turning back to Jacob. "So you're the one who's going to be taking care of our sweet girl. Sure hope you got some money to back that up."

Jacob's words still failed him, so Logan said, "No need to

worry, Lilly. He's a doctor at St. Mary's up in Athens."

"Very good, girl," Lilly cooed. "I always knew you was smart. Now, what can I get y'all to drink?"

"Two teas, please," Jacob managed to say.

Lilly looked at Logan. "And?"

"Just the tea, thanks."

"Sweetie, you're in a bar."

"We're fine," Jacob said. "We don't drink."

Lilly eyed Logan a moment. "I'll give you some time with the menu while I get those drinks."

"Thanks, Lil. And make sure those teas are unsweet."

Lilly's eyes narrowed as they darted between Logan and Jacob. It was the same look on Logan's momma's face when Logan informed her Jacob didn't drink sweet tea, like she was trying to figure out what planet he was from.

"Sure thing," Lilly finally said. She threw one last curious look at Logan before sashaying back to the bar.

Logan scanned the familiar faces around her. For some, the last few years had done practically nothing, and for others, it had done a whole lot. And not necessarily in a good way.

Jacob was a bit overdressed in this crowd, his perfectly combed blond hair, pressed khaki pants, and dress shirt standing out in a room full of jeans and T-shirts. Logan had gone with a light gray sundress and thick navy-blue cardigan to combat the early March chill. It was on the nicer side, but not altogether above the bar's standards.

"Is she always like that?" Jacob asked.

Logan brought her attention back to her date. "Lilly? Oh, she's harmless. Just likes to rattle the boys, play with them a bit. She owns a bar, so she's got to be a little feisty."

"If it's her place, why'd she call it Wade's?"

"He was her husband. He died about fifteen years ago." The day Wade McCullough died in a motorcycle accident had been a profoundly sad one in Willow Creek's history. According to Logan's late granddaddy, the three most important relationships a man could have were with his family, his barber, and his bartender. And people in Willow Creek could go a lot longer without a trim than without a drink.

Lilly came soon enough to get their orders, and Logan told stories about Wade and Lilly until the food came out.

"This looks great, Lilly. And tell Lou I said so." Big Lou was Wade's only cook. He had a gut the size of Texas and had clumsily sent the kitchen up in flames on more than one occasion, but he was easily the best fry cook Willow Creek had ever known.

When Lilly left, Logan watched Jacob anxiously as he took his first bite of the salmon, then she smiled at his moan.

"You weren't kidding," was all he said before taking another bite. Logan happily started in on her steak and mushrooms.

"I told you. Best food in town."

They said few words as they both devoured their meals.

Logan was on her last bite when she saw movement over Jacob's shoulder. The bar's main door opened, and three men came through it, all of them in matching black Willow Creek Fire Department T-shirts. The first she recognized as Wilson Oliver, a high school jock who graduated two years before her. The second had ridiculously blond hair for a grown man and was easily identified as Levi Rossetti, a pretty boy from her year, who'd always had a thing for blondes with big boobs—including her best friend back in tenth grade.

Logan's eyes traveled to the third member of the party, froze on the familiar face, and quickly bent her head down toward her plate when he turned her way. Her throat constricted and her stomach lurched, a mild panic rising in her chest. She hunched down in her seat, hand to her forehead as she attempted to hide behind it. *Please don't see me. Please don't see me. Please don't see me.*

"Well, hot damn! If that ain't Logan Kase right here in the flesh! What's it been, four years?"

And still, not long enough.

Logan pulled her hand away and pasted a congenial smile on her face as she looked up into those brown eyes.

"Cole Tucker," she said tightly. Aside from the shorter hair and bigger muscles, he looked exactly the same as he had the last time she saw him. "Has it really been that long?"

He crossed his arms in front of him, exaggerating the muscles even more. "I almost didn't recognize you. You look good. Of course, you always did, but the long hair really suits you." His voice was low, ending the compliment with a wink Logan knew was more for her date than her.

Jacob cleared his throat from the other side of the table.

"Sorry, I'm being rude," Cole said before turning to Jacob and holding out a hand. "Cole Tucker. You the boyfriend or something?"

Jacob took his hand and gave it one hard shake, not returning Cole's friendly smile. "Or something."

"Jacob is my fiancé."

Cole's smile faltered. "You're joking."

"Why would she joke about that?" Jacob frowned.

Cole shook his head, the smile coming back instantly. "No reason," he said casually. "I'm impressed, really. It's just that the Lo I knew was the last person I would have guessed to get tied down at only twenty-two. You must have done a real number on her. Congrats."

Jacob's head tilted to the side, his eyebrows drawing together. "So the two of you were friends then?"

"That's not exactly how I'd put it," Logan jumped in. "More like acquaintances, really. We saw each other at school, around town. But that was pretty much the extent of it."

Jacob's eyes flashed between the two. "Really?"

With a fake grin, Logan gave Cole a warning glare. His smile only grew, his eyes alight with what looked like intrigue at this new game they were playing.

"Sure. Small town like this, it's almost impossible not to run into people from time to time. Down by the creek, church on Sundays. The tattoo parlor over in Dublin." His eyes fell to the three black letters on Logan's right wrist.

"Right, the initials," Jacob said, eyes going to the same place. Logan fought not to pull it out of sight. "Yeah, she told me that whole story."

Cole's eyes seemed to double in size. "Really?"

Jacob nodded, his rigid posture and harsh eyes softening as he fell into a conversational tone. "I'm not really a fan of tattoos myself. But when she told me about her great-aunt and how close they were before she died, I really couldn't hold that against her."

For the second time that night, a knowing pair of eyes fell on Logan. "Great-aunt," Cole said coolly.

"Yes, what was her name again, Logan?"

Logan attempted to clear her throat, unable to look at either of them. "Caroline Elizabeth Teague."

"That's it!" he said triumphantly. "Great-aunt Caroline. What a sweet old lady. Logan told me so many stories of the two of them together. I just wish I could have met her myself."

Cole grinned. "Oh, I bet you do. She was a real hoot."

"So, you knew her?"

"Oh yeah, everyone around here knew Caroline. In fact, she was a sort of matriarch of this here town."

Logan glared at him, hating how effortlessly he could lie.

"They tried to make Willow Creek a dry town back in the day. Wanted to get rid of the bar and the liquor store, clear out any booze within the city's limits. But that Caroline, she put her foot down, got the whole town rallied against it. She was so passionate about it all, but then again she had to be or else she'd have to go a county over to get her fix. Old woman had a bit of a problem, if you know what I mean." Cole raised his hand to his mouth, tipping back an imaginary drink.

Jacob's face fell. "She was an alcoholic?"

"Oh yeah, big-time. Couldn't go more than a few hours without the stuff before she got the shakes. No wonder the old liver gave out on her in the end."

Jacob's shoulders slumped and, thanks to Cole, Logan had no choice but to nod and go along with it.

"Yup. It was either gonna be that or lung cancer from the three packs a day Caroline smoked. That woman really loved her vices," Cole said fondly. "One thing's for sure, though. She died a hero, ensuring every of-age adult in this town of his right to a good drink. Whole town's full of a right nicer lot of people because of her."

Cole smirked, and Logan imagined how good it would feel to wring that neck of his until it vanished. "Well, I've bothered you two long enough. I'll let you get on with your night." With a farewell nod to Jacob and a covert wink at Logan, he joined his friends up at the bar.

She hoped he choked on his beer.

Chapter Two

"WELL, THAT WAS interesting," Jacob said when they got back to the car.

"What do you mean?"

"You've just got a lot of...unusual people in this town. Lilly, Aunt Caroline." He shook his head. "Are you sure that guy isn't a friend of yours?"

"Who, Cole? Definitely not." Friendly was the last thing she felt toward Cole Tucker. Hatred, detestation, eternal loathing? She wasn't sure there was a word strong enough for her dislike. "Why would you ask that?"

"He seems to think he knows you pretty well," he said, glancing at her and then back to the road.

"Cole's just one of those people. Thinks he's friends with everybody. He also likes giving people a hard time, so don't let him get to you. Trust me, it's not worth it."

Jacob said nothing, and they both rode in silence back to her childhood home.

"So, what's the plan for tomorrow?" he asked after they'd pulled into the driveway.

Logan smiled. "Well, I figured while Momma and Daddy are at church we could have a nice morning in, just the two of us. And then I thought maybe I could take you to lunch—no bar this time, I promise—and show you around."

"And then dinner with your parents so you can tell them about my new job in California?"

She hesitated. "Maybe not quite yet. Let's wait for you to actually get the job first."

"I told you. With my parents' connections at San Francisco Gen, I'm a shoo-in there."

"I'm just not ready. I will be, I swear. But I just moved back, and they're so excited to have me home again. The last thing they want to hear is that the second we get married I'll be moving to the other side of the country. It's too soon to drop that kind of bomb on them."

"I get it. Honestly, I do. I just wish they knew so that we could start celebrating."

Logan put her hand on his. "We've got the wedding to start planning. Isn't that enough for now?"

"I guess, but there's not really much we can do until we set a date."

Jacob's phone rang before he could answer her. Without a word, he picked it up. "Doctor Abernathy," he muttered into the receiver. A frantic voice Logan couldn't make out was on the other end. "You're kidding." Jacob pinched two fingers over the bridge of his nose. "Can't someone else do it? I'm two hours away—" The voice cut him off.

Logan's stomach fell. She'd heard this kind of call before.

The one where Jacob dropped everything and went running back to the hospital. She tried not to hold it against him or the hospital or the patients. But just once, couldn't she come first?

"All right," he huffed. "I'll be there as soon as I can." He hung up and looked at Logan, and she felt their week together slipping through her fingers. "That was the hospital. Morgan, the guy I got to cover for me, his father has been sick lately, and he passed away just a few hours ago."

"Oh no."

Jacob nodded. "He has to take care of the arrangements and the family, so he can't do my shifts for me the next few days."

Logan slumped in her seat. "So, you have to go back."

"Tonight. I'm so sorry. I really wanted to stay here with you and your parents this week."

"I know."

He took her hand and squeezed it. "Hey, as soon as I can get a day off, I'll come down here and we can do dinner with your parents like we planned. And I'll come down other days just to see you, of course. And you can always come up to see me. It's not like you've got all that much going on here anyway."

The words stung a little, but he was right. The thought of finding anything to do the next few days without him left a gaping hole in her chest. "Yeah, we'll figure it out," she said.

Jacob squeezed her hand again. "Well, I guess we better go in and break the news," Logan said. She knew her parents would understand, but all she could see was that pissed look on her momma's face when she realized she made all that unsweet tea for nothing.

SHE'D TRIED. SHE really had.

After Jacob left for Athens, Logan had tried to resign herself to a quiet night in. She'd unpacked her bags, skimmed through the various TV channels, and had even settled into a long bath to help pass the time. But something about being back in her childhood home made her restless. The second her parents had called it a night, Logan couldn't take it anymore.

Which was why, at eleven o'clock, Logan had snuck out of the house like a teenager with her Chevy truck and was now pulling into Wade's for the second time that night.

Just one drink.

She could hear the music playing from outside, the lights within dimmed since she'd been here for dinner hours earlier. Logan walked in and found herself a place at the bar. There were a few couples dancing, a small group over by the pool table around the corner, but most were at the bar alone or sitting at a table, laughing and downing drink after drink with their loud friends.

Lilly spotted her from the other end of the bar, grinned, and walked over. "I was wondering how long it would take you to come running back. I never thought I'd live to see the day Logan Kase turned down a drink."

"Please, I've never gotten a drink from you in my life." Though not for lack of trying. Despite her easygoing attitude, the one thing Lilly had always refused to do was serve to minors. And seeing as Logan had turned twenty-one only a year and a half ago, that meant she'd never actually had a drink at Wade's.

"I know your reputation as well as anyone else in this town. And as long as you weren't getting it from my bar, I couldn't care less. Now, what do you want? More tea? Or do you not drink that anymore either?"

"Cut the jokes and get me a beer, Lil," Logan replied with a sneer.

The older woman laughed. "Rough night with the fiancé, huh?"

If you counted him promising to stay half the week and then abandoning her the first night, leaving her with absolutely nothing to do.

Lilly opened a new bottle and set it in front of Logan. She lifted it to her lips and took a greedy sip, her first in almost a year.

Damn, it was good.

She set the bottle back down, running her hands over the cold, wet glass as she frowned to herself. Jacob would be so disappointed. He made his disapproval of alcohol very clear. For that reason, Logan had made sure never to reveal her past to him and had even given the stuff up…for the most part.

She mentally kicked herself. For the two years she'd known Jacob, she'd started acting like a mature adult, going to bed early, replacing her wild nights with staying in and studying. Now, her first night back in town, she'd already succumbed to the old feelings of teenage restlessness.

But she was an adult now, and she knew better. Which was why when she finished her drink, she was going to pay her bill, get up, and go home. She could be the girl Jacob knew and loved, even if it meant fighting that urge for excitement she felt the instant she got back into town.

"Lilly, can you get us another pitcher? Wilson's really going at it tonight." Cole Tucker stood at the bar only a few seats over, fingers tapping away like little drumsticks while he waited. He hadn't noticed her yet.

Logan groaned internally. This was the last thing she needed tonight. Here she was, telling herself she was stronger than the sinful temptations that called to her, and here stood the devil himself.

His eyes scanned the bar full of people on his left side. She'd never been lucky enough to escape him before, but maybe just this once.

Please, God. Just this once.

She saw him out of the corner of her eye as he looked to

his right, and she could swear she saw him smile. *Damn.*

"Well, well, well. Back so soon. You just couldn't stay away from me, could you?"

"And you're still here three hours later. Big surprise," she said sardonically.

He came over to stand beside her, leaning his elbow on the bar. "What's the matter? You and Jack have a fight? You're not getting cold feet already, are you?" He shook his head. "I knew you couldn't be tamed."

"Jacob," she growled. "And no. We are perfectly fine."

"Right, right, of course. So then why is it you're here and your future hubby isn't anywhere in sight?"

Logan glared at him. "If you must know, he got called in to work and had to go back to Athens tonight."

Lilly set a pitcher of beer in front of Cole. "There you go, doll," she said in a sultry voice, batting her eyelashes shamelessly.

He nodded his head toward Logan. "Lilly, my love, I think I'll actually take one of what she's having and then another to top her off. On me." He winked, sealing the deal.

She didn't hesitate. "Just give me one second," she said, grinning. She grabbed the pitcher and headed around the corner where Logan assumed Levi and Wilson were sitting.

Cole sat on the stool next to her, his lips curled and chin held high.

Logan took a long drag from her beer. "You really shouldn't," she said. "I'd hate to pull you away from your friends."

"No worries. Levi and Wilson are so hammered they don't even realize I'm not there."

"So you're still playing that game, huh? Getting wasted off a few drinks with the boys and hitting on whatever girl is unlucky enough to catch your eye for the night?"

"Hardly. And I resent that comment. It takes a lot more than a few drinks to get me drunk."

Lilly set the two beers in front of Cole before she turned away to help an older man at the other end of the bar. "You mean this isn't you chatting up the girl, getting me drunk, and slowly trying to charm your way into my pants?"

Cole leaned closer. "Why? Is it working?"

He chuckled as she shoved him away. "Relax. The boys had a rough day and are letting off a little steam. I agreed to act as their sober driver. No pants-charming, no drinking."

"Says the guy who just ordered two beers." She took another sip.

"One won't kill me, and the other is for you. A peace offering after poking a little fun at your fiancé tonight."

Logan took the last swig from her bottle, set it aside, and grabbed the new one Cole offered her almost without thinking. "You're a real asshole, you know that? Spinning that story the way you did. You completely demolished the old woman he'd built up in his head."

"Some would say lying to your future spouse isn't very nice either. Tell me, were you already using the fictional dead aunt story, or did you come up with that one just for him?"

"I may have used it on a sorority sister or two." Or anyone else who'd asked about the tattoo. The events surrounding that tattoo weren't her proudest moments.

"How do you think he's going to feel when he finds out you've been lying to him? Can't be a good way to start a marriage, keeping your past a secret."

"Some secrets need to be kept," she said bluntly. "He wouldn't like the old Logan."

Cole's brow furrowed. "You say that like she's gone."

"She is." Logan pulled a five-dollar bill out of her pocket and set it on the bar. "And she's not coming back."

She stood to go, leaving the half-empty bottle on the bar. Cole frowned. "Well, don't go yet. Have one more drink with me, like old times. Or at least let me get you a real drink. We can do a farewell toast to the old Logan if she is really gone."

"No thanks," she said. "I shouldn't have even had these two. I gave up the stuff when I moved to Texas."

He put a hand to his chest. "You're breaking my heart, Lo. Don't tell me you've gone completely square."

She froze, staring him down. "I'm not *square*. I just don't need a drink to have a good time."

"I guess the old Logan really is gone. And apparently, the new one is a buzzkill."

She glared at him. "I am no buzzkill," she said. "Buzzkills

are old people who don't know how to have fun."

Cole took another sip of his beer. "I'm not convinced you do anymore. The old Logan knew how to let go."

"I let go plenty," she bit out. "Trust me."

"It's a shame. I liked the old Lo. The one who didn't care what people thought or said about her, just looked to make each day more interesting than the last."

"Yeah, well, she grew up. And now I'm going home."

Cole sighed. "It's probably for the best. You going to make it home all right, or are you such a lightweight now you need a ride after less than two drinks?"

"I can still drink your ass under the table!"

"You sure about that?" he laughed.

Logan's jaw clenched. Being called a buzzkill was one thing, but a lightweight? She had too much pride to walk away from that kind of accusation. "Yeah, I'm sure. In fact, if you're so worried about my life not being interesting enough, why don't we just make a little wager out of it?"

"You sure you want to go down this road again?" Cole asked slowly. He grabbed her wrist and turned it over gently, running his thumb over the black letters. "The last time you made a bet with me, it didn't work out in your favor."

She ripped her arm from his grasp. "I'm sure. First one to stop, pass out, or get sick loses."

"And what does the winner get? Aside from the pleasure of holding it over the loser's head forever."

"Twenty bucks?"

He shook his head. "A hundred." Logan's eyes went wide; surely she'd heard him wrong. She said nothing, and Cole went on. "You've got to make it worth my while, Lo."

"Fine. A hundred. Better warn Wilson and Levi their designated driver is about to go AWOL."

"I'm sure they'll understand when I explain the situation." Cole picked up his beer, chugging down the last of it in one turn before slamming it down on the bar. "Especially when I get to show everyone the infamous Logan Kase has gone soft on us all."

Their bartender responded instantly to the sound of the empty bottle hitting the bar and took it from Cole. "Lilly," Logan said before she could turn to leave, "a shot of whiskey for me and my drinking buddy here and keep them coming. It's going to be a long night."

Chapter Three

"SERIOUSLY, ART HISTORY? What kind of major is that?"

They were several shots in and starting to feel it. Logan and Cole sat at the bar facing each other, cheeks flushed and eyes heavy. She'd thrown her jacket off soon after they started, her skin growing warmer by the second.

"Thank you for sounding exactly like my dad when I told him." Logan forced down another shot, barely wincing at the flaring heat in her throat. "Any more of my life decisions you want to criticize?"

"Sorry, I didn't mean it like that. I just don't know what kind of jobs you can get with that."

"If I'm lucky, something in a museum or an art gallery. I want to find undiscovered talent and help get their art out there in the world."

Cole poured himself another shot. "I didn't know you were still into that stuff. That's pretty cool."

Logan snorted. "Whatever. You think it's lame." She took her shot, unable to remember which one they were on.

"No, really. If that's really what you want to do, I think it's awesome."

She studied his face. His broad grin, the light in his brown eyes. He was actually sincere. "Thanks. Now I just need to find a job."

"Yeah." Cole grimaced. "I can't really help you there. I'm not sure there's going to be much of that stuff around here."

She could tell Cole the truth, that her job searches had been geared toward San Francisco, not Willow Creek. It would be easy enough, but the thought of revealing to Cole Tucker that she was moving across the country before she let her own parents know left bile in her throat. Or was that the whiskey?

"You could ask Ms. Snyder. She might know if there's anything for you."

She hadn't heard that name in a long time. "Ms. Snyder moved to Maryland. What would she know about jobs here?"

"She moved back after her dad died." He took another shot. "She's been out of town the last few weeks, but she's in the same house since about a year ago. The art gallery's still closed down, though."

Logan felt a pang for the woman who'd been almost as much a friend to her as Carly was. Louise Snyder had owned the small gallery in town that had come to feel like a second home to Logan in her youth. At least until Ms. Snyder was forced to close up shop and move back home to take care of her sick father.

Logan picked up her shot glass and made a silent toast to

Ms. Snyder's dad and his family before swallowing it all in one gulp. She shook her head, registering the familiar sloshy feeling she got when she'd long left the boundaries of "tipsy."

"Y'know," she said with a slight slur, "I haven't been this drunk since the middle o' my sophomore year in Austin."

"I thought you said you quit when you left." Aside from the heavy eyelids, Cole showed almost no signs of his intoxication.

Logan shook her head and felt like she was sitting in the middle of a rowboat. "I stopped when I met Jacob, for the most part. I still cheated, getting a buzz here and there. But it was that party my sophomore year that me and Ashley O'Neal got completely hammered. She fell off the porch of a fraternity house and twisted her ankle. We didn't even know it was messed up 'til early the next morning, and I took her to the ER. That's where I met Jacob." Logan smiled. He should be here with her. Then again, if he saw her now, half drunk in a bar at midnight, he probably wouldn't even recognize her. He'd be so disappointed.

Cole tilted his head. "So you're really going to marry him?"

"That's the plan."

"Without him knowing anything about your past or who you really are?"

Logan rolled her eyes. "Who I was back then doesn't matter. All that matters is that he loves who I am now." She covered her mouth, trying to fight a burp attempting to force its way up. "Not counting tonight."

They were quiet for a long time, Logan waiting for Cole to take his next shot and Cole—for whatever reason—not taking it.

"I've got an idea," he finally said, his eyes lighting up. "How about we take this to the next level?"

Logan shook her head. "I'm not sleeping with you."

"Not what I was going to say. Look, ever since we were in middle school, you and I have been doing one thing."

"Making asses of ourselves," she interrupted, snorting in the process.

Cole took a deep breath. "Will you shut up for two seconds? Damn, I forgot how much you talk when you're wasted."

"I'm not wasted," she lied then stopped when she saw his face. "Sorry," she added. Cole said nothing, and Logan made a show of zipping her lips and locking them.

He sighed. "Thank you. For years now, we've been trying to prove we're each better than the other. Either with bets or pranks or whatever, the last being the night before you left. And we all know I won that."

"Yes, Cole, we are all aware." She glared at the tattoo on her wrist. The second worst mistake of her life.

"Yeah, I won fair and square, and that was supposed to be the last of it. But here we are again, doing the exact same thing. And do you know why that is?"

She blinked her eyes slowly, a subtle haze settling over

her mind. "Enlighten me."

"Because you can't finish seven years of rivalry with one drinking game." He said it like it should be the most obvious thing in the world, but Logan was struggling to keep up. "We need something that's going to show us who's the better man—so to speak—once and for all. What we need is a game of H-O-R-S-E."

Logan shook her head. "Like basketball?"

"Not a literal game of H-O-R-S-E, but in that spirit. We have a series of challenges that we take turns picking. The loser of each challenge gets a letter. First one to get a full H-O-R-S-E loses. And then we know who's better, once and for all. That way we can finally get closure, knowing the best man won."

"That sounds exactly like the kind of stuff I swore I wouldn't get into when I moved back home."

Cole laughed. "Exactly, and yet we both ended up drunk at the bar doing the exact same thing we did the last time we saw each other."

Not *exactly* the same thing. But he had a point.

"That's why it's brilliant," he said. "With this game, we can make it official. Get it out of our systems for good, and then get back to our lives."

Under sober conditions, Logan probably would see this as a bad idea. But in her current state, she couldn't really see a downside. Maybe Cole was right. Maybe all she needed to finally put all this behind her was some sort of closure.

And then, once it was all out of her system, Logan would have no problem marrying the man of her dreams, moving to California with him, and fully committing to life as a respectable and well-mannered doctor's wife.

"So what kind of stakes are we talking here? Five hundred bucks? A thousand?" Both prices were well out of her budget.

Cole grinned. "Better. If you win, I never bother you or your fiancé ever again. I won't even talk to him if you don't want me to."

She had to admit, that sounded like a pretty big win. Especially after he pulled that crap with the made-up aunt. Besides, not having Cole around to instigate would make quitting the old Logan that much easier.

"And if you win?"

"If I win, you tell your fiancé what happened the night you got that tattoo and what it really means."

>>>«««

November—Sophomore Year

"GO, RAIDERS, GO! Go, Raiders, go!"

Cole sat on the bleachers, working through a list of geometry problems, waiting so that he could give Cowboy a ride home after practice, when his phone rang in his pocket. He put the math homework aside and stood to stretch his legs as he pulled the phone out.

"Hello?"

"Cole Tucker, this is Marshall Kase."

Cole's throat tightened as a wave of panic swept through him. He couldn't think of any reason the chief of police would be calling him unless there had been some kind of emergency. Or he'd finally been able to pin one of his and Logan's games on him, only this time Cole had no idea what he'd done to get caught in the first place.

"Chief. What can I do for you today?"

There was a heavy sigh on the other end. "I just got a call from Logan. Sounds like she's gotten herself stuck in one of Old Man Carithers's fields."

"Okay…" Seriously? That was it? "Do you need me to go pick her up or something?"

"Well, now, that might be a little difficult seeing as she was driving your truck."

"My—?" He reached in his front pocket where he kept his keys and fished them out. He chuckled to himself. The key to his Bronco was missing. "Right, of course, she was," he muttered to himself. How the hell had she done that without him noticing?

"You don't sound too surprised by that."

He grinned. "No, sir." He'd learned a while back that nothing she did could surprise him.

"You at the school?"

"Yes, sir. At the football field."

The chief sighed again. "All right. I'll pick you up in ten minutes."

34

><>«<

COLE SAT IN the passenger seat of the truck pretending not to notice the way the chief kept glancing at him every few seconds. He'd never been alone with the chief before, and he couldn't remember a time he'd ever been so nervous.

Logan's dad looked ordinary enough wearing a long-sleeved T-shirt, jeans, and a Braves baseball cap, and yet the man exuded an authority that made Cole feel like he was five again. Why had he told Cowboy to get another ride home?

"So," the chief said after several minutes of silence, "you want to tell me what exactly my girl was doing with your truck?"

Cole swallowed, his throat suddenly very dry. "Oh, that. Lo said her truck was out of gas, so I let her borrow mine to go pick some up while I waited for Cowboy's practice to end." The lie came out easily enough, and he sent out a silent prayer of thanks that he'd had time to come up with it while waiting for the chief.

"That right?"

"Yes, sir."

He glanced at Cole from across the cab with narrowed eyes. "And you wouldn't have had anything to do with the twelve chickens we found in her truck after school two weeks ago either?"

"Did Logan say I did?" he asked as his shoulders relaxed some.

"No," the chief grumbled.

Cole stared out the side window and smiled. If he knew anything about Lo, it was that she'd never rat him out. It was like they had this unspoken rule ever since he put gum in her hair in the sixth grade and she'd had to chop it all off. To this day they still kept each other's involvement out of whatever mishaps they got caught in. That didn't stop their parents from suspecting, though.

After another few minutes of silence, they finally pulled into a wet field. Parked in the middle was the Bronco, and nearly every inch of black paint from the windows down was covered in thick, red-brown mud.

Logan rounded the front of the Bronco, her boots and the bottoms of her jeans getting swallowed by the mud with each step. The chief crept the truck forward and parked in a drier patch nearby.

"Hey, Daddy," Logan called when he stepped out. "Sorry to call you over here for this, but we didn't really have anyone else." She pointed over her shoulder toward the Bronco, and Cole recognized Carly's blond curls. She waved at the chief.

"Mm-hmm," he muttered, eyeing the stuck Bronco currently caked in mud.

Cole left the truck and strode up to them. Logan did a double take before she glared at her dad. "What is he doing here?"

"Well, I figured it might be best to give the boy a heads-up that his only form of personal transportation was about to get hauled out of the mud on Old Man Carithers's private property."

"I can explain…" she began.

"No need, Lo," Cole said as he threw his hands in his pockets. "I already told the chief here the whole story. About how you needed gas and I let you borrow my truck to get it."

Her shoulders fell. "Right, exactly. Me and Carly were just running to the Shell station on the other side of town. We tried to cut across the fields to get to the highway over on the other side. Just seemed faster with all the after-school traffic. It was wetter than we thought, and we ended up getting stuck."

"Mm-hmm," the chief said again. He eyed the Bronco over her shoulder. "And how exactly did it get covered in mud if you were just passing through?"

Logan hesitated. "Uh…"

"That was me, sir. Me and Cowboy were goofing around yesterday, and I still haven't gotten a chance to clean her off yet."

"You gonna tell me the drawings were you, too?"

Cole had no idea what the chief was talking about. He studied the Bronco again and noticed for the first time the collection of crude symbols that had been traced into the coat of mud. He frowned at Lo, but she was staring down at her feet, biting her lip with pink-tinged cheeks.

He sighed, meeting the chief's stare. "Yes, sir. That, too."

The chief rolled his eyes. "All right, let's just get this thing out of here." He returned to his truck and cranked it up. He whipped it around easily and started backing it up to the tail end of the Bronco.

"Thanks," Logan muttered.

Cole shrugged. "No problem. Besides," he said, pointing to the muddy Bronco, "this is amateur at best. I would feel bad getting you in trouble over this."

"Whatever. Not only did I steal your key without you noticing, but then I took your truck for a joyride, and you had no idea."

Cole nodded. "During which you got it stuck in the mud, so still not impressed. Seriously, the only thing sadder than this attempt is the fact that me and your dad had to come bail you out. It's a shame this is the best you can do."

"You really think this is the best I've got?"

"Afraid so. But I'm looking forward to seeing you try to prove me wrong." He winked before jogging over to the Bronco. When he looked back, she was still grinning.

Chapter Four

LOGAN WOKE TO the sensation of a jackhammer pounding away at her skull. With her eyes scrunched in the sunlight, she tried to remember the last time she'd felt so horrendously hungover and came up short.

When they finally adjusted to the light, Logan pried her eyes open. She was in a bed, but it took only a second's investigation to realize it wasn't hers. And it wasn't just any bed either. This she distinctly remembered as Cole Tucker's bed.

Not again, she almost cried. Logan smacked a hand to her forehead and instantly regretted it. She swore she could feel every inch of her brain throbbing. She slowly sat up and assessed the situation. The one good sign was that she was still fully clothed.

Logan grabbed her favorite pointed-toe cowgirl boots from the floor. She held them in her hands as she carefully opened the door before tiptoeing her way down the hall. She spotted the front door on the other side of the cozy living room, her only means of escape. She took one step.

"Good morning, sunshine!" Cole hollered from the

kitchen where Logan hadn't seen him. She turned around on the spot, cringing at the boom of his voice. "I was wondering when you'd finally get up."

"Keep it down or I swear I will shove the toes of these boots right into your eye sockets," she snapped.

"Geez," he said more quietly. "I forgot how cranky you are when you're hungover."

Logan glared at him, daring him to joke again. He chuckled.

"Here"—he pointed to a stool at the breakfast bar—"take a seat, and I'll get you some aspirin."

She crossed the room and set her boots on the floor before moving slowly into the raised chair. Cole set a glass of water and two white pills in front of her, which she hastily shoved into her mouth along with a gulp of water. "What happened last night? We didn't do anything...did we?"

He shook his head, and a great flood of relief washed over her. "I slept on the couch after graciously letting you take the bed."

"How did we get here?"

"Somewhere between you passing out and me puking my guts up, Lilly called Cowboy and had him come take you and me back to our place."

"So, it's still just you two here?" she asked, looking around. "Doesn't look like any women have taken over the place yet."

"That's right. Still just us."

"That's too bad." Logan took another sip of water.

"How ya figure?"

She shrugged. "I made a bet with Carly a long time ago that Cowboy would be the first of all of us to get hitched. I guess I was hoping he'd found some girl to finally make an honest man out of him."

"Ha!" Cole's laugh was loud and hard, magnifying the ache in her head and making her wince. "Cowboy would have to be capable of having a real conversation with a woman first."

"What about you? Found that special girl who makes your heart pitter-patter yet?" she teased.

He crossed his arms in front of his chest and leaned back against the counter. "What would it matter to you if I did?"

"Just curious if I need to send some poor girl my condolences," she said. He hadn't actually answered the question.

Cole's grin turned cocky. "If I didn't know you better, I'd think you sound a little jealous."

This time it was her turn to laugh. "Good thing you know me better. Though I guess it would be somewhat of a relief. Otherwise, I might feel obligated to find her and try to talk some sense into her. And I just don't have the time or motivation today."

"Whatever you have to tell yourself to be happy."

"Who's happy?" a deep voice asked from down the hall. Russell Hart, or Cowboy as he'd been known to everybody since sixth grade, stepped into the living room. He'd been a shrimpy kid back then, the nickname given by a group of bullies who made fun of him for wearing an oversized cowboy hat to school every day that year.

Now, at six-two and with at least two hundred pounds of bulky muscle, he was one of the biggest, buffest guys Logan knew and a high school football legend. The name Cowboy evoked a sense of pride and respect from the entire town. He also had a tendency to be a bit of a manwhore, but he had one of those easy personalities no one could hate even if they wanted to.

He was also Cole Tucker's best friend and therefore should have been one of Logan's least favorite people. But despite the animosity between her and Cole, Cowboy had always been a good friend to her growing up, like a brother even.

His hair was shorter underneath the old UGA cap and a few shades lighter than the last time she saw him. Judging from that and the suntan, she guessed he'd been spending a lot of time outside these days.

"Logan's happy," Cole answered as he refilled his glass of water. "Ecstatic, really. She was worried I was seeing someone and she'd lost her chance forever."

Cowboy frowned, his hand scratching the hair at the nape of his neck. "And here I was hoping she'd finally realized her secret love for me. Bummer."

"Ha-ha," Logan said humorlessly. "No wonder you guys are still single. You're not near as funny as you think you are."

Cowboy raised his hand to hide his mouth. "I forgot how crabby she is when she's hungover," he whispered. Logan punched him in the arm. "Ow! Seriously? That's the kind of thanks I get for carrying your unconscious ass from my truck last night?"

Logan arched an eyebrow. "You carried me in here?"

"After you passed out at the bar." Logan frowned. That would explain why she didn't remember much beyond her own shot glass last night. "You're lucky it was me, too. If Cole had his way, you would have ended up on the couch all night."

"So instead you put her in *my* bed," Cole interrupted. "How chivalrous of you."

Cowboy turned and glared. "That was for hurling on my favorite work boots."

"Oh, right," Cole said as he leaned back against the kitchen counter. "Sorry about that. I'll buy you some new ones."

"Great." Cowboy took the stool next to Logan. "Now just throw in that firefighter chick's number, and we'll call it even."

"I already told you she's not interested."

"Every girl is interested," he said, shaking his head.

Logan snorted. "You really haven't changed much."

"Look who's talking. Your first night back and you're already getting plastered with Cole."

"Trust me," she said, trying to fight the memory and nausea that accompanied it. "That won't be happening again."

He and Cole both laughed. "Sure it won't. Next time just remember to invite me. After four years, I expect more than a call for a ride from you."

She sighed. "It wasn't exactly a planned get-together. I would have invited you if it had been, but the whole thing just sort of happened."

"Ah, don't feel bad," Cole said. "Cowboy's just mad he's too busy to party and go wild like he used to."

"Right, like I ever got to *go wild* with you two around. Between football and your drinking bets, I was the sober one driving your asses home every night."

"Cowboy too busy?" Logan asked skeptically. "Doing what?"

"You try running a business and see how much partying you manage to get done."

"Doesn't seem to stop you from sleeping over at some random woman's place every other night," Cole said.

Logan's jaw dropped. "Hold on, you have a business? Since when?"

Cowboy looked at her. "About two years ago. I'd been working with a landscaping crew over in Macon for a year. Then when Cam finished up his degree in business, we decided to start up our own right here in town. We're actually doing really well."

"That's awesome, Cowboy," Logan said. "How did I not know about this?"

"Well, maybe 'cause you never thought to call or visit your lowly friends back home. Seriously, how do you not come back to town once in four years?"

Logan scowled. It wasn't that she never thought of coming back home, but she'd known that the best way to start over would be to completely cut herself off from the old life she was leaving behind. Especially after that last night.

"Phones go both ways, Cowboy. But you're right. Sorry I didn't keep in touch."

"That's all right. I reckon a hug'll make up for it."

Cowboy opened his arms and wrapped them gently around her. "So, you are absolutely sure you're not secretly in love with me?"

Logan pulled out of his hug and smacked him on the shoulder.

"Oh well, can't blame a guy for trying. And now that you've officially apologized, you can have this back." He dug into his jeans pocket, pulling out something small and dropping it on the counter with a metallic clatter. "Quite a rock you've got there."

Logan's eyes darted between the empty spot on her left ring finger and the engagement ring she hadn't realized was missing there. "How did you get that?"

"You threw it at me," he chuckled. "Told me to hold on to it 'cause you didn't want to lose it. That was right before you passed out in the truck and started drooling on my shirt."

Logan stared at the ring as she slid it back onto her finger, trying to digest the feeling of heavy cement settling in her stomach.

"Some fancy doctor, right?" Cowboy asked when she didn't respond.

Logan rolled her eyes. "My dad has a big mouth."

"More like Lilly," he said. "The town gossips haven't had near as much to talk about since you left, so they're just making up for lost time. So, when's the big day?"

"We haven't really—"

"While you two ladies sit here chatting, I'm going to head over to Wade's," Cole interrupted. "Make sure my bill is covered from last night, maybe get something to eat. Unless you two would rather take this girl talk over there."

"Wish I could, man, but I've got all these invoices and payments I have to get straight from last week. Next time, though."

Cole looked at Logan next. "I don't even want to think about food right now, but I could use a ride to my truck." She slipped on her boots before giving Cowboy a hard pat on the back.

"See you later, Cowboy. Let me know when you're free, and I'll make sure we get together and catch up."

He nodded, and Cole grabbed his keys from the counter before leading the way to the front door. "See ya," Cowboy called as Logan followed Cole out the door.

Chapter Five

"I CAN'T BELIEVE you still have this thing," Logan muttered as she and Cole climbed into the old, black Bronco. Aside from some extra wear and tear and the police scanner he'd installed, everything looked, smelled, and felt exactly the same as it had the last time she'd sat in it. "Surely by now you can afford something better than this pile of crap."

He shrugged, starting the thing and quickly backing it out of the driveway. "Still runs fine. Don't see why I need another one just yet. Besides," he said, "I'm working on saving up right now."

"For what?"

He turned onto Willow Creek's main street, the one that would take them through the middle of town and to the bar on the other side. "Big house."

"Why do you need a big house?"

"For the wife and kids," he said casually, keeping his eyes on the road.

"So, there is a girl?"

He looked at her, a tiny grin creeping onto his face. "No

girl…at least not yet. But one day. And it's not like I can keep living with Cowboy forever. That's why I'm saving up now so that when the time comes, I'll be ready to start my family."

Logan shook her head. "I can't believe you're already thinking about that stuff. The wife, the kids, the big house…"

"The white picket fence, the loyal family dog."

She smiled, remembering the one and only dog she'd ever had. "You know you can get a dog whenever you want. You're a grown man."

"A grown man with a rental agreement. No animals allowed while Cowboy and I are at this place."

"Oh. Still, we're too young to be thinking that seriously about the future."

"Says the one getting married."

She hesitated. "That doesn't mean I'm already stressing about kids and all that stuff." She tried to picture her and Jacob in front of the perfect house with the perfect kids, but the image just wouldn't come to her. Proof that, while she knew she loved Jacob and wanted to marry him, she wasn't ready to think about anything beyond that. "I'm just taking it one step at a time right now."

Cole opened his mouth like he was about to say something then closed it again before any sound could come out.

The rest of the short ride was silent with him looking thoughtful in the driver's seat, which left Logan trying not to think about the way her stomach felt like it could turn against her any second. Luckily, years of practice meant she had better control over her hungover tummy than most.

They finally pulled up to the bar, and Logan relaxed when she saw her truck safe and sound. There were a few other cars and trucks, some of the nonchurchgoers who'd come in for an early lunch—and probably at least one who'd never left last night.

"Well, thanks for the ride," she told Cole as she undid her seat belt. "I guess I'll see you around."

"Oh, we're not done yet."

"What the hell do you mean, *we're not done yet?* I'm going home. I'm hungover and tired." Not to mention in desperate need of a shower.

"Soon," he said. Without another word, he was out of the Bronco and making his way across the parking lot to the door. He stopped at the top of the porch steps, looking back for a split second before going inside.

Logan rolled her eyes, grumbling as she climbed out of the Bronco and marched toward the bar's entrance. The blinds were open, allowing sunlight to brighten up the place tremendously. Logan scanned the bar's few inhabitants, soon finding Cole sitting in a booth on the far left wall.

He was scrutinizing a lunch menu in his hand and appeared to be in deep thought. She crossed the bar and stood by the booth.

"What are we doing here?"

He said nothing, nodding to the seat opposite him. Logan grunted as she gave in and sat across from him. He put the menu down. "Clearly, we are getting lunch."

She slumped back in her seat. "Didn't you hear me say I couldn't even think about food right now, or do you just not care?"

The corner of his mouth tilted up. "I did hear you, and it gave me a great idea for our second challenge."

"Second challenge?" she cried. "When did we even have a first challenge?"

"Maybe you should quit drinking. You have a horrible memory when you do." Cole pointed to the wall-sized chalkboard behind the bar. Like always, it was covered with the prices for various alcoholic drinks, but the section on the end where the specials usually were had been wiped clean. Now in its place was a T-grid with *Cole* written on one side and *Logan* on the other in Lilly's flowy script.

"What is that?"

"Scoreboard," he said, sitting up taller. "For our game of H-O-R-S-E."

She groaned. She vaguely remembered a drunken conversation from last night involving a series of challenges. And worse, she remembered agreeing to it.

Worse still, she remembered the terms.

"We take turns picking the challenges, and the first one to a full H-O-R-S-E loses," Cole went on.

"And you've got Lilly keeping score." Why hadn't she

just stayed home last night like she'd originally planned? "Why does your name already have an H?"

"That would be from the drinking last night."

"Cowboy said I passed out."

Lilly appeared at their table as if out of nowhere. "You did, but not before this one got sick all over my floor," she said with a pointed look at him. "The way you two left last night, I thought for sure you'd be ready to dig your own graves by now."

"Don't you ever sleep?" Logan asked.

"Oh, honey, I'll sleep when I'm dead. Besides, what else have I got to do all day? I'd much rather be here where the action is. Not to mention the men." She winked at Cole.

Logan frowned. She loved Lilly to death, but sometimes she was just too much.

"So what are you two doing back here already?"

"You mean aside from admiring you, Lilly?" Cole asked, much to her amusement. "We are here to eat."

"All right, doll. What can I get you?"

He looked back down at the menu in his hands. "I'm thinking a bacon cheeseburger with all the works, onion rings, French fries, and a milkshake. And the same for Lo here."

"You expect me to be able to eat all that?"

"I expect you to try," he corrected. "First one to finish without getting sick wins. Unless you want to go ahead and forfeit the challenge."

"*That's* the challenge? Eating a bunch of junk? But I'm hungover," she whined.

Cole laughed. "The whole point of a challenge is that it's supposed to be difficult. Unless you don't think you can handle it, which is fine with me since it just gets me closer to winning the whole thing." He glanced at her tattooed wrist. "Have you decided how you're going to tell him that everything he knows about you is a lie?"

"Fine," she growled. "But when I win, you get to cover the bill."

He laughed. "Hell, if you win, I'll cover lunch and our entire bar tab from last night."

"Deal."

Ten minutes later, Logan sat with a smug smile as she forced down the last sip of her chocolate shake.

Cole stared like he'd just struck out two batters only to have the third step up and hit a grand slam. "I thought you said you couldn't eat all that," he said once he swallowed.

"When you have to play it cool at breakfast after a night of drinking so the chief of police doesn't get suspicious, you figure out how to get it all down and keep it down." Logan proudly rubbed her midsection. "Carly used to call it the Iron Stomach."

He shook his head. "You hustled me. That shouldn't count."

"Whatever. You're just mad because my name is still clean." She pointed to the scoreboard where Lilly had just added a letter on Cole's side. "And you are now officially a ho."

"Good burn. You get that one from a ten-year-old?"

"Nope. Unlike you, I'm clever enough to come up with that one all on my own," Logan said. She took a small sip of water to help wash the taste of chocolate shake from her mouth as Lilly set the check between them. Logan slid it across the table to Cole.

He took it, pulling his wallet from his back pocket. "Not sure *clever* is the word for it."

"You're just jealous of my mad eating skills."

"No point denying that." He set a stack of cash on the table. "The next challenge is yours, so I suggest you make it a good one. I wouldn't want to beat you simply for your lack of imagination."

Logan rolled her eyes. Cole would be lucky if she took this thing any further. She couldn't lose a game she refused to play, and for Logan, losing this bet was just not an option.

December—Sixth Grade

COLE WAS WALKING to his dad's hardware store downtown after school when he saw it. Sitting on a thick, brown limb at least fifteen feet in the air was a pink camouflage bookbag he'd instantly recognized belonged to Logan Kase.

He'd first noticed Logan about a week ago. He was at his

locker one morning when he'd heard Zach Prescott picking on a stick of a girl less than half his size. He was teasing her about her dad being a cop. Apparently, Mr. Kase pulled Zach's dad over and slapped him with a DUI charge. Zach started yanking her books from her hands and calling her and her dad names.

Cole was about to step in when the girl pulled her arm back and punched Zach right in the nose. She'd held her head high, not even looking sorry, when the nearest teacher dragged her to the principal's office. He didn't think he'd ever seen a girl that tough before.

He'd watched her a lot after that—in the gym before school, passing her in the hallway, across the cafeteria during lunch—each time feeling this weird sense of respect. How had he never noticed her before? She looked just like any other girl, but there was something about her that said one wrong move and she'd chew some guy up and spit him out.

It only fascinated him more.

Cole gazed up at the backpack in the tree again. There wasn't a doubt in his mind that this was Zach Prescott's idea of revenge for making him cry in front of half the sixth grade. Clearly, he wasn't smart enough to know when he'd met his match.

Cole shrugged off his coat. He'd climbed trees like this one a hundred times growing up, so getting this bag down would be easy enough. Then he could bring it back to the school's lost and found and she'd be none the wiser.

The afternoon breeze was cold and strong, whipping his thin shirt all around and causing a number of brown leaves to fly into his face as he started to climb. He tried to go slowly, taking one branch at a time in order to keep his balance.

"Hey, you!"

Cole nearly slipped. He froze midclimb and peered down over his shoulder. Logan Kase stood at the bottom of the tree, hands on her hips and long hair flying around her. She glared up at him. "What do you think you're doing?"

"What's it look like?" he called down to her. "I'm getting your bag down."

"Why?"

What did she mean, *why?* "In case you didn't notice, some jerk put it up a tree. I'm just helping you get it down."

She crossed her arms over her chest. "Well, maybe I don't want your help."

His mouth fell open. Seriously, what was wrong with this girl? Any other girl in their class would be grateful for the offer. Heck, they usually got smiley and giggly just talking to him. He'd never been chewed out by one before.

Not that that should have surprised him. It had taken him all of twenty seconds to realize she wasn't like most girls their age.

Cole ignored her and continued to climb. His tennis shoes had a good grip, but the cold air was making his fingers cramp before he'd even made it halfway.

There was a rustle of leaves and the sound of scraping bark beneath him. Logan was scurrying her way up from branch to branch like a thin, human-sized squirrel.

"What are you doing?"

"Getting my bag."

He rolled his eyes. "You're gonna fall and break something. Get down and just wait for me to get it."

"Why? So you can tell everyone I needed a boy to help me? I don't think so." They both climbed higher. Shoes scraped on bark again, and Cole's heart stuttered as he saw Logan slip and only just catch herself.

"Be careful!" he shouted. Why couldn't she just accept his help like a normal person? "I told you to just wait. I've almost got it." He was perched on the branch just below the bag. He let go with one hand, reaching up as high as he could. His fingers brushed the bottom corner, still not close enough to grab it.

Logan pulled herself up onto the branch beside his. "And I told you that just 'cause I'm a girl doesn't mean I can't take care of myself, Cole Tucker."

Logan stretched up on her toes, her fingers extended toward the pink backpack. They clamped around the bag's fabric before she lowered herself onto flat feet.

The bag shifted and started to fall toward her. She swayed; Cole reached out and steadied her.

His foot slipped, and then he was falling.

He wasn't sure which of them screamed, the sound echoing in his ears even after he hit the cold, unforgiving ground.

His arm was broken, the doctor said an hour later while his mom cried beside him in the emergency room. He was put in a cast once the swelling went down. By lunch the next day, almost every one of his classmates had signed it. Everyone except Logan.

Where he'd expected to get some sort of "thank you" or "get well soon" or maybe even a "my hero" from her after practically saving her life, instead she'd spent the entire day completely ignoring his existence.

Friends swarmed around his lunch table, sharing the story of his bravery, but Cole wasn't listening. He was too busy glaring at the irritating brown-haired girl across the lunchroom, already planning his retaliation. *Let's see just how long she can ignore me then.*

Chapter Six

LOGAN LET OUT a breath as she pulled into her parents' driveway. Her dad's truck wasn't there, which meant they were probably getting lunch or visiting with a sick church member.

Wherever they were, she thanked God her parents weren't home. She'd narrowly avoided the onslaught of questions like *Where've you been?* and *Why do you smell like grease and stale booze?*

The first thing Logan did when she got inside was strip down and throw her clothes in the washer, hoping to get rid of the evidence from last night. Next, she ran straight to her bathroom, allowing herself only a few quick minutes in the shower as opposed to the long, hot bath she'd been craving all morning.

Once her hair was clean and her skin smelled of fresh body wash, she cut the water off and raced to get herself dressed and her hair dried. Then Logan settled onto her still freshly made bed and pulled out her laptop.

She opened her usual job search websites and set to work, looking for anything interesting and art related in the San

Francisco area. She spent over an hour combing through the options and coming up short. Well, it wasn't like she needed a job right away. Carly's wedding wasn't for another two months, and she and Jacob still hadn't set a date for their own wedding yet. Which meant she still had some time. Something would come up eventually.

Her phone rang and broke her concentration. She stared at it until Jacob's face filled the screen before she picked it up.

"Hello."

"Hey, babe. I just left the hospital and thought I'd call to check in, maybe apologize a few more times for missing out on this week with you."

Logan grinned. "I told you it's okay. You can't help what happens at work. You don't need to apologize."

"I'll make it up to you," he said, accompanied by the sounds of his Lexus starting. "I'll be back out there as soon as I can. But with Morgan out for the next couple weeks, it looks like I'll be taking on some extra shifts."

"That's okay," she said, trying to hide her disappointment. "You don't have to stay out here if you're busy. We can just do dinner or something one night when you're free."

"Between mine and the extra shifts I took on, my schedule is going to be pretty swamped. I'll try to make sure I'm free one night so we can do dinner with your parents."

"Great. Just let me know what day. Momma and I can cook dinner. You and my parents can get to know each other better—"

"We can finally tell them about moving to San Francisco," he finished for her.

Logan hesitated. "Um, yeah…maybe."

"Logan, you've got to tell them eventually. And the longer you put it off, the harder it will be later." She could hear the agitation in his voice.

"I know, I know. You're absolutely right," she muttered. "So how did your night go? It seems pretty late for you to just be getting out now."

"I know. It was a madhouse in there, completely slammed. I ended up staying to help a bit longer, and before I knew it, hours had gone by. I was lucky to get out when I did."

"Oh no. You poor thing," she said, her eyes now scanning a very short list of art-related positions near Willow Creek just for fun.

"Yeah, and you wouldn't believe the crazy stuff we saw—" Logan clicked on a link for an elementary school art teacher a few counties over while Jacob relayed the details of his shift.

After two years of these after-work calls, she'd mastered the art of pretending to listen. Jacob got so wrapped up in his own stories, all Logan had to do was mutter the occasional and well-placed *oh* or *mm-hmm*. She wasn't completely ignoring him; she liked to think of it more as multitasking. She made a point to actively listen every once in a while, to get the general idea of the story he was telling.

"So I ordered a CT for the guy…that's where you scan a specific part to—"

"Mm-hmm," she muttered offhandedly as she read through another page of job postings. After a few more minutes of listening and searching, Logan declared this particular job search to be a lost cause. She closed out the webpage and pulled up her e-mail. She skipped right over most of them but stopped on a very promising-looking YouTube video sent by one of her sorority sisters. Before she knew it, she had gone through almost ten more videos and had all but forgotten the voice on the other end of the phone.

"Logan, did you just laugh? Did you even hear what I said?" he asked loudly. "I had to refer the man to an oncologist who'll end up telling him he may only have a few weeks to live."

Crap. Logan closed the YouTube video of hilarious dog fails. "I'm sorry. What kind of cancer did you say he had again?"

Jacob sighed. "It doesn't matter. It wouldn't mean anything to you since you're not a doctor."

She ignored the jibe. She knew he didn't mean to insult her. He was tired after a long shift and had every right to get upset since she really hadn't been listening.

"So," he said, his voice sounding a bit deflated, "how was your night? Do anything fun?"

She closed her laptop and sat up straighter on the bed. "Not really," she said, which was kind of the truth. Getting drunk and waking up in Cole's bed was anything but fun. "Just a boring night in with my parents."

Now that was a lie.

"That doesn't sound boring at all. That actually sounds really nice."

"And so far, I've spent all day looking at job sites, but I still can't find anyth—"

"I'm sure you will," he cut her off. The car suddenly got quiet as the engine hushed. "Listen, babe, I'm at my apartment now, and I'm exhausted. I'll call you later, okay?"

"Yeah, sure. I'll talk to you then."

He yawned. "I love you."

"Love you, too." The phone went silent as he hung up.

Chapter Seven

HALF AN HOUR after her phone call with Jacob, Logan was putting her now-clean clothes away when she finally heard her dad's roaring truck pulling into the driveway.

She met him at the bottom of the stairs. Marshall Kase wore a pair of khaki slacks and a soft, red polo. His dark hair was graying and thinning out at the top, and beneath his shirt sat a moderate-sized gut.

He shook his head as soon as he saw her, wrapped strong arms around her, and muttered a short "good luck" in her ear. Then he kissed the top of her head, and then turned to go up the stairs she'd just come down. She had no idea what that was all about or why she needed luck and chalked it up to exhaustion after several hours of visiting with church members and his desire to get out of his Sunday clothes and into a comfortable pair of jeans.

Logan found her mom in the kitchen. Cindy's hair was a thick, straight curtain of graying brown that fell just past her shoulders. She was a thin woman, had been all her life, despite her love of beer and having carried a child for nine months. She still wore her pale green dress while she put away groceries. No doubt she'd had to stop at the store after promising some people a few more of her famous apple pies.

She gave Logan a small smile.

"Hey, sweetie. You were up and out awfully early this morning. We missed you at church," she said, not looking at Logan as she busily put the butter away in the fridge behind her.

Logan grabbed the flour and sugar from the counter and carried them into the pantry closet. "Yeah, Carly wanted me to check on some wedding stuff while she's still out of town. So I decided to get an early start." She kept herself from making eye contact. She couldn't even count all the times she'd gotten away with stuff like this over the years, and she'd become quite good at it. Of course, this would be the last time she'd have to if she just told Cole where to stick his stupid bet.

"Oh, that's nice. So then you weren't out all night, God knows where, after getting drunk at Wade's?"

And then sometimes it didn't matter how good a liar she was. Logan turned around to see her mother practically seething. "That…may have happened also."

Her mother slammed her hands down on the counter. "Logan Brynn! You can't keep it together just one night?"

Logan's tongue felt heavy as lead in her mouth. No wonder her daddy had escaped upstairs without so much as a word. After twenty-five years of marriage, he knew better than to hang around when her mother was on the warpath. "Momma, I can explain."

"Oh, good!" her mother yelled. "I would love to hear your reasons for sneaking out and getting trashed your first night back in town. And with *that boy* no less!" she spat.

"How do you even know about that?"

"Well, apparently, Judy Carmichael saw you two there last night, thick as thieves, and told the entire Methodist church this morning at service. And you know how they like to gossip." She huffed. "It wasn't long before word spread to the Baptist and Presbyterian congregations, too. And now it's all over the whole town."

Logan fought to hold back her snort. Only Judy Carmichael would admit to being out at the town bar the night before worship service.

Her mother scowled. "I swear Pastor Joe was staring me down in service this morning." She took the eggs in her hand and spun around, shoving them not so gently into the fridge. "I would say I've never been so humiliated in my life, but then hearing about your latest escapades from appalled church members was a regular occurrence before you left for school. I suppose I should be used to it by now."

"Momma, it's not that big of a deal. I just went to get one drink. I didn't even know he would be there." Momma's lips parted, but Logan held her hand up. "Yes, admittedly, things did get out of hand. I shouldn't have let him talk me into all those drinks. But, Momma, it was the last time, honest—"

Her mother's hands clenched. "You say that every time, and I am tired of hearing it." She laid her palms flat on the counter, her shoulders tense. "I thought you were done with Cole Tucker."

"I am, Momma."

"You know," she sighed, pinching the bridge of her nose between her fingers, "some mothers dread the day their little girl gets married. But I swear that day cannot get here fast enough. For whatever reason, Jacob makes you better, and that is exactly what you need to be. Maybe when you're married to him you can finally get past all this nonsense and settle down. Be the girl you were supposed to be all these years."

Without another word, Momma stormed out of the kitchen. Seconds later Logan heard feet stomping up the stairs and down the hall followed by a door slamming.

Her mom was furious, but Logan didn't care. Instead, she made her own flaring exit as she forced her way across the kitchen and out the door to the garage. In only a minute, she was in her truck and barreling down the narrow gravel road. Already, the familiar roar of the engine was calming her anger.

Why did she even try to explain that she hadn't meant for it to happen? It didn't matter to her mother. Just like it didn't matter how well Logan had done over the last couple years, how hard she'd been trying to be the lady her mom expected her to be. Why even bother? She would never be the daughter her mom wanted.

It was all Cole Tucker's fault. It was like a superpower he had, convincing her to do stupid things. Like tossing back shot after shot as if they were old friends. So what if she'd told him she wasn't that girl anymore? He wouldn't take no for an answer, didn't care that she was trying to do better. He didn't care about anyone but himself.

She thought of the two of them laughing together at Wade's that morning and the night before. For a little while there she'd forgotten how much she hated him, and while her guard was down he'd dragged her into yet another one of his stupid games. She wouldn't make that mistake again.

She was going to remind him exactly who the hell he was dealing with.

Logan's hands tightened on the steering wheel as she drove past a road sign informing drivers that Willow Creek Park was only a few miles away, the memory of her and a naked Cole Tucker flooding her mind as inspiration struck like lightning.

Before she even registered what she was doing, Logan had pulled her truck over on the side of the road and was sending Cole Tucker a text.

She knew exactly what their next challenge would be.

May—Freshman Year

COLE READ THE note one last time then folded it and shoved it back in the pocket of his swim trunks.

No more than half a mile off, he could hear his friends and classmates laughing and screaming at Willow Creek Park Beach. It was a small beach, even for the small town. But it was just big enough for his class to get together and celebrate another school year coming to an end.

Somewhere over there, Savannah Wainwright would be sneaking away from her friends and following the narrow trail that led to the dock.

He'd been talking to Savannah a lot the last few weeks. She was cute, sweet, maybe a little ditzy sometimes. Okay, so she wasn't going to help break the dumb blonde stereotype anytime soon.

It was just some harmless flirting. He never thought it would amount to anything, certainly not a skinny dip in the lake. But hey, when opportunity knocked, who was he to deny it entry?

Even if the only reason he'd been flirting with Savannah in the first place was to get *her* off his mind.

Cole scanned the water by the dock, the gravel road that cut through the trees, and then the woods surrounding him. He stripped down to nothing, tossing his clothes beside the dock, and waded into the water.

His chest was hammering, not because of the cool water enveloping him or the fact that he was naked for anyone to stumble across, but because just thinking about Logan Kase made his heart race and his jaw clench at the same time. Everything she did irritated him, and yet he still woke up in the middle of the night dreaming about her. Her soft, golden skin, the way her nose crinkled when she laughed, and her eyes that had become his favorite shade of blue.

Christ, what the hell was happening to him?

Sometimes he just wanted to throttle her, like two months ago when she'd put something in his Coke that turned his teeth black. But then she'd looked at him with those same blue eyes and a victorious smirk, and all that anger had disintegrated. Well, almost all of it.

"I see you got my note."

Every muscle in Cole's body clenched, and his heart skipped a beat. He turned slowly toward the source of the voice.

Logan stood by the dock with his T-shirt and swimming trunks slung over her shoulder. Strands of dark hair framed her face where they'd fallen out of her short ponytail. She had one hand raised to her hip, and he could just make out her dark bikini through the thin tank top that hugged her every curve.

Cole's hands jerked forward to cover himself below the water. Okay, so naked in the lake was not the best time to think about Lo's body.

Wait a second. "Did you say *your* note?"

There it was, that smirk that made him want to choke

her and pull her closer all at once. "Pretty good, huh? Let's just say I've got a friend with a criminal talent for forging people's handwriting."

She could only mean Carly. As far as he knew, she'd never included anyone else in their pranks before.

The side of his mouth curved upward, and he forced away any trace of worry or discomfort. "If you wanted to see me naked, Lo, all you had to do was ask," he crowed.

"Oh, I didn't do this for me," she said with an equal grin.

"What—?" Cole went silent. The sounds of screaming and voices he'd heard coming from the beach were growing louder.

"Yeah." She glanced at her watch-less wrist. "I'd say they should be here anytime now."

"Who?"

She shrugged. "No one special. Just our entire class."

Cole moved forward, stopping when the water was only a few inches above where his hands still carefully covered his groin. The voices were coming closer. "All right, you had your fun. Got me real good. Now give me my clothes."

"I don't think so."

"I'm warning you, Logan." Just then a crowd of almost a hundred kids broke through the trees. Several pointed and laughed when they saw him standing alone in the water.

"I swear to God, Kase, you better give me my clothes back!" he yelled this time. Thank God the water was murky.

"Or you'll do what?" she called back to him. Their entire class had to be standing behind her now.

"Or I'll make everything I've done to you up to now look like a joke," he growled.

Logan shook her head. "You're going to have to do a lot better than that if you want these back." She pulled his swim trunks and T-shirt off her shoulder and dangled them in front of her. "Maybe something like... 'Logan is smarter and better than me in every possible way. She's ten times more awesome than I'll ever be.'"

He pulled his hands out of the water and crossed them over his chest. "Seeing as I'd hate to lie in front of all these people, I'm not gonna say that."

"Then I guess you get to hide out in the water for a while."

"That's how you want to play this?" He glared at her, not waiting for an answer. His hands fell to his sides. "Fine."

Whatever Logan had been expecting, he guessed from her wide eyes and gaping jaw it wasn't him walking out of the lake buck naked in front of her and their entire class.

There was an uproar of catcalls and whistles as he strode out of the water and onto dry land. Cool air caressed his skin, and he felt all eyes on him, but he didn't care. He had tunnel vision, blinded to everything around him except Logan's face.

She was staring at him, her eyes roving down over his face and chest. When they drifted even lower, her lips parted and she sucked in a quick breath.

She didn't fight him when he tore the clothes from her hands and started pulling them on. Her eyes had turned darker than he'd ever seen them.

He'd been wrong. *This* was his favorite shade of blue.

Chapter Eight

LOGAN LEANED AGAINST her truck as the Bronco came down the gravel road, its headlights shining painfully in her eyes. It was dark, which meant no one would be around to witness the event, which Logan was grateful for. She'd almost immediately regretted texting Cole with the location of their next challenge, but it would only look worse if she backed out now.

She was supposed to be at home with her parents for an uneventful evening in. Night after night, over and over, until she married Jacob and could get out of this town. Instead, she was out at the Willow Creek Park dock waiting for Cole Tucker.

He parked the Bronco several feet from her truck and stepped out, leaving it running and the headlights shining brightly on her.

"What took you so long to get back to me?" she called out as he approached the dock. "I texted you three days ago."

He strolled up wearing jeans, a dark blue shirt, and a thick jacket. "I've been at the firehouse the last three days. Some of us have to work for a living," he muttered, his breath just visible in the chilly night air. The cold wasn't unbearable, being March and all, but it wasn't the air she was concerned about. The lake, on the other hand, would still be freezing this time of year. Which was kind of the point.

Cole studied the area. "You mind telling me what we're doing out here?"

Logan shrugged. "Sure, and while I do, you can start taking your clothes off."

His head jerked around to face her, a tiny grin spreading across his face. "You trying to see me naked, Lo?"

She let out a bark of laughter. "Please, there's nothing there I haven't seen before," she said, nodding to the area hidden by his jeans. "Keep your underwear on. We're just going swimming."

This time he laughed. "In this weather, are you crazy? We'll get hypothermia!"

"Something tells me you won't last that long." She started pulling off her coat. "We both go in the water, the first one to come out loses."

He huffed, pulling off his own coat as she started to take off her boots. "I'm a firefighter, Lo. I don't do well with cold."

She smiled. She set her boots and then her socks on the hood of her truck before pulling her sweater over her head and exposing her black bikini top. If she'd been wearing a bra and underwear instead of the bathing suit she had on under her clothes, she would have felt weird stripping down like this in front of Cole Tucker. A bathing suit was a lot less scandalous than jumping into the lake in her underwear.

She sucked in a breath as the cold air hit the skin of her bare stomach and arms. "Hence, the challenge," she said once she could speak.

He gave her a cocky grin. "Good thing I love a challenge."

"Exactly. Now stop whining. You said I could pick the next one, so suck it up and take your clothes off," she said, cringing at how anxious she sounded.

"Yes, ma'am." He pulled his long-sleeved T-shirt over his head and revealed a plain white shirt underneath. Logan scanned the area around them one last time before she unzipped her jeans and pulled them down. She clenched her jaw, trying not to let Cole hear her teeth chatter.

When he was down to a pair of boxers and his white T-shirt, he placed his clothes with hers on the hood of the truck. Then he threw his hand out, letting Logan lead the way.

The ground was cold as she crossed to the dock with bare feet. She stopped there, contemplating for a second if she should walk in or jump.

While she was still debating, Cole walked past her to the end of the dock. He sat down slowly, careful to keep his feet from dropping into the water just yet. His back was illuminated by the Bronco's headlights as he turned to Logan.

"I say we lower ourselves in at the same time, to the

shoulders," he said. "Just try not to get your hair wet or you really will get sick."

Logan, unable to come up with a better idea, walked down the dock and sat next to Cole. She took a second to pull her long, dark hair up into a messy bun on top of her head.

She ignored the goose bumps rising on her arms. She needed to win this one. Cole would have an *R* added to his name—surely enough for him to admit she was better—and she would let herself be done with his stupid challenges.

Cole stretched his legs out, letting them hover over the water. "On the count of three," he said. Logan nodded. When he reached three, she forced her arms to lower her body into the water. The shock of freezing water was painful as it traveled up her body, but she wouldn't let herself stop. Cole did the same beside her.

Logan was immersed in the cold water, her muscles cramping, as her lungs froze. Her left hand held on to the edge of the dock, but with the shock of cold water, it provided no strength to hold her up. She barely felt Cole's hand grab her other arm and pull her up an inch or two before her head could dip under the water. She finally managed to move her legs and hold herself afloat in the water without Cole's help.

"It's not that bad," she said through chattering teeth.

He chuckled two feet away from her. "Liar."

She closed her eyes, trying to imagine herself snuggled up

on the couch with a thick blanket and a roaring fire beside her.

"What are you thinking about?" Cole's shaky voice whispered after several seconds, pulling her back to their reality. Logan opened her eyes to see Cole watching her, his chin just above the water and one arm hanging from the dock a foot from hers.

"Fire," she whispered. "A nice, big, hot fire."

There was an almost imperceptible nod. "Hmm. A beach in the Bahamas, the white sand scorching my feet," he said between shallow breaths.

Logan let out a soft moan. A hot beach sounded so good right now. She closed her eyes. "Wade's, with the heat blasting and half a dozen shots of whiskey burning in my stomach."

"And the lovely Lilly putting an *H* under your name," he said dreamily.

Logan ignored him and tried to focus on her warm daydream. Her entire body was shaking beneath the water. She could barely pull air into her lungs, and her muscles were stiff.

"So this fiancé of yours, what is it he does again? Something incredibly dull to match his personality?" he mumbled with a tight jaw.

"Actually," she forced out, "he's a doctor. He works in the ER. So no, not dull at all. Quite the opposite, since he saves lives every day."

He rolled his eyes. "I might be impressed if I didn't risk my own life every day running into burning buildings...often saving someone else in the process, I might add. What's the worst that could happen to him—he catches a cold?"

Logan's eyebrows would have lifted in surprise if her forehead weren't frozen. "You really don't like him."

"Why would I? The guy acts like he's got a stick up his ass."

"You don't even know him," she said, suddenly very aware of the platinum engagement ring that felt like ice on her fourth finger. "He's a great guy."

"I bet he's not so great when he finds out the truth about that tattoo."

"Good thing he isn't going to find out." She could feel her stomach muscles shaking violently, and she shifted to pull her legs up to her chest. She was closer to Cole now. But given the small amount of heat that came with the proximity, she didn't care. She struggled not to move closer just to increase that warmth.

"You know," he said softly beside her, "you could have it removed."

Logan shook her head as much as she could. "Maybe if I had a couple thousand dollars lying around."

"I think you've grown attached to it. That you like seeing my name on you every day," he said with his crooked smile, no doubt trying to unnerve her, distract her, so that he could win. Didn't he know that she wasn't like all the other girls, that his charms didn't work on her?

She smiled back. "If only to remind me how much better my life is without you."

He was about to say something but then closed his mouth, his brow wrinkling. "What do the rules say regarding time-outs?"

"Time-outs?"

He nodded. "Like a pause in the challenge."

"There are no pauses." She laughed, and that, at least, seemed to warm her a little.

"If we can just pause for ten seconds—"

Logan shook her head. "If you can't take it anymore then just give up. It's only one letter anyway." And, God, did she need him to give up. She didn't know how much more of this she could take. They couldn't have been in here talking more than five minutes, but it felt like it had been hours.

"All right," he said, looking grim. "You asked for it."

She stared at him, hopeful that he would start to pull himself out of the water, but Cole Tucker didn't budge.

Asked for what? She couldn't get the words out, every inch of her too numb. Feeling only slowly started to return as the water around her grew noticeably warmer.

Chapter Nine

"EW!" LOGAN SCREAMED as she fought to pull herself up out of the water. Cole followed only a second behind her.

"I can't believe you!" she yelled, wrapping her arms tightly around her. "Did you seriously just pee in the water? While I was right next to you?!"

He pulled himself up onto the dock and into the shining headlight beams, bouncing up and down as he tried to warm himself. "Relax. You do realize that every time you get in that lake you are swimming in urine and blood and other unmentionables."

"That's disgusting!" She stared at him, also hopping up and down. The air was a lot colder this time around, and the soaking bikini she wore did nothing to help. She wasn't sure how Cole was managing to keep his dripping wet shirt on, as cold as it had to be.

"It's the truth. And I told you I wanted a pause; it's not my fault you wouldn't give me one."

"You couldn't just hold it like a normal person?"

"Have you tried holding it in cold water? It's not easy!"

"That doesn't mean a grown man should just let it out when he's less than a foot from someone!" she growled and started marching up the dock.

"Where are you going?" Cole asked, following close behind her.

She grabbed her clothes from the hood of her truck, not bothering to look at him. "I'm going home to take a very hot shower and wash off whatever *unmentionables* I'm currently covered in."

He grabbed Logan by the arm and started dragging her to the passenger side of the still-running Bronco. "Your truck won't heat up fast enough before you get sick." He pulled the door open for her. "Get in."

She wanted to argue, but then the hot air from inside the Bronco hit her. She jumped into the seat, and Cole slammed the door behind her. He raced around the front, grabbed his clothes, shoes, and her boots from the truck, then hopped into the driver's side. His shirt and boxers were clinging to him, and Logan could only imagine how she looked in her very cold and wet bikini.

She shoved her hands up to the air vents and rubbed them together in the blasting heat. Cole turned to pull something out of the back behind their seats. Soon, she was covered by a large, warm wool blanket. She let out a sigh and wrapped it around her, snuggling into it.

Cole pulled out another blanket for himself. Next, he grabbed two thermoses and handed one to Logan. "Coffee," he said when she just stared at him. "To get us warm."

She opened it, hesitating only a little at the thought that it might be a prank. It wouldn't be the first time he'd offered her a sullied drink.

"Why do you have all this stuff?" she asked. She doubted that he just happened to carry two warm blankets and two thermoses full of hot coffee with him all the time.

"I had a feeling we'd need it," he said, separating her clothes from his on the seat between them.

And he'd left the Bronco running the whole time, making sure it would be nice and toasty for them. "You knew what the challenge was?"

"I didn't know for sure, though the thought did cross my mind."

She pulled the blanket even tighter around her. "How did you know?"

"There are only so many possibilities when you tell me to meet you at the dock in the middle of the night."

"Then why didn't you wear a bathing suit or something that would keep you warm?" Almost anything had to be better than thin, cotton boxers.

"And ruin your obvious attempt to see me in my underwear? I'm not heartless," he said with a wink before he handed Logan her jeans and T-shirt. "You need to change and get out of your wet suit."

She stared at him. She knew he was right, but there was no way she was changing in front of him.

So instead, she pulled the blanket even tighter around her and crawled into the open space in the back. She had to shove a few things aside—a fishing pole, a toolbox, a paint-ball gun.

"Seriously." She snorted, unable to stop herself. "Aren't you a little old for paintball?"

"Paintball is a man's sport. And the fact that you don't know that makes it pretty clear you've never played before."

It was true, she hadn't. Not that she'd give him the satis-faction of confirming it. "Whatever." Despite the objects in the back, there seemed to be enough space for her to change comfortably, as long as someone kept his eyes to himself.

"No peeking," she muttered, leaning over the seat and twisting his rearview mirror to the side so he couldn't see.

"Nothing I haven't seen before," he reminded her. And there it was. The first reference to what happened the night of the big farewell bonfire.

"But something you will never see again." She lay down in the back, trying to stay covered and out of sight as she struggled to get out of her bikini and into her jeans and sweater. Getting dressed in the back of Cole Tucker's Bronco while he sat a foot away in the front seat—just one more to add to the long list of things she would never tell Jacob.

Unfortunately, she hadn't thought ahead enough to bring a bra or pair of underwear, which only made the situation worse.

When she was finally clothed, she grabbed the blanket

and crawled back into the front seat where her coffee thermos awaited her. She took a long sip once it was open, looking over at Cole. He'd changed clothes, too. His wet boxers and shirt sat on the seat between them.

Logan picked them up carefully between her thumb and forefinger and threw them into the back.

Minutes passed in silence as they allowed the heat of the truck to warm them up. The radio was playing some of the country songs they'd grown up listening to.

"I should go home," Logan finally said when Dierks Bentley's "Feel that Fire" ended. She'd finished her coffee, finally feeling warm enough to get out of Cole's truck and into her own. She grabbed her boots from the floor in front of her and started putting them on.

"Too bad," Cole said. "I was thinking we could go down to Wade's and you could buy me a drink in honor of my win today."

Logan shook her head. "I wasn't kidding when I said I was done with all that. I may have slipped up the other night, but that can't happen again." The further she fell back into her old ways, the harder it would be for her to crawl back out when she needed to.

"It's just one beer, Lo."

"No, it's one beer *with you*. And we both know that one beer with you will turn into another and another until one or both of us is wasted." She pulled her jacket on over her shirt. "Being drunk or making a bet seems to be the only way we can stand to be in the same room." It was certainly the case for her.

"We're sober right now."

"Yes," she said patiently, "but we also just jumped into the freezing cold lake to see who could stay in the longest. We're not the types to just go to the bar and kick back one beer together. We're not friends, Cole. Maybe we were at some point, but not now. Not anymore." Not after that night.

Logan opened the door beside her and climbed out with her wet bikini in hand, leaving the blanket and the thermos behind.

"Well, I'll be at Wade's anyway since I have to tell Lilly to add a letter to your name," he said through his now open window. "Swing by if you change your mind."

"I won't." Logan climbed up into her truck. As soon as it started, she watched Cole slowly turn the Bronco around and drive up the narrow gravel drive that led back to the park's main entrance.

Why had she let herself get into this? There was a reason she'd avoided this town while she was gone, and now all her hard work was unraveling. This competitive drive she had around Cole was not good for her, and the sooner she grew up and ended it the better.

She could always refuse to humor him and his challenges. But knowing him, he'd consider her refusal to play as a forfeit. That left her with only one option.

Winning.

As soon as she won the challenges, she could be done with Cole, and he would never bother her again.

Just a few months. After that, she'd be free and clear of this town and Cole Tucker. She'd finally get to be the girl Jacob needed her to be.

And she'd be happy.

September—Junior Year

COLE STOOD AT the workbench inside the otherwise empty barn, holding the rod of a branding iron in one hand and a propane torch in the other. Old Man Carithers's signature C glowed bright red at the end. His grip tightened on the rod as he cut off the torch. He waved the iron around the open space above the workbench, watching the trail of red it left in its wake.

"Cole Tucker!"

He jumped, the red-hot iron slipping from his hand and, thankfully, onto the barn's cement floor.

"Jesus, Kase!" he yelled as he bent down to pick the iron rod up by the middle. "Don't you know not to scare a guy holding a hot iron? I could have burned myself."

He turned to find her standing in the open doorway, hands clenched into fists. Her hair was a mess, and her eyes were wild and fiery as her chest rose and fell rapidly. She looked like a Valkyrie or one of those fierce Amazons they'd learned about when covering mythology in middle school. Beautiful and pissed.

"You'll wish you had when I'm done with you," she growled, stomping over to him and shoving him hard in the shoulder.

"Take it easy." He set the iron down on the workbench behind him and turned back to her.

She shoved him again. "Don't you tell me to take it easy! Where is it?"

Cole wiped his sweaty forehead on his arm. "Where's what?"

"You know damn well what. The note. The one Carly and I were writing in Spanish. I know you have it, so just give it back!"

His head tilted. "Now why would I go and do that?"

"That note has personal information you have no right reading!"

He bent down, shoving his face close to hers as the corner of his mouth curved upward. "You mean you didn't leave it there on the floor just for me to find? I wish I'd known that before I read all about your little crush on the new kid."

She gasped. "I knew it! You just couldn't mind your own damn business, could you? How many people have you told?"

He gritted his teeth. "You really think I'd do something

like that?" On the contrary, the last thing he wanted to do was tell the whole school Logan had a crush on Ryan Baker. Ryan was a spoiled rich kid who was used to getting whatever he wanted. He wasn't right for Lo, and he sure as hell wasn't good enough.

"I know exactly what kind of guy you are, Cole Tucker. I bet you've already told half the school by now."

"Not sure why I'd need to. Anybody could tell you like him the way you're fawning over him all the time."

"I am not!" Her scream echoed through the barn. "Just give it back!"

He stood tall, his arm reaching back behind him. If she wanted a reason to be angry with him, he'd give her one. "Fine, you want it so bad?" he asked, pulling a small, folded piece of paper from his back pocket. "Take it."

He lifted his hand overhead. Logan rose on her tiptoes trying to reach it, but it was too high. She punched him again. "I mean it, Cole Tucker. Hand it over or I will kill you with my bare hands." He held the note higher, and she tried to jump for it.

He lowered his arm and held out the note to one side and to the other, then back again.

Logan continued grabbing at it as he proceeded to pull it away at the last possible second, leaving her hands clutching nothing but air.

"You're going to have to do better than that," he taunted.

He held the note behind his back, and she lunged forward. He turned to the side just as she tried to reach around him. She lost her balance and stumbled into the workbench behind him.

A piercing scream sent painful tremors up his spine and straight to his heart.

"Logan!"

The smell of burning cotton and flesh singed his lungs. He reached for her, the folded paper he'd been holding forgotten as it fell to the floor.

Chapter Ten

I T WAS AMAZING how easily time seemed to stand still in Willow Creek. And even more how everyone supported each other, whether friend, family, or neighbor, because that was what people did in this town. Like one impressively large family. Logan hadn't realized until now just how much she'd missed that.

She'd just left Macy's Market with a bag full of groceries for her momma. Following the sidewalk back to her truck, she took her time as she gazed through the storefront windows of the dozen or so shops and boutiques that still looked the same as when she left.

Even Tucker's Hardware Store, from what she could tell staring at it from across the street. Logan hadn't been inside it since eighth grade, but it boasted the same display of tool kits and power drills and the like as if she hadn't been gone the last four years.

At one familiar green door, she stopped. She'd been wrong. This one had changed drastically for the worse. The large window to the right was dirty but still proudly carried the name Willow Creek Art Gallery in black, elegant lettering. The lights were off and the space inside was empty. On the door was a sign that read Out of Business.

It broke Logan's heart to see it like this, the one place that had felt like her home away from home. She'd spent most afternoons here after school, much to her mother's pleasure, since she'd hoped it would keep her wild girl out of trouble.

That November in her senior year when Ms. Snyder told her she was packing up and moving to Maryland, Logan had lost more than her after-school sanctuary. She'd lost a very dear friend. Logan had kept in touch for a while, but when she left Willow Creek, she left just about everything that reminded her of it behind, too. Including contact with Ms. Snyder.

When she reached her truck, Logan threw the small bag of groceries her mom asked her to pick up into the passenger seat. Just as she was about to place the key in the ignition, her phone beeped in her pocket, alerting her to a new message.

She pulled it out and glanced at the screen. A text from Cole. It was Saturday, more than a week since she'd last heard from him that night at the dock.

Logan tapped the screen to open the message.

Fairfield Woods 1 hr.

Logan sighed, her head dropping back against the headrest. The last thing she needed right now was one of his challenges. Carly was getting back to town today. Logan was supposed to meet her and Jacob for dinner tonight, and she really needed to go home, shower, and get her hair and makeup ready. And she still had no clue what she was going to wear.

Can it wait a day? Almost immediately, her phone beeped again.

Forfeit? That H will look a lot better with an O next to it.

Logan groaned. She had no choice, really. She could either do this and win or condemn her relationship with Jacob and ruin any chance she had of proving to her mother that she could be the daughter she always wanted.

She glanced at her watch. There were still a few hours before she absolutely had to get home and start getting ready. Fine, she would do this. But only because it was for the greater good. As soon as she won this challenge, she would be one step closer to besting Cole Tucker once and for all.

Logan tapped on her phone, her competitive fire already starting to flare up inside her.

Fine. 1 hour.

SHE WAS MORE than a little concerned when she saw that not only was Cole's truck not parked on the outskirts of the thickly wooded area where she was told to meet him but that there were at least ten other vehicles that she didn't recognize. She pulled off onto the side of the road and across the grass to park by the extensive line of trucks, cars, and Jeeps.

A crowd of men gathered just at the edge of the woods, all wearing head-to-toe camouflage.

What had she gotten herself into now?

Logan ignored the pit in her stomach as she approached. She recognized most, if not all, of the men standing around chatting in front of her.

She grinned when the big guy in the middle turned to face her.

"'Bout time, Lo," Cowboy said, cutting through the crowd and giving her a giant bear hug. "We've been waiting for you."

"I didn't know you would be here," she said as she hugged him back. She pulled away only to find several others from her high school class lining up to hug her and ask how she'd been—Roy Finnick, Justin Fisher, and even Levi Rossetti. They all looked just about the same as they had four years ago, give or take a few pounds.

She recognized a few others who'd graduated in the years before and after her. It was hard to come across a stranger in a small town like Willow Creek, and they all seemed to have stayed updated on her while she'd lived in Texas, thanks to her mom and dad and the town gossips, she was sure.

"Where's Cole?" she asked once the catching up came to an end.

"He's marking off the boundary lines with flags," said Wilson Oliver, one of Cole's firefighter buddies he'd abandoned at the bar two weeks ago. "Should be back any minute."

"Cole says you're gearing up with us," Justin Fisher said in his Southern drawl, though it came out more like a question.

"Um...I guess so." She had no idea what he was talking about.

He nodded, a grin lifting his freckled cheeks. "Cool. We've never played with a chick before. This should be fun."

Logan turned to Cowboy, still close by her side. His white-blond hair was hidden beneath a camo Bass Pro Shop hat instead of his usual black UGA cap. "Play?"

Cowboy's eyes narrowed. "Cole didn't tell you?"

She started to shake her head when several of the guys' attention turned to the Bronco pulling onto the grass near them. Seconds later, Cole Tucker stepped out in full-body camo, his eyes landing on Logan.

"I see our guest of honor is here." He reached back into his truck to pull something out and then tossed it straight at Logan, who caught it easily enough. It took her only a moment's examination to realize it was a rather large camouflage shirt. "You ready to see what kind of shot you are?"

"Are we going hunting?" she asked slowly. Some of the guys chuckled.

"Let's gear up," Cole called out. Everyone turned on the spot, heading to their trucks or cars. Cowboy was now at the back of the Bronco, shifting around boxes and tools and fishing rods as he looked for something specific. "Here," Cole said as he placed a large gun in her hand.

Not a real gun, she realized. A paintball gun.

She rolled her eyes. "You made me come down here to play paintball with you?"

"You said you've never played before, so I thought we could change that. And if we knock another challenge out of the way while we do it, all the better."

"But I don't know how to play. I don't even know any of the rules."

He took her hands in his and held the gun up for her, moving her right hand and index finger into place. "The only thing you need to know how to do is pull the trigger." He dropped his hands from her gun, turning to grab his own out of his seat in the Bronco.

"As for the rules," he said, turning back to her, "we usually play teams. Blue versus red." He indicated the red band now wrapped around Roy Finnick's upper arm.

She stared at Cole. Did that seriously mean the only difference between shooting the enemy and one of their own guys was that small strip of color?

He grinned. "Don't worry. Since this is your first time, we'll have some special rules in place for you."

"What kind of rules?" she asked. She didn't like the idea of special treatment, but she also knew how intense most of these guys could get when it came to their sports. She did not feel comfortable being thrown headfirst into a game she'd never played with them. Especially when she really needed to win this challenge.

"You are free to shoot whoever you want, red or blue team, but they're not allowed to shoot you."

"They're okay with that? Doesn't seem fair."

Cole shrugged. "We all agreed it would add an interesting twist to the game. You're the wild card. It'll keep us on our toes. And if you manage to hit anyone, they're out."

Logan liked the sound of that. Wild card. Maybe that would be her official paintball name. Not that she was ever playing again after today. This was purely for her and Jacob's relationship.

"What about you?" she asked Cole. "Can you shoot just anybody?"

He chuckled. "Trust me, that wouldn't be fair for the other guys. No, the only person I can shoot is you. And you are the only one who can shoot me. The first one of us to get a clean shot at the other wins."

"Okay," Logan said, rolling her tense shoulders. "That doesn't sound so bad."

"Glad you think so." He pointed to the large shirt she'd tucked under her arm. "Go ahead and put that on. Otherwise, you'll just be an easy target."

She glanced down at her bright yellow shirt and frowned. They would see her coming from a mile away in this thing, not to mention she really didn't want to get paint all over it. She placed her gun on the hood of the Bronco before pulling the yellow shirt up over her head, leaving behind her thin white camisole. There were a few playful whistles behind her, but Logan ignored them as she unrolled the camo shirt and pulled it on over her head.

Fortunately, this shirt would do a lot better job of hiding her in the woods. Unfortunately, the thing swallowed her whole. It had to be one of Cole's. It smelled like him—which, even she had to admit, could have been worse—and the sleeves and hem fell several inches past her hands and hips.

Cole took the end of one of those sleeves in hand and started rolling it up to her wrist. Then he did the same with the other. "We all get a few minutes to scatter through the woods, but when you hear the horn, that means it's time to move your ass. They'll start coming at you quick if you're not careful."

Logan's eyes shot up to meet his. "I thought you said they couldn't shoot me."

"They're not supposed to, but it can get pretty confusing out there once we get going. Things happen. But don't worry. Only my shot will count against you."

She didn't like the sound of that. "Where's the gear?" she said, looking around them. She didn't see anyone pulling out pads or protective equipment, and some of the guys were already running out into the thick trees. "Don't you guys wear vests and stuff?" she asked hopefully.

He shook his head. "We're men, Lo. We don't wear that

stuff."

"I'm not a man, and I want a vest. Or at least some goggles."

Cole's eyebrow rose. "Are you telling me you're scared of a little paintball?"

"No," she said, turning her nose up. "But I'd prefer not to go to the emergency room when you accidentally shoot me in the eye." She also didn't feel like having large red welts all over her skin when she met Jacob for dinner tonight.

"I won't shoot you in the eye," he muttered. He turned around and pulled something else out of his seat in the Bronco and then turned to hand it to her. "You can wear the goggles, but that's it."

She quickly shoved on the protective eyewear that looked more like clear sunglasses. She looked like a dork, but it was better than showing up to dinner with an eye patch.

"Wait a few seconds and then start running. And remember, as soon as the horn blows it's hit or be hit," he told her.

He took off at an angle through the trees, gun in hand, and soon disappeared.

Logan sucked in a deep breath then took off with her gun in the opposite direction of Cole, heading deep into the woods.

Chapter Eleven

"NOT BAD, LOGAN." Levi rubbed the spot on his shoulder that was now covered in white paint. "Looks like you may be a natural."

She had to agree. Especially when she'd already taken out three other guys. Granted, it had mostly been due to her good luck, but their paint-splattered shirts didn't lie.

"You sure you've never played paintball before? You're too good a shot to be new at this," Wilson said offhandedly, studying the white paint on his red armband where she'd shot him only seconds after hitting Levi.

Logan nodded innocently. It was true she'd never played paintball. But she had held a gun before and shot them on several occasions. Her dad was the chief of police, after all. It wasn't like he was going to let his daughter grow up without knowing how to protect herself. It had been a long time, though, and Logan had forgotten the adrenaline rush that came with pulling a loaded trigger.

"Look," Levi said quietly. "I saw Cole wandering not too far from here, so keep your guard up. Don't tell him," he said with a grin, "but I'm betting on you."

"Thanks," she said as he and Wilson turned to head back through the woods. She wasn't sure what he meant by betting on her, but she took his advice seriously all the same.

She made her way deliberately through the trees for several minutes. Her eye was on the ultimate prize now. If Cole Tucker really was close by, she was going nail his ass and show him just who he was messing with.

The leaves rustled behind her, and Logan turned on the spot, gun raised in the air as she pointed it directly at the noisemaker.

The squirrel sat frozen on the ground in front of her, staring up at her with wide, beady eyes. She let out the breath she'd been holding, lowering her weapon and pushing forward.

As much as she hated to admit it, Cole had been right. Not only was paintball kind of fun, but it was a lot more stressful than she'd expected.

Logan stilled, her eyes darting to a large fallen tree a good ten feet off to her side. It didn't seem large enough to hide an entire person, and she wouldn't have thought much of it if she hadn't just heard something thumping directly behind it.

Logan took slow, careful steps toward the fallen tree, glancing in all directions for any oncoming assaults. When all was clear and she was close enough to the tree, she took a running leap over it, aiming several shots at the other side of the large tree trunk.

She only stopped when she realized her paintballs had hit

nothing but tree bark and dirt. But she swore she heard—

A loud pop and something small and painful rammed into Logan's side. She hissed, glaring down at the large white paint spot just above her left hipbone. The skin underneath was already starting to sting.

"Dammit!" she cried just as Cole Tucker landed with a heavy thud on the ground in front of a tree only a few feet away.

"Oh, Logan, haven't you seen enough movies to know not to fall for that one?"

Clearly, she hadn't.

Cole chuckled. "Too bad. I was kind of hoping you'd at least give me a run for my money. It almost feels like it was too easy."

Logan didn't say anything as she dropped her gun on the ground and lifted her shirt and camisole to see the damage. Just as she expected, the skin just above her hip already looked red and swollen.

Cole came closer, and Logan flinched when he raised his hand to her injured side. But instead of touching the welt, his thumb lightly traced the crescent-shaped white scar a good inch below it.

She looked up and found Cole only inches away now. He didn't meet her gaze, his eyes busy studying the roughly healed skin beneath his thumb.

"Christ," he said with a forced laugh. "I remember that one like it was yesterday."

"Trust me, so do I." She'd never told anyone the story of her scar or the day she'd been stupid enough to fall onto a red-hot branding iron.

"I still feel awful about what happened," he said.

Cole had always been a jackass, but occasionally he'd let a different side of himself show, leaving her with no idea whether she should hug him or smack him to make him snap out of it. He clearly hadn't lost his touch.

"You have no idea how terrified I was, seeing you hurt like that." His voice sounded normal and unaffected, but his eyes told her how badly it still haunted him. "I called the police station to let your dad know I was bringing you to the hospital. And when he saw me carry you into the ER, I thought he was going to murder me right there."

Cole's thumb brushed it again, and Logan closed her eyes as she tried not to show him how good his touch felt on the sensitive patch of skin.

"You're lucky I didn't tell him what really happened. Even if it was just an accident, he would have kicked your ass," she said, opening her eyes again in time to see him smile.

Cole's eyes shifted up to hers. "All those times, and you never ratted me out. Why?"

She shrugged. "Not really my style." There was a short, awkward silence, Cole's hand still on her hip as he stood what *should* have been too close for her to be comfortable.

She was about to say something—what that was she

didn't know—when Cole moved his hand from her scar and lightly flicked the tender welt where the paintball had maimed her.

"Ow, asshole!" she hissed, shoving him away.

He chuckled. "Only three more letters and you're toast. I'm pretty sure that makes us tied now."

Logan's glare hardened as she picked up her gun and aimed it at the center of Cole's chest, shooting him point-blank.

"Jesus!" he yelled, taking several steps back and holding his hands up as a shield. "What was that for?"

Aside from confusing the hell out of her?

"Now we're even," she said sharply, throwing her gun back down.

Cole laughed as she pulled her phone from her back pocket to check the time. Great. She had a voice mail from Carly. She'd completely forgotten in all the chaos that she was supposed to be meeting Jacob and her for dinner soon.

"Shit." She listened while she mentally calculated how long it would take her to get home, showered, and ready to go.

"Hey, it's Carly. We just got off the plane and we're exhausted, but we cannot wait to see you and Jacob at dinner tonight. We have so much to—"

Logan cut the message short and shoved her phone back in her pants pocket. She said nothing as she turned in the direction Levi and Wilson had gone and started walking.

"Where are you going?" Cole called after her. She could hear him running up behind her, and a quick glance revealed he'd grabbed the gun she'd left, along with his own.

"I'm supposed to have dinner with Carly tonight, and I'm going to be late."

"That's right, they were getting back in today." Logan gave him a side-eyed glance. How did he know when they were coming back? "What? We keep in touch."

"Since when?"

"Me and Carly are practically best pals now," he teased. "Is it just you two girls?"

Logan hesitated. "More like a double date."

"Oh yeah? Word around town is that your boyfriend hasn't been back to see you since he got called away to work. Got something special planned? Two weeks seems like a long time without any action."

Logan shook her head. "Don't see how that's your business."

"That's a yes." His steps fell behind. "Probably shouldn't let it get too heated, though. I'd hate for him to see the giant bruise on your ass and get the wrong idea."

"What bruise on my—" There was a loud pop again, and Logan stopped in her tracks as a painful, stinging sensation started to spread across her right cheek.

Oh, he really was an asshole.

Cole was bent over in hysterical laughter a foot behind her. Instead of looking back at him or the large spot of paint she knew had just ruined her jeans, Logan held her head high and walked away with silent dignity as she fought the urge to rub her pained bottom.

>>><<<

April—Junior Year

COLE'S LEG BOUNCED as he watched the second hand slowly tick. His history teacher, Mr. Hill, sat with his feet kicked up on his desk while reading a political magazine. He didn't seem to care that his students were whispering to each other instead of reading the pages he'd just assigned.

But Cole didn't need to listen to know what they were all talking about. He'd heard plenty already. Still, he couldn't completely block out the chatter surrounding him, low voices muttering the words *Ryan Baker* and *Logan* and *prom night*. Cole's hands clenched tighter.

He'd been in class all of twenty minutes before the news spread to him. Ryan took Lo's virginity after prom Saturday night. He'd rented a swanky hotel room with minibar and in-room Jacuzzi and everything to mark the special occasion.

He hadn't even finished getting dressed before he dumped her.

Cole stared at the ticking clock, every muscle in his body rigid. Christ, he couldn't imagine how Lo must have felt. He didn't want to. He was too focused on his rage.

The bell rang, and Cole was the first one out of his seat.

He stormed out of the room and started scanning the halls. He made it ten steps before a hand clamped his arm and pulled him to the side.

Cowboy stared down at him with tight lips, his shaggy blond head only an inch or two taller. "So you've heard." He sighed, his hand still on Cole's arm. "Who'm I kidding? You'd have to be deaf not to. He's been bragging about it to half the guys in school."

Cole's hands balled into fists.

Cowboy's hand moved to Cole's shoulder. "What do you want to do?"

"I want to beat him within an inch of his life, make him bleed until there's almost nothing left in him."

Cowboy's brow softened and his lips relaxed. He'd never told Cowboy just how much Logan meant to him, partly because he wasn't certain himself. But the way Cowboy looked at him, he had to at least suspect Cole's feelings were more than he'd been letting on over the years.

"Whatever you need to do, brother, I've got your back."

There was really no question why Cowboy was his best friend.

Cole led the way to the small quad where he knew Ryan and his friends usually spent their lunch period, Cowboy close on his heels. Together they threw open the doors leading to the outside area. He searched for Ryan but instead saw Logan and Carly with Harper Maddox, the introverted blonde who was currently the top of their class. He headed straight for them.

Carly grabbed Lo's arm. "Let's just go."

Logan turned and bumped right into Cole's chest. She stumbled back, and he reached out with two hands to steady her. She looked up at him through flooded eyes.

She blinked and the tears fell. Cole's thumbs rose to her cheeks and wiped the streaks away. She stared at him with wide eyes.

"Where is he?" he gritted out.

Her forehead creased. "Who?"

A bark of familiar laughter from the far side of the quad made Logan's shoulders tense, and other voices joined in. Cole shot past her in an instant. The crowd cleared a path for him as he approached, Cowboy following behind him.

Ryan's grin vanished the second his eyes met Cole's, and he raised his arms between them like the little chickenshit he was. "Look, man—"

Cole's fist shot out and connected with Ryan's nose with a satisfying crunch. Ryan stumbled back, and Cole was on top of him, his fist ramming into the guy's face over and over. Blood roared in his ears, nearly drowning out the sound of Ryan's screams. Pain lanced through his knuckles and hand, but he ignored it as adrenaline surged through him.

Voices shouted around him, but only one cut through to his senses. "Cole, stop!"

With a strength even he didn't know he had, Cole raised

his bloody fist and backed away. Logan was standing beside Cowboy, her breaths coming almost as quickly as his.

Vice Principal Hardwick cut through the crowd that had surrounded them and grabbed Cole by the arm.

Cole refused to meet Logan's eyes—he didn't want to know what he'd see there—and said nothing as Hardwick led him away from the crowd and down to his office.

Chapter Twelve

"I'M SORRY I'M so late."

Jacob stood from his chair, took Logan's coat, and gave her a quick kiss. "That's okay. We've had a lot to catch up on since they last came out to Austin, and Carly's been telling me all about Cancun."

Logan turned to Carly with her biggest, brightest smile.

"How's my favorite bridesmaid?" Carly asked as she wrapped her arms around her.

"Not as good as you seem to be." Logan squeezed her tightly before she stepped back and got a good look at her. Her hair was a darker shade of blond than she was used to, and her bronze skin glowed against her white dress. Though that was probably thanks to the Mexican beach she just got back from.

But more than anything, Carly radiated pure joy. "I can't believe you're getting married in six weeks!" Logan said.

"I know!" she squealed. "It came so fast." Behind her stood the man who had made Logan's best friend the happiest she'd ever been.

"Darren." Logan held out her arms.

His grin was just as big as hers. "Hey, Lo." He accepted her hug, holding her tight and even lifting her off the ground. It was hard to believe this was the same awkward kid who'd had a massive crush on Carly for years in high school. Sure, he still had the same red hair, freckles, and impressively fit body, but back then he'd been so shy around girls. Especially Carly.

He could hardly even get the courage to talk to her. But after he heard they'd both be going to OFTC, he'd somehow worked up the nerve to suggest they carpool to the campus. A few weeks later he'd managed to ask her out on a date. And now, after almost four years with Carly, he was one of the happiest, most outgoing men Logan knew.

It was like finally getting the girl of his dreams was all the confidence he'd needed.

Once the hugs were over, the four of them sat down at their table—Logan trying her best not to wince at the sharp pain on her right butt cheek—while Carly and Darren finished telling Jacob about their beach trip.

"So, Darren, how has work been?" Logan asked.

"It's really good. We've been so busy this past year, I was lucky to get the last two weeks off, especially with the honeymoon on top of that. But I think my dad is just happy his best employee is sticking around town for a while." According to Carly, Darren had become Willow Creek's top mechanic, and people from towns over came to Whitehead's Auto Repair to get their cars serviced by him.

"That reminds me," he said to Jacob, his eyes lighting up. "I've got that '70 Chevelle we've been talking about out in the parking lot."

Jacob smiled. "Could we go take a look right now?"

Since when did the two of them talk about cars?

Both guys looked to their fiancées, eyes pleading.

"I don't mind," Carly said, glancing at Logan. "It'll give us some time for girl talk."

Darren kissed her cheek. "Thanks, honey. We'll be right back." With that, he and Jacob both stood, talking animatedly about horsepower and torque.

How had she not known Jacob was into cars? She was going to marry the guy, for crying out loud. How much else did she still not know about him?

"Ow!" Logan yelled, her left hand jumping to her arm where Carly had just pinched her. "What was that for?"

"What the hell is wrong with you?" Carly whisper-shouted, though it sounded more like genuine curiosity than anger.

"Me? You're the one going around pinching people for no reason."

"Look me in the eye and tell me you were not late for dinner because you've been playing paintball with Cole Tucker."

"What?" She eyed her best friend skeptically while simultaneously trying her damnedest not to rub the sensitive welt on her ass. "How could you possibly know about that?"

Carly rolled her eyes. "Well, for starters, I know for a fact that Cole's monthly game of paintball with the boys was today because Darren has been playing with them for the last year but couldn't go today because of the trip. And second," she added with a laugh, pointing at Logan, "you've got red paint behind your ear."

Logan's hand automatically went to her ear. After Cole shot her, she'd passed Cowboy on the way to her truck and was forced to give him a hug. His shirt had been covered in red paint from, she assumed, being taken out *Platoon* style during the game. The camo shirt Cole lent her had been covered in red paint, and she'd clearly failed to get it all off her neck in the shower.

"I wasn't off the plane even five minutes when Lyssa called me saying you and Cole have been at it again," she went on.

Logan scowled at Carly's sister's gossip. "Look, it's not as bad as it sounds. It's just a bet to see who can win the most challenges. If I win, he has to leave me and Jacob alone. You should have seen him the night he met Jacob, going on about the tattoo parlor and Aunt Caroline."

"Uh-huh," Carly said. "And what does he get if you lose, Logan?"

"I—" She hesitated, her voice lowering considerably. "If he wins, I have to tell Jacob about the tattoo."

"Oh, shit." Carly's hand jumped to cover her mouth. She closed her eyes. "Why in hell would you agree to something like that?"

"I may have already been drunk when we made that bet. But it doesn't matter because I'm beating him…or at least I was. Technically, we tied after the paintball game. But it's okay because I get to pick the next challenge, and I'll make sure it's one I win. Cole Tucker is going down. And then he'll finally leave me alone." Logan couldn't help the grin on her face that popped up anytime she thought about beating him.

Carly glared until Logan began to squirm. Then her friend's face transformed. She looked more like a doctor preparing to tell her she only had months to live. "I can't believe you're still doing this to him."

"Doing what?" Logan asked. The last she checked, Cole was the one trying to ruin her life.

"Dragging him along like this. It's not fair to him, Lo," she said gently.

"What do you mean, *not fair to him?* I'm not dragging anybody along."

Carly's head tilted. "Are you trying to tell me that you still don't see how crazy he is about you?"

Logan's mouth fell open. Carly had to be joking. "Crazy about me? We hate each other!"

"God, you're so blind. How can we all see it but you?" she asked. "He's had a crush on you for over ten years, Logan. Everyone knows that."

"No, he's been making me miserable for ten years, ever

since he fell trying to get my backpack out of that stupid tree. That doesn't mean he likes me."

"He was trying to get your attention."

Logan shook her head. "What about when he pantsed me in eighth grade right in the middle of PE? Is that how guys treat girls they like?"

Carly sighed patiently. "In eighth grade, yes. Boys are idiots until they grow out of it."

"Except that Cole kept pulling stuff like that 'til senior year."

"Well, Cole was a bigger idiot than most. But he was also crazy protective of you. No one would even try to mess with you because they were afraid of what he'd do. Why else do you think he attacked Ryan Baker after the prom?"

"Prom was just an excuse. He hated Ryan long before that."

"Because he was dating *you*. Look, I know you don't want to hear this, but take it easy on Cole. He's a nice guy, and I rooted for you two for a long time. If you really don't care about him like that, then cut ties and let him move on. But…"

"But?"

"But—and I say this with only love in my heart—if the reason you can't stay away from him is that you really do like him, you should probably take some time to figure out what you want before you walk down the aisle to the wrong man."

Logan sucked in a sharp breath. "The wrong man? You

think Jacob's the wrong man?"

Carly's lips parted, her eyes growing wider. "Hold on a minute. That's not what I meant."

"I thought you liked Jacob." What was happening? This was not how dinner with her best friend was supposed to go tonight.

"I *do* like Jacob. I mean, he can come off a bit self-centered sometimes and maybe a tad condescending, but he's a nice guy, and you like who you are around him. I like him because you like him, and you were pretty certain that he was the one you wanted."

"Then why did you say you'd rather I be with Cole— who, by the way, doesn't even see me like that." That much she knew for certain.

"That's not what I said." Carly reached for Logan's hand. "I just want you to be with the person who makes you happy," she explained. "No matter who it is. I admit, there was a time when I thought that person would be Cole. I knew how much he cared about you. Everyone did. The only person who needed to see it was you."

Logan shook her head. No way they were having this conversation when her fiancé was standing just outside the restaurant. "If you thought Cole liked me and was so great for me, why are you only just now telling me?"

Carly shrugged. "I guess I thought that you'd figure it out when you were ready, that it would be because you felt the same way about him. The night of the bonfire, I assumed everything that happened was because you realized he had feelings for you and maybe you'd realized you felt it, too. But then you left town and never came back."

"What happened that night was not because Cole had feelings for me."

"How can you know that? You said you barely even remembered what happened."

"Well, I lied." She remembered the events of that night and the next morning all too well, and she had no plans to rehash the details now. "Trust me, he'd made it perfectly clear what happened that night. We both got drunk and made a stupid decision, one I will regret for the rest of my life. But that's all it was," she said pointedly. "And as soon as this bet is over, I am marrying Jacob because he makes me happy, and he is the one I want to be with."

Logan was breathing quickly, and she refused to say anything more until she was sure that Carly believed her. Carly was silent for a moment before she finally nodded, her voice quiet and firm as she said, "Okay."

Chapter Thirteen

LOGAN AND JACOB waved as Darren and Carly drove away from the parking lot. All through dinner, Logan had tried to pretend that the argument between her and Carly had never happened. That was the good thing about best friends. Usually, they could fight one minute and be totally normal the next.

But this time was different. For the first time that Logan could remember, she found herself unable to let their argument go.

"I meant what I said," Carly whispered as she hugged Logan goodbye. "I love you, and I'm here for you, no matter what happens. I just want you to be happy."

Logan had hugged her back stiffly but said nothing in reply and, eventually, Carly released her and made her way to the Chevelle with Darren. Even as they drove away, Logan was still grinding her teeth.

What she needed was someone to take her mind off it. She turned to Jacob, wrapping her arms around his neck as she pulled him in for a slow, seductive kiss.

"What do you think about getting a hotel room here for

the night?" Her voice was low and husky. "We could finally spend some quality time together, just you and me"—she kissed him again—"and a bed."

He grinned. "That sounds perfect," he said, and Logan felt her worry easing already. She needed him desperately, needed to feel his skin on hers. Needed him to prove what she already knew, that he was the right man for her, that she'd made the right choice.

"Unfortunately, I have to get up early tomorrow for this shift I took on."

"Another shift," she groaned, pulling out of Jacob's arms. "All you do is take on more work. And you and I never get time to spend with each other."

He shook his head. "I know. But think how good all this overtime is going to look to the head of emergency over in San Francisco. When they see how much I'm willing to take on, they'll be desperate to hire me. Then as soon as they do, we can have all the time together we want."

"It's been months, Jacob," she said quietly. She placed a hand on her forehead, hardly believing they were having this conversation in a parking lot.

"I know, babe. But I can't tonight. Next time we're to-gether, I promise. We'll do dinner with your parents, and then the two of us can get a nice suite a few towns over." He slowly took her in his arms, kissing her forehead gently. "Somewhere really special."

"But I want you now," she whined, not caring how awful

it made her sound. Was it too much to ask to be with the man she was going to marry, as in actually *be* with him? "We could do it in the car."

"You're joking, right? You wouldn't really make love to someone in a car in the middle of a parking lot, would you?"

Yes. "Of course not. I'm just messing with you," she said, forcing a smile. "I've just really missed you these two weeks, is all."

"I know, and I'm sorry." He pulled away from her one last time, kissing her chastely on the lips before he opened the door to his Lexus. "I'll call you tomorrow," he said. "I love you."

"I love you, too," she said quietly, not bothering to hide how miserable she felt. She wanted him to feel guilty for not giving her the relief and assurance she really needed right then.

Jacob closed the door and started the car, backing out of his spot and pulling out onto the road. Logan just stood there, watching him go.

A drink. That was what she needed right now. As Logan made her way to the truck at the back of the parking lot, her mind was already made up. She would stop at Wade's tonight on her way home.

Just one beer.

But as she drove, Logan rethought her plan. What if Cole was there when she got to the bar? She'd already admitted to him that they would never be one-drink people when they were together. They'd drink and drink until one of them came up with a bet or challenge and the other would automatically accept it.

Then they'd both do something stupid like in tenth grade when they woke up hungover in the middle of Mrs. Garrett's yard after spending the night cleverly cutting dirty words out of the brand-new sod for all the neighbors to read as they passed by.

Or worse, she'd wake up in Cole Tucker's bed again, like she had the last two times they'd been drinking together. Granted, the latest time she'd woken up with all her clothes on and the assurance that nothing had happened the night before.

She wished she could say the same for the first time she woke up in Cole's bed. Her stomach twisted and her cheeks warmed as the memory tried to come crawling back.

No, she wouldn't stop at Wade's. Instead, she'd go home and take a nice, hot bubble bath before she climbed into bed for a long, desperately needed night of sleep, and try not to think about the man she hoped to wake up next to every day for the rest of her life. Or the man she swore never to wake up next to again.

August—Morning After the Farewell Bonfire

COLE BLINKED SEVERAL times as his eyes adjusted to the

early morning light pouring in through the window blinds. He was lying on his back with his hand splayed low on his abdomen, cool air stroking his bare chest. He stretched and felt the soft, thin fabric of a bedsheet draped over his naked hips.

A hushed sigh filled the room.

His eyes shot open and flew to the other side of the bed. She was there, curled up on her side. The bedsheet sat low on her hip, exposing the smooth, tan skin of her back pulled tight over curves of muscle and bone. A tiny freckle on the back of her right shoulder rose and fell with each breath.

Logan Kase was in his bed. The space beneath his ribs constricted. He'd never seen anything so beautiful in his life. He ran his hand through the ends of her hair, torn between letting her sleep and the desire to take her in his arms again and relive the most incredible night of his life. He compromised by gently tracing a finger down the line of her spine. She shuddered and moaned in her sleep, and the sound flooded his body with waves of need.

He kissed the freckle on her shoulder and slid out of bed. He grabbed some fresh clothes from his dresser and headed to the bathroom down the hall, closing the bedroom door behind him.

Memory after memory resurfaced as hot water rained down over him, washing away years of doubt and missteps and leaving behind a blank page on which they could write their future. The bonfire. Red Solo cups. The buzz of a tattoo needle. The dark look in her eyes when he drove them back to his place. The feel of her in his arms. The way she clung to him. The cry of his name on her tongue as his lips trailed over her skin.

He couldn't stop grinning. It was as if he'd won the lottery, only he doubted that would come close to the euphoria of the night he'd spent with her, the girl of his dreams. His Logan.

Cole dressed and returned to the hall, stopping outside his bedroom door.

"Carly, thank God," a voice hissed inside.

His hand froze inches from the doorknob. He leaned closer. "Carly, this is serious! I'm at Cole and Cowboy's new place, and I need you to come get me, fast. I…I made a huge mistake."

Cole's hand fell.

"I'll tell you later. Could you please just hurry up?"

He couldn't breathe. He felt like he'd taken a heavy blow to the gut and his lungs refused to suck in air. How? How could he have been so wrong about last night?

The room went quiet except for the sounds of hurried movement. Not knowing what else to do, he inched the door open. Lo sat on the edge of his bed, pulling on one of her boots. Her hair was in wild disarray, her shirt and jean shorts wrinkled. She stared up at him through wide eyes.

She was unbelievably gorgeous, only now it felt like a slap in the face.

Mistake. That one word was like a knife carving out his insides, but he refused to let her see it. He pushed everything down and forced himself to smile. He leaned against the doorframe.

"Leaving so soon?"

"I have to go home. My plane leaves this afternoon," she said quietly. She finished pulling on her boot and stood. She pointed to the bed. "About last night—"

"That was fun, huh?" he rushed out before he had to hear her say the M word again. "I've got to say, Lo, I didn't know just how wild you really were 'til last night."

"Yeah." She glanced back at the mess of sheets behind her and rubbed her hands over her arms. "Right, fun."

"And don't forget the tattoo. I still can't believe you actually went through with it."

Her brow creased. "Tattoo?" Her gaze fell to her wrist. "Oh, God." Her fingers worked to tug off the bandage, revealing the three etched letters surrounded by angry red skin.

CET. "That," he said, forcing a grin, "was our wager. And as you can probably tell, you lost the bet."

Her face blanched, and he could practically see her own voice echoing inside her head.

I made a huge mistake.

"As for this," he said, indicating the bed, "don't beat yourself up about it. Girls throw themselves at me all the time. It's nothing to be ashamed of. Consider it your going-away present."

She flinched. He'd wanted to hurt her, make her feel even a fraction of the pain he was burying, and judging by the moisture pooling in her eyes, he'd hit his mark. So why did it only make him feel worse?

Logan crossed the small space between them. She shoved her finger hard into his chest. "This never happened," she told him through clenched teeth. "And if you ever tell *anyone* that it did, I will find you and kill you myself."

Cole's grin slipped. Did she really hate the thought of being with him that much? "Jesus, Lo, lighten up. What's the big deal? It was just sex."

"Fuck you," she muttered before shoving him out of the way. She escaped through the door and down the hall. The front door slammed, and all the anger and pain he'd pushed away came bubbling up at full force. It was drowning him, suffocating him from the inside.

He couldn't take it. It was too much.

His fists clenched at his sides and before he knew what he was doing, he turned and lashed out at the wall with his fist.

Chapter Fourteen

LOGAN'S STOMACH GRUMBLED as she pulled into a parking spot at the Willow Creek Police Department. It had been hours since she ate thanks to the excruciatingly long fitting she and the other members of the wedding party had to go to that morning, and her body was taking its frustrations out on her in the form of embarrassingly loud growling.

She'd been running errands and getting everything ready for Carly's wedding for several days now—all while avoiding any direct contact with the bride herself since she still wasn't talking to her after their fight at dinner—and had barely found any time to sit down and relax. So that morning when Daddy mentioned meeting him for lunch at Wade's, she'd eagerly accepted his invitation. And right now, she could think of nothing better than a giant plate of fries.

Logan was about to jump out of the truck when her phone started ringing. Jacob.

"Hey, everything okay? I thought you were working today." She hadn't talked to him much in the last several days, and she'd tried to tell herself it was simply because she was busy and not because she was still bitter after he'd turned down her advances after dinner.

"Everything's fine. I just got some time during my lunch break and wanted to call and check in, see how your day is going."

Her lips curled into a small smile. "Oh, it hasn't been so bad. Just the normal wedding stuff...standing around in an uncomfortable dress for hours, dealing with Carly's little sister Lyssa, who makes Stalin look like the Dalai Lama."

"At least you're not stuck at work dealing with incompetent coworkers. If I hear one more nurse try to tell me how to do my job...I mean, I didn't go through med school and a residency all to have a tech school graduate think she knows more than I do about medicine. And don't even get me started on some of the half-brained idiot rednecks I've seen today! One guy actually had an arrow stuck in his—"

"Jacob, as much as I would love to hear your story, I'm supposed to be meeting my dad for lunch right now."

She could practically hear him perking up on the other end of the line. "Yeah? You going to tell him?"

"Absolutely not."

He took a deep breath, most likely preparing his usual line. "You're going to have to tell him eventually, Logan. And sooner's better than later."

"I know. But wouldn't it be better to tell them when they're together? If I told him and not her, there's no way Daddy wouldn't crack and tell Momma before I could. He hates lying to people."

"At least give him a hint that it's coming. Maybe if he has a heads-up he can support you when we tell her over dinner Friday night. And then, it will all be over and done with, and we can start planning our future together."

Future. She was having a hard enough time getting through the present right now. "Maybe. I'll see what I can do."

"Great," Jacob said, sounding distracted now. "My break is ending, and the patients are coming in fast today. I'll call you tonight, okay? Love you."

Logan hung up the phone, already regretting having answered it in the first place. She was starving and wanted fries and time with her dad. The last thing she wanted to do was think about San Francisco and the way her parents were going to react when she finally told them.

Her stomach growled again.

Logan jumped out of the truck and started making her way across the parking lot. She was almost at the main door when a familiar face came through it.

"Cole?" she called, grabbing his attention from the phone in his hand. It shouldn't have been surprising to see him here—the firehouse was directly across the street from the police station—but the fact he wasn't wearing his black WCFD T-shirt meant he wasn't on duty. Instead, he was in a white T-shirt and an open, button-up green-and-white-plaid shirt with the sleeves rolled up to his elbows. "What are you doing here?"

He smiled, putting the phone away in his back pocket. "I was actually just here to see the chief. We usually get lunch on one of my off days each week."

Logan's mouth fell open. "You're kidding."

His smile grew as he ran a hand through his short, dark hair. "Nope. It started about a year after you left. We ran into each other at Wade's one day, got to talking. When we finished, he asked if I wanted to meet up with him again the next time I was off. It's kind of a thing now."

How the hell did her dad and Cole Tucker have a thing? "But he hates you."

"I'm not so sure about that. In fact," he said, placing his hand on her shoulder like he was bracing her for bad news, "I might even go so far as to say he likes me. I came by to see if he wanted to do lunch today, but he said he already had plans with you. So we'll just do it another day."

Okay, so technically it was her mom who hated Cole, while her dad just got tired of all the bullshit and trouble Logan got into because of him. But to hear that her daddy might genuinely like Cole felt like complete and utter betrayal.

Well, this certainly threw off Logan's mood. Her dad and her enemy were pals now, huh? They probably laughed over drinks while they talked about her and the trouble she used to get into. That thought upset her more, given all the times her daddy got so angry he'd actually cussed her out for all the stupid shit they did.

As a churchgoing man, Marshall Kase almost never swore. When Logan was little, she'd never heard her daddy mutter so much as a *hell* or *damn*. But as she and Cole started going at it more and more over the years, she heard her father shout every cuss word he knew, at every decibel, on a regular basis. He never swore at anyone else. Logan just seemed to have a way of bringing that side out of him.

Which gave her an idea.

"Why don't you come eat with us? That way you two can still do your thing, and I can still spend some quality time with my dad."

Cole shook his head. "No, I don't want to ruin your time. I'm sure you'd both enjoy it more if I wasn't there. But thanks for the offer." He tried to pass Logan, but she stepped in front of him again.

"Oh no, I insist," she said. "And then when we're done, I get to put an *R* under your name on the scoreboard."

Now he looked intrigued. "I see. So, this is about our next challenge then?"

"Mm-hmm." She hadn't had much time to think about their challenge this week, which was why she couldn't ignore it when this one landed at her feet all wrapped up with a pretty bow on top.

Cole took a step forward, his eyes narrowing. "And what makes you so sure you're going to win?"

"Because we're about to do something I've been doing

for a very, very long time." She smirked. "It's simple. First one to get Daddy to swear is the winner."

His head tilted as if considering it. "Seems like someone's got an unfair advantage."

She merely shrugged.

"All right, fine," he said. "You're on."

Chapter Fifteen

"IT WAS VERY nice of you to invite Cole along," the chief said after Lilly brought them their drinks and took their orders. He sounded pleased about it, but Logan couldn't ignore the way his eyes narrowed. "I didn't know he was off today until he stopped into the station."

Logan smiled. "My pleasure. I just didn't realize how much time you two have spent together lately," she said, arching an eyebrow. "Seeing as you never told me."

Her dad shrugged, picking up his Coke and taking a sip. "What's to tell? We come to the bar, we eat, and we talk about sports and work. That's it." So they didn't talk about her and Cole and embarrassing stories from when they were growing up? Good. That would make Logan's mission today only that much easier.

"It's true," Cole said from his spot between them. "I've tried to get my dad to come along, too, but it's not easy for him to leave the store like that."

"Plus, there's that little thing where he doesn't like either of us," she said.

"I'm pretty sure it's just you he doesn't like."

Logan stared at him. "Both your parents hate me...and my parents by association."

Her dad grimaced. "You can't really blame him, baby girl," he said. "As far as I know, you're still the only person he's ever had to ban from the hardware store."

"Yeah, and why was that again?" She glared at Cole. "Oh right, because *someone* decided to pour a gallon of pink paint on my head in the middle of the plumbing aisle." Logan still flinched anytime she smelled paint fumes. Her dad, of course, had been furious.

She looked at her father now to see if the memory had upset him, but he only shook his head. "Kids, can we just try to keep this civil? I know you two have a past, but I think it's best if we don't dredge it all up again."

Lilly came out then carrying the three plates of food to their table with a smile and a wink at Cole. She set the chicken sandwich and fries in front of Logan, gave a steak with veggies to Cole, and handed the chief his usual grilled Reuben.

"Sure, Dad, if that's what you want." Logan took a long sip of her water. "I just thought you might be interested in hearing about the time in seventh grade when Cole messed with the brakes on my brand-new bike, and I rode it right into the bottom of the creek."

Cole's eyes narrowed. For the last ten years, they'd had a silent understanding that they would never rat the other out for something they did, and this was the first time Logan was breaking that code. Desperate times and all that.

Her dad's eyes slowly shifted to Cole before coming back to her. "You mean that blue and green one you told me was stolen? You never told me that was because of him."

"There's a lot of things I never told you about, Daddy. Like the town carnival senior year when he shoved me in a Porta-Potty and left me locked in there for three hours."

Cole laughed. "Oh yeah, I remember that one. It was right after Big Lou was in there for twenty minutes."

"And there's the time Cole put superglue on my seat in American history junior year and I had to walk out of class in my underwear." The chief did not look impressed. "Or the time he *stole* all my underwear from my room and put them on display in the boys' locker room in ninth grade."

Her dad turned on Cole, his face growing darker. "You did what now?"

Cole raised his hands. "In my defense, it was only after your daughter tried to tell all the girls in our class that I had a micropenis."

"Logan!"

She glared at Cole. "Well, if you weren't such a manwhore by then, maybe they would have believed me."

"Or maybe they didn't believe you because less than a month later you stole all my clothes at the beach and everyone saw me naked."

"Oh, please," Logan said. "You were just looking for an excuse to expose yourself to every girl in school."

"At least I didn't offer Michael Davis a blowjob to do my chemistry homework for me."

Her dad's red face whipped around on her, and she could practically see the torrent of expletives ready to burst through his lips.

"That was a rumor *you* started!" she yelled at Cole.

"Enough," her dad's firm voice boomed out over theirs. Logan looked at him hopefully. Getting him upset like this sucked—especially when it had to be done by divulging just how reckless and immature she'd been growing up—but it would be worth it when she won the challenge.

The chief's eyes shifted between her and Cole, who both sat silently, waiting. "Now I don't know why you have decided to start telling me all of this now. But I can assure you that there is very little about you two that would surprise me at this point," he said with a sigh.

Cole smirked and grabbed his bottle to take a sip of his beer. She was running out of chances. She had to pull out the big guns.

"Cole and I had sex the night before I left for school!" she shouted before she could stop herself. The rest of the bar went eerily still as everyone inside gaped in their direction.

Cole spluttered and choked, coughing as he tried to avoid eye contact with the chief. Logan was breathing heavily, her hands gripping the edge of their table and trying not to stand up and run out of Wade's like a red-faced, yellow-bellied coward.

With a tight jaw, Daddy took in a deep breath and let it out slowly. Staring down at his plate, he said, "If you two are done, I'd like us to finish this meal in silence."

Logan glanced at Cole, not sure what else she could possibly do. She'd pulled out all the stops, used every trick she knew, and it still hadn't been enough. How the hell was she supposed to win now?

Cole, on the other hand, did not look shaken. Instead, he took a bite of his steak and chewed as he held a finger up at Logan, wearing a cocky grin.

"You know," he said calmly once he finally swallowed his mouthful, "Adam and I were just talking the other day about Coach Sanchez over at the high school, and he seems to think he's got a real shot at getting them to the state championships this year."

"Bullshit!" The entire restaurant looked their way as the chief yelled. "The only way Willow Creek is getting its ass to state is with a new coach! Now I know your brother is the assistant coach and looks up to Mark Sanchez—and I have all the respect in the world for that man as a person—but, as a high school football coach, Sanchez is a grade-A, shit-for-brains idiot."

Logan stared at her father, completely lost for words. Seriously? Word straight from the horse's mouth that his baby girl had slept with Cole years ago wasn't enough to start her daddy on a tirade of curses, but *that* was? She didn't know whether to be amazed or insulted.

Logan's heart sank as she turned her head to find a very smug look on Cole's face. "I was pretty sure you'd say something like that," he told the chief before winking at her. "If you'll excuse me, I have something very important to take care of."

Cole stood from his seat and crossed the floor to the bar. He said a few words to Lilly, who looked Logan's way before shaking her head and picking up a piece of chalk.

"What's that about?" her dad asked.

"We were trying to see who could get you to swear first. And, obviously, I lost," Logan said, almost growling as she watched Lilly add the *R* to her name.

"You mean to tell me this was all part of that bet y'all have going?"

"You know about that?" She expected him to be furious, but he didn't look at all upset by the fact that there was a bet or that he'd clearly just been used in it.

"Of course I know about it. Everyone knows about it, not to mention that I come in here at least twice a week for lunch. Half the town has money down on who's going to win. Including me."

Logan's jaw dropped. "Daddy, there is no way Momma let you bet money on this!"

The chief huffed. "I'm a grown man who can make his own decisions." He watched Cole circle the bar, high-fiving people and boasting his victory. "And besides, what your momma doesn't know won't hurt her. So as long as we keep our mouths shut, you win, and I get my money back, she'll never have to find out," he said with a smile.

"You bet on me, Daddy?"

"Of course I did. You're my baby girl, and I know for a fact you can run his arrogant ass into the ground."

She couldn't remember a time her daddy had been so supportive. He'd always sided with her momma when Lo acted up. But knowing he bet money on her, on the girl she used to be—she wanted to wrap her arms around him and never let go.

Instead, she smiled at him and took a bite out of one of her fries. At least with the challenge over she could eat her meal and enjoy the time with her dad rather than continue yelling her personal secrets to half of Willow Creek.

Daddy leaned in close. "You were just kiddin' about all that stuff earlier, right? About you and him having...you know. You just said that for the bet, right, to upset me?"

Logan hesitated. Could she really be this lucky?

"Of course, Daddy. You know I wouldn't do anything that stupid."

His eyes shot to the tattoo on her wrist. Eventually, he smiled. "I knew it," he muttered, letting out a puff of air. He took a bite out of his sandwich. They ate in silence for a while as Cole continued to tell Lilly and the other patrons the story of his success as if they hadn't heard half of it being yelled from only a few feet away.

The chief just wiped his mouth with his napkin. "Now

about those other things you two mentioned—"

"It was a long time ago, Dad," Logan said. "Just let it go."

"Fine." He shrugged. "Just promise me your mom doesn't hear about my part in this. Or else I'll be sleeping on the couch for a week."

"So, you're not mad about the bet?"

He took another bite of his sandwich. "Don't see why I should be, as long as you aren't doing anything stupid or dangerous that could get you killed."

"You don't think I'm just going to mess everything up with Jacob?" It was what everyone else was thinking. Her mom, Carly. Even Cole knew she'd be screwed if she lost this bet and Jacob found out the kind of girl she really was.

"I'm not going to lie to you, baby girl. It could rough up the waters between you two. But I also think he has a right to know who you are and the truth about your past. That's how it's supposed to be going into a marriage. You both need to be able to accept the girl you are, not just the girl you've been trying to be."

He made it sound so easy, and yet she knew that nothing about Jacob knowing the truth would be easy. "But what if he can't accept that side of me?"

He held his hand out to her on the table and she put her own in it. He squeezed. "If he can't accept all of you," he said, "he was never the right one to begin with."

Chapter Sixteen

"I F SHE TRIES to change my seating arrangement one more time, I swear I will strangle her with the cheap, fake pearls she insists I wear on my wedding day!"

Logan winced as Carly's shrill voice pierced her eardrum through the cell phone. She'd never heard her sound so pissed. Logan had been on the job search website again, this time looking for positions around Willow Creek that could give her some extra cash and experience. She would have asked Ms. Snyder if she knew of any nearby openings, but she was still out of town.

Logan was growing restless, search after search leading to nothing but dead ends. She felt trapped in a cycle she couldn't escape from and was on the verge of running to Wade's for a drink she knew would take some of the edge off. So when Carly had called two minutes ago, she was more than happy to slam the computer shut and focus on anything else.

"Well, isn't it normal for a woman not to get along with her mother-in-law?" Logan asked.

"It's not that we don't get along. We do. But if she keeps

trying to micromanage *my* wedding, I think I might kill someone." She sighed. "Does it ever feel like that with Jacob's mom?"

"Honestly, I've only ever met Jacob's parents once, and that was for about ten minutes."

"You're kidding."

"They were in Dallas for something, and Jacob took me up there to meet them. He introduced us and told them we were getting married. They said their congratulations, and then a few minutes later they had to leave or they'd miss their flight."

"Wow, I wish Darren's mom could live across the country…just for a few months. It must be so nice to be able to plan everything without a pair of judging, opinionated eyes over your shoulder."

"I guess," Logan mumbled. Truth be told, she hadn't done much of any planning at this point. She still hadn't even set a date. It wasn't her fault; she'd tried. But anytime she attempted to sit herself down and make any actual decisions about this wedding, she'd find something else that seemed to need her attention more presently.

"How's the big bet going?" Carly asked carefully.

After a week of not talking to each other, Carly had shown up at Logan's front door two mornings ago with a box of their favorite doughnuts from Byrdie's bakery and café downtown and a huge apology. They'd easily forgiven each other before devouring their deliciously fattening breakfast while Carly begged for all the details from the different challenges so far.

"The same. I've still got one more letter than him." Logan had been avoiding Wade's the last few days, not wanting to see the scoreboard and the very clear *HOR* under her name.

"And you haven't heard from Cole? He gets to pick the next one, right?"

Logan's stomach tightened, something it had been doing more and more lately. She was used to having a physical reaction to the name or thought of Cole Tucker. When she first got back to town it was easily a feeling of dread or disgust. But in the last week or so, that yucky feeling had started to morph into one of an addict about to get his next fix—a feeling she hadn't associated with Cole Tucker since she was a kid plotting her latest revenge. It left her unsettled.

"Not since lunch at the bar. But between his schedule at the fire station and whatever he does in his free time, it could be a while before I do," she said with a frown. "And it's not like his life revolves around our bet."

"Mm-hmm," Carly said.

The doorbell rang downstairs. Logan pulled her cell phone from her ear and checked the time.

"Shit," she muttered. "Carly, I have to go. Jacob just got here for dinner, and I'm not even close to ready."

"Okay, have fun, and tell Jacob I said hey."

"I will. Bye."

Logan raced to her closet.

➳➳➳❮❮❮❮

"MRS. KASE, THIS is the best meal I've had in a long time," Jacob said, wiping his mouth with his napkin.

Momma smiled with delight. Her dark hair was perfectly done, and she was wearing her favorite light blue dress. Logan didn't doubt that her mother had put more effort into her appearance tonight than even she had. "Aw, thank you, honey. And I told you to please call me Cindy."

"Yes, sorry." He smiled brightly at Logan, clearly pleased with how well the evening was going. It was sad that this was the first time the four of them had sat down together for a dinner.

"I'm not even sure the last time I had a home-cooked meal," he went on. "With me working most nights and neither of us being much of a cook, Logan and I usually go out to a restaurant when we're together."

"It's true. Unfortunately, Logan did not inherit my love for cooking," her mom teased.

"Or your talent, it would seem."

Momma was beaming.

The topic of Carly's wedding—was Jacob going, was he in the wedding party, how did he like Carly and Darren?—managed to take up a good twenty minutes of conversation.

The chief sat at his end of the table, nodding, but otherwise adding nothing to the conversation, too focused on devouring his chicken, potatoes, green beans, and dinner roll. He was already working on his second plate when the subject turned to Jacob's reasons for not consuming red meat, alcohol, or anything with refined sugar. At that point, her father just stared down at his plate, shaking his head. Luckily, Jacob didn't notice.

"Tell me about Logan," Jacob said as he pushed his empty plate away from him. "What was she like as a kid?"

There was a collective silence as three pairs of eyes shifted around the room. "What is there to tell, really?" her mom said, moving the potatoes around on her plate with a forced smile. "She was just a normal, sweet little girl. Spent her time around the house mostly, helping me with this and that."

"And taking care of Aunt Caroline, of course," Jacob added.

Logan grimaced as both of her parents looked at him, equally lost.

"Right," Logan jumped in. "Great-aunt Caroline, whose initials I got tattooed on my wrist after she passed."

"Yes, of course," her mom said. "Aunt Caroline…"

"Teague."

"Yep, Caroline Teague. My grandmother Jeanette's sister. That's right," she said, nodding. Daddy rolled his eyes and took another bite of his green beans.

"Do you have any other family here in town?"

"Oh, no, just us," her momma said. "I've got some extended family up in Virginia that we try to go visit every year, but other than that we don't see much of them. Marshall's sister Lynn is up in New York, though, and they stay in touch. Her daughter, Darby, is just a few years younger than Logan."

"What about your family, Jacob?" The chief grabbed his sweet tea and took a sip. "I don't think we've heard much about them."

"Yes, tell me all about them. I can't wait to meet everyone," Momma said.

Jacob smiled. "Well, my mom and dad are both surgeons in San Francisco. That's really all there is to my family. I'm an only child like Logan, so there are no brothers or sisters to tell you about. And my parents didn't stay very connected with the extended family. Other than my grandparents, I don't think I've seen anyone else in maybe ten years."

"Oh, that's a shame," her momma said.

Jacob shrugged. "It's not that bad. I think, if anything, it's just made my mom, dad, and me feel closer. And as much as they work, it's not like they would be able to contribute much to a big family."

"So, was it your parents who made you want to become a doctor?"

"Yes, ma'am…I mean, Cindy. Seeing all the good they did to help people, I knew I wanted to do exactly what they did."

"It takes quite a commitment to get through that kind of education," the chief said with approval. "Did you ever consider taking a different route, trying something else?"

"No, sir, not really. I've never felt like there was any other option. I've always wanted to do something good in this world, to save people's lives."

Momma smiled. It was the answer her parents wanted to hear, but it was also a far cry from the truth. Logan knew well enough that Jacob's love for his job was due more to the income than anything else. If her parents only knew the number of patients he'd accused of being redneck, hillbilly idiots, they'd start spouting Bible lessons on the Golden Rule right here at the dinner table.

It had never really bothered Logan before. It was just one of those things she learned to accept about her significant other. It was how he was raised, after all, no fault of his own.

But for some reason, watching him work his way into her parents' hearts at dinner with how much he cared about his patients was really grating on her nerves, especially when there were other people out there who really did care and deserved her parents' praise a lot more than Jacob at this moment.

"And what schools did you go to?" her dad asked.

"Stanford and then to UCSF med school. After that, I completed my residency at Dell Med in Austin before I took the job at St. Mary's." Jacob calmly took a sip of his water. He didn't seem at all bothered by the third-degree.

"What made you choose to go to Dell Med?" Mom asked. She took a bite from her barely touched plate before she set it aside, resting her elbows on the table while she listened.

He smiled at her. "My parents thought it would be a good idea. They have some connections with the faculty and made it happen. Not that I can complain. If I hadn't been in Austin, I wouldn't have met Logan."

"Aw, that's lovely. So, now that you're in Athens, you'll be staying for a while, I assume."

Jacob's eyes lit up, but Logan gave him a sharp look.

"Actually, Mom—"

"I've applied for a job at San Francisco General," Jacob's voice came in louder. "We'll be moving there as soon as I get it."

"Jacob!" Logan yelled across the table. She suddenly wanted to throw her dinner plate at her fiancé's head.

Her mother's startled eyes turned on her. "You...what? San Francisco?"

"I'm sorry, Momma. I've been trying to find the right time to tell you. And I planned for a gentler delivery than that." She glowered at Jacob, who shrugged like he didn't understand her anger. How could he possibly have thought that blurting it out like that would be okay?

The chief set his fork down for the first time, abandoning the food on his plate. "Now, Jacob, you said you applied. But what makes you so sure that you'll even get this job?"

"My parents have friends on the board of directors, so it's all but a done deal. We just have to go through the formalities."

"Is that how life works for you?" Dad asked, his voice unforgiving. "You want something and your parents just go off and get it for you, just like that? Is that how you plan to take care of my daughter? Having your mom and dad call in favors for you?"

"Daddy." Logan said his name softly. She couldn't blame him for being angry, but that didn't give him the right to take it out on Jacob. "It's not his fault. I'm the one who kept putting off telling you guys."

Her mom stood quickly, grabbing her and the chief's plates from the table. "I'll just take these into the kitchen," she murmured.

"Here, Momma." Logan picked up her own plate. "Let me help you."

"No, no." Without looking at anyone, she took Logan's plate from her hand. "I've got it, honey. You just stay seated, and I'll be out with dessert in just a minute." She picked up Jacob's plate last and left the dining room.

Logan took one look at her father, who closed his eyes and nodded toward the door. She followed her mother into the kitchen. Her mom let the plates fall loudly into the sink as her hands gripped the edge of the counter.

"Momma? Are you okay?"

At the sound of Logan's voice, her momma stood tall and ran her hands over her face. "I'm fine, baby." She turned around, smiling at her. But Logan could see where her eyes were turning red with tears. "It's just a bit of a shock is all.

California is a long ways away, and I feel like I only just got you back."

Logan stepped around the island and put her hands on her mother's arms. "I know, but I'll call you every day. And it's just a plane ride away. I'll come visit you all the time."

"Like you have the last four years?" The words slapped Logan across the cheek, and her momma's face fell. "I'm sorry. I didn't mean that."

Logan's heart ached, but she had no right to be upset. Her momma was right. She hadn't once visited home when she lived in Austin. How could she be trusted to visit when she was on the opposite side of the country?

"You know why I stayed away before," she said quietly. "But I promise you, nothing'll keep me away this time." Not even Cole Tucker. Logan couldn't be that selfish again, not when it came to her mom and dad.

"And besides, you guys can come out to us anytime you want. Jacob makes plenty of money as it is, and the pay there will only be better after this promotion. We could fly you two out and give you the vacations y'all never really got to have before."

Her mom nodded. "We'll see. Now do me a favor and grab some silverware while I get this pie," she said, taking out the fresh apple pie she'd made only a few hours ago just for Jacob.

"When you said Jacob didn't drink sweet tea, I didn't realize it was because he doesn't eat sugar at all." She frowned. "It's a shame. I bet he would have really liked this."

"Don't worry, Momma." Logan pulled open the silver-ware drawer and grabbed a handful of spoons and forks before going to the freezer and pulling out the half gallon of vanilla ice cream. "I'm pretty sure he'll make an exception tonight."

At least he would if he didn't want one of her pointed leather boots shoved up his ass while he drove home.

>>>>><<<<<

"I THINK THAT went really well, don't you?" Jacob asked, rubbing his stomach as Logan walked him out to his car. "Although, I think I could have done without the three slices of pie you practically shoved down my throat."

"What the hell is wrong with you?" she whispered, turn-ing on him and forcing him to stop dead in his tracks. "You had no right to spring it on them like that. I was finally ready to ease them into it. And then you go and pull a bullshit move like that one?"

His eyes widened. "I know, but I thought it would be easier for you this way. If I didn't just tell them, you'd probably still be trying to figure out a way to do it nicely without hurting their feelings."

"Easier for me?" she cried out. "I don't care about how hard it is for me. I wanted to make it easier for them! After everything they've put up with over the years, they deserved at least that much."

His brows came together. "Put up with? What's that supposed to mean?"

"Nothing," she sighed. "I just really wanted to tell them myself. You had no right to do it for me like that."

"You're right. I'm sorry. But, hey, at least they know now. So you don't have to stress over it anymore."

When she said nothing, Jacob took a step closer. He wrapped his arms around her slowly and pulled her in close. "So," he said with a devious grin, "what do you say we get that hotel room you were talking about last week? I don't have to work again until Sunday. We could get a room tonight and spend all day tomorrow coming up with reasons not to leave it."

"I have a better idea," she said, pulling out of his embrace. "Why don't you go get a hotel room and then spend tomorrow trying to figure out why the only one willing to have sex with you tonight is your hand."

Logan turned to go back into the house.

"Ah, come on, babe. Don't be like that. I was just trying to help you."

"Go home, Jacob," she called over her shoulder.

Once she was inside, Logan stood at the window by the door and watched as Jacob backed his car out of the driveway and sped off. She let out a sigh. She didn't think she'd ever been so relieved to see him go.

Chapter Seventeen

LOGAN SQUIRMED, FEELING several pairs of eyes studying her but refused to return their gaze. She shifted in her seat, picking at the fabric of her new pink dress. There was a time when she thought about dresses and high heels with nothing less than an all-consuming loathing and swore never to wear either in public.

Now, however, it was more like a mystified appreciation. She still preferred a good pair of worn blue jeans and a comfy shirt. But since she'd reached puberty, even Logan had to admit that the somewhat painful combo had its uses. Not that any of those uses included sitting in a church pew and listening to Pastor Joe greet them all while she was gawked at by just about every woman over sixty.

Logan hadn't stepped inside Willow Creek Baptist Church in years, but the building was still the same. From the light blue walls, dark blue carpet, and row after row of wine-red pews, to the ridiculously high ceiling with huge golden chandeliers. Floor-to-ceiling windows perfectly framed the row of sun-lit magnolia trees. A breeze ruffled the white and purple blossoms and called invitingly for Logan to join them in the clear, sunny day that existed beyond the sanctuary's four blue walls.

Logan shivered as the building's monstrous air conditioners kicked on. She glanced at her mother sitting to her right wearing a warm, pale blue cardigan over her cream-colored dress. On her mother's other side, in what used to be Logan's spot at the end of the pew, sat the chief.

"I forgot how cold it gets in here," she muttered under her breath, rubbing her bare arms. The chief smiled. Her mom gave a slight shrug but otherwise made no indication she'd even heard her.

Logan said nothing as she turned her attention back to the pastor, who'd just invited them to stand and sing along with the choir.

She felt the distance between her and her mom since their disastrous dinner with Jacob like a chasm. She'd hoped her efforts to surprise Momma at church this morning would help fix that void, but her mother's cold shoulder so far left her feeling empty.

That emptiness became even more real when her stomach growled and she realized she'd been so focused on getting to church on time that she'd forgotten to eat anything. She crossed her arms over her stomach to stifle the noise and sang a little louder, hoping to drown out the sounds of her starvation.

She spent the next several verses trying not to think about how hungry she was or how badly she wanted her momma to hug her or, at the very least, acknowledge her existence.

As the music minister led them into another hymn, Logan finally took a chance to observe the members of the congregation the way they'd been observing her since she walked in.

Most of them she'd already encountered around town or down at the bar, but there were a few she was seeing for the first time since moving back.

She turned to glance at the back of the room where the Tuckers usually sat. She immediately recognized Mr. Tucker, standing tall in his black slacks and white dress shirt, his wife next to him. She was more than a foot shorter than her husband, her dark blond hair pulled back from the smooth, minimally made-up face that reminded Logan so much of her youngest son.

Logan eyed the empty pew beside Mrs. Tucker and frowned, searching the rest of the congregation. She wasn't sure why she'd expected Cole to be here, but the realization that he may not be left a heaviness in her gut, almost like disappointment. Or maybe that was just her stomach eating itself.

At the front of the church, the music minister led them straight into a third song. Logan scanned the crowd one last time for her least favorite Tucker, her eyes finally landing on a head full of short, brown hair and familiar build in khakis and a light blue dress shirt. He was in the third row, his back toward her. But she was sure it was him; she'd recognize just about any part of Cole Tucker from almost any angle.

The weight in her stomach eased, only to settle back in heavier. A tall brunette Logan didn't recognize stood next to him. While she couldn't see the woman's face, Logan could tell from her physique and the way her olive-green dress hung on her slender, tanned frame that she was gorgeous. Not that there was any reason this woman shouldn't be pretty, but wouldn't it have been fairer for the rest of them if notoriously sexy Cole Tucker had a girlfriend who ended up being a plain Jane...or better yet, a total cow? Or maybe she was one of those really pretty girls who had absolutely nothing in the way of brains or personality.

Cole Tucker's stupid, bimbo girlfriend.

Whoa, where the hell had that come from? She didn't think she'd ever thought such ugly things about a stranger before, so why on earth would she start now? And why did the weight in her stomach get heavier and heavier each time she thought the G word?

To be fair, Cole had made it clear he didn't have a girlfriend when she first came back into town. So it wasn't completely insane for the sight of him with this tall, Amazonian beauty—as far as she could tell from the back, at least—to throw her off so much. She just hadn't been expecting it, that's all. Of course, it had been three weeks since Cole admitted he was single. More than enough time for that to change.

The music ended and Pastor Joe asked everyone to sit. A few seconds behind everyone else, Logan followed suit and sat in the pew and turned her focus to the sermon.

>>>><<<<

LOGAN STOOD OUTSIDE by the green lawn in front of the parking lot, grateful for the first time for the ridiculous heels that made it easier to see over half the heads in the crowd that came pouring out of the main doors.

She'd offered to meet her parents outside after they finished chatting and catching up with all the usual people.

"No point, really," the chief had told her. "Your mom's already made plans for us for lunch and then to visit a few people who missed church this morning." Logan could tell he was struggling not to roll his eyes. "We probably won't be home until evening."

So, basically, they'd planned an entire day out just to avoid her. Ouch.

Daddy gave her a sad smile before pulling her into a one-armed side hug. "Why don't you go home, baby girl? Enjoy having the house to yourself for a while."

Logan nodded.

"Sure. You guys have fun, and I'll see you later." She'd pulled out of her father's hug and slowly made her way out of the sanctuary. She'd had every intention of leaving then, but before she knew what she was doing, she'd stopped by the grass and started watching as, one by one, people emerged from the building.

She waited for one person in particular.

It wasn't creepy, she told herself as she searched patiently for the girl in the olive-green dress. Just a healthy curiosity.

She'd tried to focus through Pastor Joe's sermon; honestly, she had. But time and time again she found her mind wandering to the girl sitting with Cole. Who was she? And why did they sit together all comfortable and familiar looking? She tried not to stare but found herself unable to look away when he draped his arm behind her across the back of the pew. She just wanted to see the girl's face, and then she could leave it alone. She spent almost the entire hour watching them, her eyes practically boring holes into the back of the girl's head, and still, she never turned. Not once.

"Looking for someone?"

Logan jumped at the quiet sound of Cole Tucker's voice in her ear, his hands catching her as she fell back into his chest with a shriek. She whipped around to see him laughing at her.

"Don't *do* that!" she yelled, punching him hard in the bicep. She grinned to herself when he winced just a tiny bit. She hadn't seen him exit through the main door, which meant either he came out a different way or her search for the girl in the green dress had gone to a scary, mind-consuming level.

Cole stopped laughing as he rubbed his arm, but his smile remained. "I didn't know you were in there until I saw you walking out. Were you with your parents?"

She nodded. "I wanted to surprise them. What about you? Sitting in the usual Tucker pew?" she asked, feigning ignorance and disinterest.

"Nah. I usually sit up near the front now. Helps me focus." So he wasn't going to mention the woman he was sitting with. Two could play that game.

"Usually? You come a lot on Sunday mornings?"

He shrugged. "I try to whenever I'm not at the station. Makes my mom feel better, and it's kind of become a Sunday ritual, going to church and then heading out to my mom and dad's house. They like to call it our family day. Keith and Adam try to make it, too, when they can."

"Aw," Logan said with a genuine smile. "A Tucker Family Day. That sounds so cute."

Cole shook his head. "No. There is no aw-ing with my family. We usually just spend the day arguing over who ate all the cornbread and shouting at whatever game we're watching on TV."

"Oh, come on. It can't be that bad." Logan wished she had a big family she could spend the day arguing with. Hell, right now she just wished the family she did have would talk to her.

"So, what about you?" Cole asked. "I assume you're out here waiting for your mom and dad. What've you got planned with them?"

She grimaced. "Actually, my mom and dad have plans to get lunch and then go visit some church members, so it looks like I'm probably just hanging out at the house today. Maybe I'll catch up on laundry or clean or something."

"What?" he said, crossing his arms over his chest. "That doesn't sound like the way to spend an afternoon on a day like this."

Logan shrugged. It certainly wasn't how she'd hoped the day would go. "Bet Tucker Family Day isn't looking so bad now, is it?"

Cole eyed her for a second. "You know what, I have the perfect solution. Just what we need to liven up this day."

"A challenge?"

"You know me so well," he said, grinning. He grabbed her hand. "Come on, let's go."

Logan pulled her hand from his grip. "Hold up. You're not about to use me as an excuse to get out of spending a day with your family."

"Not an excuse," he said, still smiling as he took her hand again. This time she let him pull her along with him. "Just a reason to enjoy it."

Chapter Eighteen

I F SOMEONE HAD told Logan a few years or even a few weeks ago that she would be spending a Sunday afternoon with Cole's family—even if only for a bet—she would have laughed in their face. And yet, here she was, standing in front of the Tucker's dark green front door.

"So, here's the deal," Cole said beside her. "We both go in together, and the first one to call it off and walk out loses. Simple as that."

"I don't know." She wasn't sure how long she'd be able to withstand the inevitable glares and judgment, not to mention the possible beratement when one of them brought up her and Cole's hostile history. In a way, this challenge was more daunting than anything else either of them had come up with so far.

"Trust me, this will be no less painful for me than you. At least if you're here, my mom might be too shocked to remember her usual rant about how I still haven't brought home a real girl to meet them."

Logan frowned, remembering the woman sitting next to him at church. She forced herself to focus. This was not the time to wonder about Cole's relationship status. "Couldn't I have at least gone home and changed first?" she asked, glancing down at the pink dress and heels. "I look ridiculous."

His eyes raked over her. "Not on your life."

Her stomach fluttered, and she glanced at him by her side. His face lit up with an encouraging grin. "You ready?"

No. She felt a tremor of anxiety similar to the one and only time she'd met Jacob's parents, only this time she knew that these parents already hated her. How exactly was she here and not the girl in the green dress? Or any other girl for that matter. Surely, she wasn't his first choice of who he'd like to spend the day with. But it wasn't some other girl, it was Logan. And for some reason, that fact made her smile back at him.

She nodded.

Cole put his hand on the doorknob, her own hands shaking though she was failing to come up with a single place she'd rather be at this moment.

And that scared the hell out of her.

"Mom, Dad?" Cole called as he opened the door and stepped in. Logan reluctantly followed him into the foyer. She took in the room's light green walls and the dark wood floors. It was large, warm, inviting. She tried to imagine Cole growing up here as a boy. How had she gone more than ten years knowing him and never once stepped foot in his house?

Her eyes swept over to the stairs on her left and froze.

Hanging on the wall over the steps was a large oil painting of a single sunflower. She'd not only seen it before in Ms. Snyder's gallery, but it had been her favorite piece to ever hold residence there.

There was something about the detail of the brushwork and the focus on a single flower that drew her in every time she saw it. It was as incredible as she remembered. But what she didn't understand was how it had ended up here in the Tucker house, of all places.

Heavy footsteps came from the back of the house. "Cole, that you?" Mr. Tucker's voice called. "We were wondering what was taking so long. Keith and Adam are out back waiting for you."

Logan whipped around just as Mr. Tucker appeared from a hallway in the back with a wide grin on his face Logan didn't think she'd ever seen and found surprisingly endearing.

The older man stopped in his tracks. "Oh," he said slowly.

Logan's heart beat chaotically. "Hi, Mr. Tucker."

His eyes darted between her and Cole for a moment. "Hello, Logan," he finally said, focusing on her. "I didn't realize you'd be joining us today."

"Logan mentioned after church that she didn't have any plans, so I thought I'd invite her along," Cole said casually.

She took a deep breath. "I'm sorry. I told Cole this was probably a bad idea. I don't want to intrude."

Mr. Tucker's questioning look transformed into a friendly smile. "No intrusion. We've got plenty of food. We can certainly share with one of Cole's friends."

"Careful, Dad. You might offend her. Lo here has made it very clear that we are not friends," he teased.

She rolled her eyes, and Mr. Tucker said nothing. Instead, he turned and called out over his shoulder, "Suzanne, better set another place at the table. Cole's brought a…guest."

"I would hardly call Cowboy a guest at this point, the way he cleans out my entire pantry each time he's here," Mrs. Tucker yelled from what Logan assumed was the kitchen. "If I'd known he was coming I would have made double of everything."

"Not Cowboy," her husband called back.

There was a sound of dishes clattering together. "Is it a girl? Did my baby boy *finally* bring one of his girls home to meet us?"

Cole gave Logan a *told-you-so* smirk. Logan returned it with a *just-how-many-girls-have-you-had?* one.

Before anyone could answer her, Mrs. Tucker came around the same corner her husband had. Her mouth fell open. "What are you doing here?"

"I—"

"I invited her," Cole stepped in. "She didn't have plans, and I thought Tater could use the female company."

"Did someone say my name?"

Logan looked up to find the last person she'd expected to see at the top of the Tucker staircase. Though the olive-green dress was gone, this girl was without question the same one Logan had spent the entire church sermon staring at. Finally seeing her face only confirmed Logan's suspicions. She was gorgeous, her long, dark hair perfectly framing her prominent cheekbones and jaw. But instead of the dress Logan had thought flattered her tall, slender frame, she now wearing jean shorts and a T-shirt that made her look stunning in that girl-next-door sort of way.

The girl stared down at them. "Logan?" she squealed.

"Tater, is that really you?"

The girl bounded down the steps two at a time and crashed into Logan with a painful hug. Multiple feelings flooded Logan at once: excitement at seeing the girl she'd come to know very well in her final year in Willow Creek, wonder at how she could possibly have grown so much in the last four she'd been gone, and a combination of embarrassment and relief that the girl she'd been obsessing about all morning was only Cole's little sister.

Logan stepped back to get a better look at her. "Oh my God! You look amazing, Tater!" Gone were the glasses she'd worn in middle school, leaving behind a beautiful, tall, tan young lady. She still had the same deep accent and spray of freckles across her nose from when she was a kid.

She had to be a junior in high school, at least, though she looked much more mature. And she may possibly even have been tied with Cole in the looks department. "Sorry, I mean Tatum. I know you hate that nickname."

She shrugged. "Nah, Tater's fine. Especially compared to the other nicknames I've heard over the years."

"Bad?"

"Well, there was Fried Tater, Tater Tot, stuff like that. And then the ever-popular Tater Salad," she huffed.

Logan grimaced.

"I've missed you so much!" Tater practically shrieked. "I can't believe how long it's been."

"Henry, would you go get the boys and tell them lunch is ready? And you three can go ahead and sit at the table," Mrs. Tucker said, not looking at all impressed by the happy reunion in front of her.

"Come on," Tater said, pulling Logan by the arm to the back hallway. They took a left into a beautiful blue dining room with a large table already set for six. Tater sat in what Logan guessed was her usual seat, patting the chair next to her.

To Logan's surprise, Cole moved to pull the chair out for her to sit before going around the table to take the seat across from her. "I didn't realize you two were so close."

Tater grinned at her brother. "Oh, me and Lo go way back," she said. "Ever since I helped her put glow-in-the-dark paint stuff on some of your clothes."

Cole's mouth fell open. "You helped her? What are you, some kind of traitor?"

"Oh, that was nothing," she sneered. "There was also the time we shrank all your boxers."

"You said that was an accident."

Tater ignored him. "Or my personal favorite, when I put a laxative in your Coke right before your date with Melissa Walsh."

Cole's eyes went wide. "That was you?"

Tater laughed. "It was her idea, not mine," she said, pointing at Logan. "Though it was my idea that she spend the whole day with her mom so she'd have a solid alibi."

Her brother shook his head and said very slowly, "I will kill you."

Tater stuck her tongue out just as two grown men Logan immediately recognized as Adam and Keith Tucker walked into the room.

"Who's Cole killing?" Keith asked. He was the middle brother of the three and, according to the chief, had started his own construction company. He was tall just like the others, with dark hair and a bit of scruff on his face that suited him. He took the seat beside Cole. "Because, given their history I'd be willing to bet it's this stunning vixen sitting before me," he finished with a wink that Logan couldn't help but smile at.

Adam grabbed an extra chair from the wall behind him and pulled it up on the other side of Cole before plopping down. Unlike the rest of the Tucker children, Adam had lighter hair like his mother. And he was by far the bulkiest.

Adam had been a high school football star in his own day and went on to become one of Willow Creek High's assistant coaches.

"Could we maybe hear how the infamous Logan Kase came to be eating lunch at our humble table before you kill her? I bet it's a really good story."

"It's not," Cole said dryly. "And I'm not going to kill her. At least not today."

Keith perked up. "Oh good, it would be a shame to kill someone looking as lovely as she does today," he said. "And I do mean that with all sincerity, Lo. We all knew you'd age well, but we had no idea how well. I mean, in that dress…" Keith whistled as he made a show of observing her legs under the table.

Logan's cheeks flooded with heat just as Cole punched Keith hard in the arm.

"Ow!" he yelled, rubbing the spot. "Don't tell me you're getting jealous."

Cole shrugged. "Not at all, just a friendly reminder that you've already got a girl…I believe you call her your *wife.*"

"What about Adam?" Keith cried, pointing an accusing finger at his older brother. "He's the one with a kid on the way. Aren't you gonna hit him?"

Adam's head shot up. "Did I say anything?"

"You were thinking it!"

Cole glanced at his two brothers before punching Adam in the arm for good measure.

"Dammit, Cole!" Adam yelled before hitting his brother back. Logan watched in stunned silence as the three of them proceeded to strike each other over and over.

Tater looked disgusted. "You see the kind of adolescents I have to deal with."

"How on earth do you manage?" Logan asked, watching the three boys with amusement.

"Oh, that part's easy. Daddy!"

"You boys better knock it off before I give you something to really get upset about!" Mr. Tucker yelled from the doorway. "Now get your lazy asses up and come carry the food out for your mother like gentlemen."

They each stopped and glared at Tater before they stood and did exactly as their father said. Once all three had passed with slumped shoulders, Mr. Tucker gave Tater a wink before following behind the boys.

⇶⫷

"MRS. TUCKER, IS there something I can do to help?"

Logan stood in the kitchen doorway watching as Cole's mom worked over the sink, rinsing and shoving dishes into the dishwasher.

Lunch had gone surprisingly well, much to Logan's relief. Of course, that was mostly because the boys, Tater, and Mr. Tucker ended up talking the whole time. Keith and Adam showed her pictures of their wives, who were busy planning a baby shower and couldn't make it to lunch that day. Otherwise, the majority of the Tuckers hadn't given her presence a second thought.

Mrs. Tucker, however, sat quietly through the entire meal and spoke only when someone complimented the cooking. Logan felt sick with each icy glare of distaste the woman kept throwing at her almost as much as her own mother's silence all weekend. Cole's mom made it perfectly clear that Logan wasn't welcome at their table, and Lo would have left right in the middle of the meal just to escape the discomfort if Cole hadn't put one of their challenges on the line.

After Mr. Tucker urged Cole, Keith, Adam, and even Tater to help him with an old truck that wasn't working right, Logan felt almost sick at the realization that she was about to be left all alone with Mrs. Tucker. Cole had been no help, simply giving her a sympathetic look before heading out the back door.

"I'm nearly done with the dishes," she muttered, glancing at Logan over her shoulder. Almost as if it pained her to say it, she asked, "You ever make a pie?"

Logan's chest lifted a little. "I used to make them all the time with my momma."

Mrs. Tucker nodded. She put the last of the dirty dishes in the dishwasher and closed it. "You get a bowl out of that cupboard"—she pointed to the one in the corner—"and I'll get the stuff for the crust."

Logan did as she was told, and the two of them silently started work on mixing the dough for a pie crust.

"I noticed the sunflower painting on your staircase. I recognized it from the art gallery in town Mrs. Snyder used to run. It was one of my favorites."

Mrs. Tucker grunted.

"I actually graduated with a degree in art history because of that gallery. I used to go there almost every day after school until she closed it down."

Nothing.

Logan stopped cutting the butter, flour, and shortening, swung around, and leaned against the counter. "Look, Mrs. Tucker. I know you don't like me but—"

"It's not that I don't like you." She huffed as she grabbed a bowl full of peaches from the end of the counter. "You just make me nervous."

"Nervous?"

"What exactly is going on between you and my son?"

"I'm not sure what you mean." Surely, she didn't think they were romantically involved. They could barely stand each other.

"Cole is reckless around you. Growing up, he was always getting into trouble or dangerous situations that I'm almost certain was because of you. Now he's a grown, responsible young man. The kind of man I always hoped he'd be, and I'm so proud of him for that.

"But with you back now, I'm scared he's going to go

back to being that crazy, reckless boy he was." Mrs. Tucker put down the peach she was peeling and looked Logan straight in the eye for the first time all afternoon. "I already have to worry about him risking his life every day at work. I don't need any more anxiety keeping me up at night."

For the first time, Logan saw a bit of her own mother in Mrs. Tucker. "I didn't realize you worried about him so much."

Mrs. Tucker laughed. "How could I not? When he would come home drunk in the middle of the night, thinking I couldn't hear him stumbling around downstairs? Or when he dislocated his shoulder trying to ride a bull bareback for no reason, according to him?"

Logan remembered that one vividly. Not her best moment. The whole thing had been a joke; she'd never intended for him to actually do it. But once he got the idea, he'd been stubborn.

"Or," Mrs. Tucker went on, "there was the time when the school nurse called to tell me there was a rumor going around that my youngest boy had chlamydia. That was a day I'll never forget."

Logan tried not to laugh and failed. "In my defense, I didn't say which STD it was, only that he had one." She stopped, taking a deep breath before turning serious. "I know we can be crazy and do stupid things, especially back then. And I'm sorry. I never realized how hard it must have been to watch helplessly on the side."

"I know for a fact your mother felt the same way." Cole's mom frowned, her eyes drifting to the window above the kitchen sink. Logan followed her gaze, spotting the truck and the four Tucker men bickering with each other around it. Ironically, Tater seemed to be the only one actually working under the hood.

"I've just never understood it," she said, watching her kids. "The relationship between you two. You swore you hated each other. But you were loyal, no matter what happened between you. I've been teaching for over thirty years—siblings, best friends—and I've never seen anything like the bond you two have. I just wish I knew what it was."

Logan continued to stare out the window. Cole's hair was messy, his dress shirt gone, leaving only a white T-shirt that now had about as much grease on it as his hands. He was smiling, not the way he usually did when he was acting cocky or flirtatious. But a real smile that reminded her of the kids they used to be.

"Honestly," Logan muttered, grinning at the sight of Cole grabbing Keith in a headlock. "I'm not sure we know what it is either."

When Mrs. Tucker said nothing, Logan turned to find the woman staring at her. Not knowing what else to do, Logan turned her eyes back down to the bowl of pastry dough she was cutting. She silently willed the rush of blood in her cheeks to disappear.

"So," Mrs. Tucker said after a moment's silence. "Tell

me about the kind of art you like."

LOGAN COULD NOT stop laughing.

She was sitting in the Tuckers' living room, her strappy heels kicked off, and her feet pulled up under her on the couch. Tater sat next to her on the sofa, bent over, and clutching her stomach as tears of laughter spilled from her eyes. Keith was on her other side. Mr. Tucker sat in a chair, while his wife was poised on the arm, her own arm draped over his shoulders. Adam was in the other chair by himself.

"So, he would walk around naked?" Logan squealed in disbelief. "Like completely naked?"

Mrs. Tucker nodded. "He swore he was going to be like that survivalist on TV. And apparently, that meant walking around the house and yard without a stitch of clothing on. Sure gave the neighbors a good sight."

The room filled with yet another burst of laughter. It started to ebb after several seconds, only to pick back up the second Cole walked into the living room. He looked around warily. "What's going on here, Dad? I thought you were coming in to see what was keeping Adam and Keith so long with the beers."

Mr. Tucker wiped at his eyes. "We got a little distracted. Besides, the truck is a lost cause. I'll call Darren first thing in the morning to take a look."

Tater patted the small space on the couch between her and Logan. "Come sit. We were just telling Logan some of our favorite stories about you."

Cole visibly stiffened, his eyes darting to Logan, who was doing all she could to not laugh. "What have they told you?"

"Not much," she lied, shaking her head.

Adam nodded. "Yeah, unless you count the bedwetting. Or when me and Keith used to dress you up in Mom's old clothes and make you look like Dolly Parton."

"And the time you ate an entire dinosaur cake on your fifth birthday and thought you were dying 'cause it turned your shit blue." Keith laughed and looked at Logan. "Took us four hours to get him to stop crying."

"Oooh! What about that song he sang nonstop all summer at Aunt Kayla's lake cabin?" Tater shouted, and the five of them—even Mr. Tucker, much to Logan's amusement—burst out in a familiar Britney Spears hit. Logan doubled over, laughing.

"Okay, that's it," Cole said, shaking his head. He crossed the room abruptly, grabbing Logan's hand and hauling her up to her feet. "Sorry, guys, but I promised Logan I'd have her back home soon. So we should get going."

Her bottom lip stuck out. "Are you sure we can't wait a little bit longer? We're having such a wonderful time."

"I'm sure," he said, glaring at her. His hand still holding hers, Cole pulled her across the room, yanking her strappy heels up off the floor and dragging her into the hallway.

Logan stopped him short again. "But what about the pie your mom and I made?"

"Don't worry, hun," Mrs. Tucker said, getting up from her seat and coming over to them. "I'll make sure to send a piece over to you. And don't forget to send me a save the date as soon as the wedding is set." She opened her arms, wrapping Logan in a warm hug. "You'll make a beautiful bride."

Logan smiled, hugging her back. "Thank you, Mrs. Tucker. I had a great time."

"I told you, call me Suzanne."

Before Logan could say anything, Cole was hauling her away. "Bye, Suzanne!" she yelled as he dragged her to the Bronco, shaking his head.

They rode in silence for several minutes, Cole unusually quiet. But she didn't mind. She smiled in the passenger seat, her mind still replaying her afternoon.

It wasn't until they'd pulled up next to her truck in the church parking lot that she finally spoke. She shifted in her seat, fiddling with the dress that was all wrinkled now, then looked up to see Cole observing her.

"What?"

"Nothing," he said. "I'm just kind of amazed. I didn't think they'd take to you that well, but somehow you won them over."

Logan grinned. For reasons she didn't understand, that statement made her entire body feel light as air. "I liked them, too. And that's what you get for using your family for a bet."

"What about when you involved the chief?"

"Whatever. The point is, you couldn't take it." She leaned over and poked his chest. "You pulled us out of there, and now *you* get a big fat *R*."

Logan did a little victory dance in the passenger seat of the Bronco. "That means only two letters left, and then you lose."

He watched her, failing miserably at looking upset. He sighed. "Well, even if it cost me a letter in the process, I'm glad you had a good time."

"I really did," she said slowly. "Thanks for the invite. It was definitely better than staying at home alone."

"You know," he said, looking down at his hands, "you're welcome back anytime."

Logan grinned, imagining another Sunday afternoon with the Tuckers. "I think I'd like that."

He looked up. "But no more childhood stories. You've already got too much dirt on me."

She shrugged. "We'll see."

She grabbed her shoes in hand and slid out of the Bronco before turning back, leaning in through the open door. "I just have one question for you."

"Yeah?" Cole asked, getting a cocky grin as he leaned across the cab, closer to her.

Logan shifted her weight from one bare foot to the other

on the hot pavement. "Did you really have a crush on Velma from *Scooby-Doo?*"

The cocky grin vanished. He sat back in his seat, his head falling back on the headrest. "I was eight."

"Still," she said with a laugh, "didn't most boys go for Daphne?"

His head snapped up. "Velma was the smart one. I like to think it showed maturity."

"Uh-huh." She shut the door and turned, waving over her shoulder. "Bye, Cole."

"See you later, Lo."

Chapter Nineteen

"I STILL CAN'T believe you forgot to tell me that you spent an entire Sunday afternoon with the Tuckers and lived to tell about it... What about this one?" Carly asked, holding up a long, slim, peach dress. Logan considered it for a second before shaking her head. Her friend frowned and put it back on the rack.

Logan turned to the collection of dresses in front of her, skimming through them. "Henry and Suzanne actually liked me by the end of it. He even lifted the ban at the hardware store."

"It's true," Tater said as she sifted through her own row of brightly colored dresses. "Mom even sent Daddy over with some pie for her that night." Tater had been there, too, wanting to know if there was any way Logan could help her pick out a dress for prom in a couple weeks—it wasn't exactly something she could ask her brothers for help with. Logan had been more than happy to accept. "The chief looked so shocked to see us, I thought he was going to pass out."

Actually, Logan's dad had been three innings into a

baseball game on TV when Mr. Tucker came knocking that night. When the chief saw who was at the door, he scowled at Logan from his recliner in the living room and asked, "What did you do this time?"

"He nearly did pass out when Mr. Tucker invited him to go fishing this Saturday. I can't even remember the last time I saw Daddy so excited."

Carly moved to a new rack. "Do you have a specific color in mind, Tater?"

"She looks amazing in green," Logan offered.

"I don't really do bright colors. I like simple, but I don't want it to be boring."

Carly pulled out a short, black and white dress with a full skirt. "What about this one? It's short and cute, but the black and white gives it a classic sophistication. And the white will really pop with your tan. I dare anyone to say it looks boring on you."

Tater's eyes glittered just looking at it. "Definitely add it to the stack."

This was why Logan had invited Carly along. Logan had never been the girly type, or terribly good with fashion, which was why she was so lucky to have Carly. Instead of going to the mall or getting her nails done, Logan had always preferred playing in the mud and chasing Cole Tucker around with whatever implement of torture she chose that day. Her lips curled up at the memories.

She'd found herself thinking about Cole a lot lately. Especially in the last week since lunch with him and his family. She looked forward to whatever challenge she chose next, but even more, she anticipated when she'd just see him again. It made absolutely no sense.

Maybe she'd been wrong. Maybe the two of them could be friends after all.

"Why are you grinning?" Carly asked, staring at Logan.

"No reason, just thinking about what a perfect night this will be for Tater," she said, turning to the girl in question. "Who are you going with?"

Tater shrugged. "No date. My best friend, Chelsea, and I decided to go stag together. Figured we'd have more fun that way."

Carly laughed. "See, now that's the way to do it. Why didn't we have the sense to think of something like that?"

Tater winced. "Bad dates?"

"You could say that." Carly continued looking through more dresses. She pulled out a thin, pale blue one. "What about this color for your bridesmaid dresses, Lo?"

Logan glanced at the dress, her teeth pinching the soft flesh of her cheek. She tried to envision Carly and a few of her sorority sisters in light blue dresses at her wedding, but just like always, she couldn't picture any of it. Not the bridesmaids, not the colors, not the flowers. Nothing.

Carly still held up the dress. Logan's cheeks felt warm, and the more she tried to visualize her wedding, the hotter her skin grew.

She turned to the stack of dresses they'd already picked out for Tater. "Well," she said, hefting them up and ignoring her best friend's question, "what do you say we get to the fun part and you start trying some of these bad boys on?"

LOGAN COULD FEEL Carly watching her as they stood outside the dress boutique waiting for Tater to pay.

"You want to tell me what was going on back there?" Carly asked quietly.

"What do you mean?" Logan said, adjusting the rolled-up sleeves of her plaid flannel shirt.

"The way you keep changing the subject anytime I mention your wedding."

"It's not a big deal," she said. "I guess I just haven't really been in the mood to plan anything ever since Jacob told my parents about San Francisco. Momma's still not talking to me. Daddy's putting on a brave face for both of us, but I can tell it's bothering him a little, too. And then between your wedding and the move and the job hunt, the future is just so overwhelming right now." She conveniently left out the panicky feeling she got any time she so much as thought about the details of her wedding.

"Oh, Lo." Carly pulled her into a hug. "Don't worry, sweetie. Just give them some more time. They'll come around to it. I'm sure they understand this is what's best for you right now. And as for the future and the wedding, you've got plenty of time to figure all that stuff out. And if you need help with anything, I'm always right here." Carly patted Logan on the back, and some of the residual stress ebbed, but only slightly.

"I know. Thanks, Carly."

Tater came out of the small downtown boutique clutching a garment bag. "I love it!" she squealed as she ran to them. "Thank you both so much for helping me with this. You have no idea how much I needed it."

Logan laughed. "If you're anything like me, I do."

Tater was on the verge of saying something when she spotted someone far off. "Is that...Cole!" she yelled across the street. Logan felt a jolt in her stomach, and sure enough, she turned to find Cole Tucker coming out of Macy's Market with several grocery bags in hand.

Tater waved, and Cole started making his way over.

"Now, why does seeing the three of you together make me so nervous?"

"Don't look at me," Carly said. "I'm a neutral party in this rivalry."

He peered at Tater, waiting.

She sighed. "If you must know, they were helping me shop for a prom dress."

"Really?" Cole looked skeptical.

"Yes, really," she said, holding up the garment bag. "Believe it or not, not everything revolves around you." Tater glanced at her watch and her shoulders fell. "Crap, I should go. I have a big test in history tomorrow I need to study for, and I wanted to go to the hardware store to show Daddy my dress." Tater smiled at Logan and Carly. "I'll see you guys later. And thanks again for all the help."

"No problem, Tater."

"Yeah, we had a blast. And you better call me so we can figure out what time you need me to come over and do your hair," Carly said.

Tater's eyes went wide. "But it's the weekend before your wedding. Are you sure?"

"Yes, I'm sure. By then, I bet I'll be begging for the distraction."

"Okay, thanks," she said. "I better get going."

"Wait, don't you want to show me your dress?" Cole asked.

She scowled at him. "You don't deserve to see it. Bye, guys." She waved, then crossed the street on her way to the hardware store.

Cole's eyes followed his sister until she was several shops away.

"What are you up to today?" Carly asked, eyeing the grocery bags filled with sodas and several kinds of chips and snack foods in his hands. "Please tell me all that junk isn't just for you and Cowboy."

"It's for the guys at the station."

"That's the kind of crap you guys eat when you're on

duty?"

He snorted. "Not usually, no. And I'm not technically working today. But we've got a game of poker going tonight, and I offered to bring snacks."

"You guys play poker? That's so cute," Logan said, trying to picture it.

"Well, when you're stuck in the station for three days with no emergencies, you get bored. And when you're as good as me, it can help to pay the bills from time to time."

"You drive a fifteen-year-old truck and still share a two-bedroom rental with your best friend. You don't have to be that good to pay those bills."

Cole smirked. "Whereas you're a real cardsharp, I bet," he said, voice flat with sarcasm.

"As a matter of fact, my dad taught me how to play when I was sixteen. And I beat him most of the time. I bet I could beat you."

"Is that an official challenge?"

"Maybe it is."

He shrugged. "All right, let's go."

Logan's smile fell. "Wait, what…you mean right now?"

"Why not? We've already got a game set up. Unless you've got something planned tonight?" he asked, eyes traveling to Carly. Logan had all but forgotten she was there.

Carly shook her head, watching Logan silently.

"No…but what about the guys? They won't want me crashing."

He laughed. "On the contrary, I think they'll find your presence highly entertaining."

Logan's skin buzzed. She'd be lying if she said she didn't want to spend her Thursday evening in yet another challenge with Cole Tucker. But it was that very enthusiasm that made her hesitate.

"I don't know," she said, the weight of her best friend's gaze like fifty-pound dumbbells on each shoulder. "I rode here with Carly, so my truck is back at the house."

"I can give you a ride, Lo. It's not a big deal. Let me beat you at poker, and then I'll have you back home before curfew," he teased. "Unless you're scared to play me."

She huffed. "Please. When have you ever known me to be scared of anything?"

"I can think of at least once," he said slowly, his eyes hard on hers. It made her skin itch.

"Go ahead, Logan." Carly sighed. "I need to stop by the store to get stuff for dinner tonight anyway."

Logan's eyes darted between them. "Fine, but only because someone needs to bring you down a peg," she told Cole.

Carly stepped over and gave Logan a quick hug. "Be careful," she whispered.

"It's just poker."

Carly pulled back, her voice still low. "You know what I mean." She pointed at Cole. "And you," she said loudly. "You better make sure my best friend doesn't get arrested or you'll have me to answer to."

"I promise, no additions to her already extensive criminal record tonight." He laughed.

Carly hugged him. "That's my boy. I'll see you guys later."

Logan watched as Carly crossed the street over to Macy's Market. *Be careful.* The words felt heavy in her stomach.

"You ready?" Cole asked. Almost instantly, the weight in her gut vanished.

She nodded. "Here, I can carry some of that," she said, pointing at the bags in his hands.

"Nah, I got it. I feel bad enough that I'm about to take all your money and win my easiest challenge yet. The least I can do is spare you the heavy lifting."

She laughed. "You seem awfully sure of yourself."

"Oh, honey," he said with a sickly sweet grin, "you have no idea."

❧❧❧❧❧❦❦❦❦

"HERE, THIS ONE'S on me."

Cole Tucker pulled a wad of cash out of his pocket, including all of Logan's poker money, and set a five down on the bar. Lilly handed Logan another beer and frowned. "It's all right, doll. You'll get him next time."

Logan twisted the top off and took a gulp, relishing the cold drink as it traveled to her stomach.

Unfortunately for her, Cole had not been exaggerating about his poker skills. And even worse, she was now fairly certain that her daddy had been taking it easy on her all those years. She hadn't just lost; she'd failed miserably.

She'd wanted to go straight home after, feeling sluggish with a belly full of bland, greasy pizza from Sherman's Slice. She wanted to relax and lick her wounds. But Cole had insisted on stopping by Wade's to update the scoreboard and spread his good news.

So instead of a long, warm bubble bath, Logan was settling for ice-cold beer.

"Don't look so sad, Lo," Cole said as he sat on the barstool beside her. He took a drag from his own bottle. "At least we know, for future reference, that you really suck at poker."

"Bite me."

"If it helps, it's not completely your fault. I can just tell when you're bluffing is all."

"Bullshit," she shouted over the music and bar chatter.

He chuckled, pointing at his temple. "Ah, you forget. I've watched you lie since the sixth grade, can even hear it in your voice. I know your tell, Logan Kase."

She rolled her eyes, taking another long chug from her beer and nearly finishing it.

"Whoa. Slow down, cowgirl." He called to Lilly down at the other end of the bar. "Can we get one more here, Lill? Thanks."

Lilly reached for another beer behind the bar, but Logan waved her off. "Can we go now? As much as I love watching you brag about your win, I do have other things I could be doing."

"Like what?"

Like trying to find a job, like trying to plan her wedding, like calling her fiancé for the first time in three days. "Can we just go?"

Cole sighed and pulled out a five to cover his own beer. "Fine, I suppose you've suffered enough for one night. Keep the change, Lilly."

Logan drained the last of her bottle and hopped down from her seat, glad to get away from the noisy crowd that frequented the bar this late at night.

They drove silently, for the most part, Cole tapping his fingers on the steering wheel and Logan humming along with the music. Before long, they pulled up in front of her house. Cole put the Bronco in park and waited.

She stared out the window in front of her. She hadn't been lying when she said she wanted to leave the bar, but the truth was, she wasn't quite ready to go home either. And now the thought of all that awaited her inside pressed down on her, making it impossible to move. First, there would be her momma wondering where she'd been and why Cole Tucker, of all people, was dropping her off. Then she'd have to call Jacob because they had barely spoken since the dinner with her parents, and she knew it wasn't right, but couldn't bring herself to get over how he'd acted. And when Jacob asked what she'd been doing tonight, she would have to lie to him.

Logan felt the same rising heat from the boutique flood her skin.

"Hey," Cole said.

She glanced at the clock; they'd been sitting silently for several minutes.

"Want to do something fun?"

Her eyes narrowed. "Is this another challenge?"

"Not a challenge," he said. "Just a little mischief."

She did like mischief.

Carly's words of caution echoed in her mind. Had Carly guessed the night wouldn't end with poker? Probably. Was she concerned about whatever trouble Logan would almost inevitably get into? Maybe. But then why didn't Logan believe that?

Maybe Carly was just worried her friend was getting too deep into her old ways. Contemplating this undoubtedly nefarious scheme of Cole's, she was a little worried about it herself. But the fact of the matter was, Cole was offering her an escape from the real world that waited for her inside. Even if only temporarily.

"Okay, what did you have in mind?"

Chapter Twenty

"WHY WE ARE sneaking onto Old Man Carithers's property in the middle of the night?" Logan whispered.

"I told you, it's a surprise." Cole led the way through the woods out by Harrold Carithers's barn. Logan hadn't had any idea where he was going when he pulled off the road and onto a worn trail through the woods. He'd driven slowly, with his headlights off, using only the patchy bits of moonlight shining through the clouds to light his way. She'd asked several times where they were, but it wasn't until they'd left the Bronco and started walking the rest of the path that he'd told her.

She squinted, her eyes focusing on what looked like a clearing up ahead through the trees. "Please tell me we aren't here just so you can steal a couple chickens again."

"It was twelve chickens. And no, that's not why we're here."

"Then why?" she asked as they came up to the edge of the woods. A couple hundred feet away and down a small hill sat Carithers's familiar old barn.

In front of the barn, Logan could just barely make out the chicken coop, and in the back sat a large fenced-in pasture several acres wide. It wrapped around to the front and ran parallel to the gravel drive that led from the road to the barn.

"Now keep quiet and follow me."

Logan did as he said, following closely behind and not saying anything until they were coming around to the front of the barn.

She froze. "What's that?"

"Doghouse," Cole muttered as he moved to the barn door.

"You mean he finally got that guard dog he kept talking about?" she whispered so as not to disturb the dog she could now hear snoring inside.

"Relax." He pulled something out of his pocket and started messing with the lock on the door. "Moses may technically be a guard dog, but he's about the laziest, sweetest one you'll ever find. He's just here to look scary." Cole knelt down and rapped the shingled roof. "Ain't that right, Moses?"

Inside, the dog groaned before falling back into heavy snores.

Cole managed to open the padlock and remove it, pulling the barn door open and then disappearing inside. Logan silently followed.

She hadn't been inside the barn since the branding iron

incident, and never had she been here at night. It was dark inside, the air filled with the sounds of loud huffs and heavy thumps. With each breath, she took in the smell of hay and some other distinct smell she couldn't immediately identify. Her gaze shifted around, trying to make out the source of the sounds and smell.

She took a step forward and heard something large shift to her right. "What was that?" she whispered.

Light flooded the barn. Logan looked to her right and nearly jumped out of her skin at the sight of the massive brown and white horse penned up just over a foot from her.

Slowly turning away from the gigantic animal that had nearly given her a heart attack, she took in the rest of the barn. She saw the workbench by the front corner of the barn with a few different tools scattered across its surface just like it had been the afternoon she'd fallen onto the branding iron and Cole had to take her to the emergency room. She shuddered.

There was a loft above her with what looked like hundreds of bales of hay, which explained the smell. And running along each side of the barn was a row of stalls, each with a thousand-pound animal tucked away inside. Seven in all, she quickly counted. Some, like the one beside her, stood still as they chose to either watch or completely ignore her. Others paced back and forth anxiously.

Logan looked around again, searching for Cole, but she didn't find him. She did, however, see a door wide open down at the other end. From where she stood it looked like some kind of closet, and she thought she heard Cole moving around inside it.

She turned back to the brown and white horse.

"Hi there," she said carefully, not sure if this one was a boy or a girl—or if it was the type to try to bite her fingers off if she touched it.

The horse reached its neck out and sniffed the air between them. Slowly, Logan stepped forward, raising her hand to the animal's head. The horse barely reacted as her hand came to its face, and she placed her palm on the spot between its eyes. To her relief, it didn't freak out and try to bite her. Instead, the horse leaned into her hand.

She grinned as the horse nuzzled her palm. "You're not so scary," she whispered. Of course, it helped that the horse was stuck in its stall and Logan was safely outside of it.

"That's Cheyenne," Cole said, his voice coming from a couple stalls down where a large dark brown horse had been pacing. She wasn't sure when he'd moved from the closet to the stall or why he was even in there in the first place. But, honestly, she was too busy marveling at the horse in front of her to care.

Logan turned back to the horse, moving her hand up to scratch behind her ear. "She's pretty."

"She especially likes it when you rub the spot at the base of her neck. She can't reach it herself very well."

Logan took a deep breath, eyeing the horse. As if Cheyenne had understood him, she turned on the spot, bringing her neck and side up to the edge. Before she could chicken out, Logan reached over the low door and into the stall, patting the horse's neck. Again, the horse leaned into it.

"Whoa!" she gasped, taking in the horse's large belly. "Are they supposed to get this fat?"

Cole chuckled from within the other stall. "She's not fat; she's pregnant." He stepped out of the stall and closed it again behind him. "Come on," he said. "Let's get you a saddle."

"Why would I need a saddle?"

"Unless you want to ride bareback—which I don't recommend—you're going to need a saddle."

"*Ride?* I can't ride a horse," she screeched.

He shook his head. "It's easy. I would put you on Cheyenne, but she's due any day. Pixie's just as gentle; she'll go easy on you."

"No, you don't get it. Horses and I are not a good mix." Not since she'd tried to ride one at her cousin Darby's horse farm one summer and was bucked off, nearly breaking her arm. Logan tried to imagine herself up on top of an animal ten times her size again, trying to keep it under control beneath her. All it would take was one throw and she'd be a goner. "I can't, Cole."

"All right, fine," he said softly. He turned back into the stall he'd just left and came out with the massive, dark brown horse in tow. "You can ride with me then."

"What?" she asked, almost as shocked as when he'd mentioned her riding alone. "On one horse?"

The barn filled with the echo of clomping hooves as Cole walked the horse to the open barn door and patted it on the neck. "Yeah, Rocky's already saddled up and ready to go. This way we didn't waste the trip and you can still have some fun."

Logan hesitated. "I don't know."

"Hey," he said, coming over to her and placing his hands on her upper arms. His eyes were hard on hers. "I'll be in control the whole time. All you have to do is sit back and enjoy the ride."

She eyed the horse, who'd amazingly stayed exactly where Cole left him, shifting his weight every few seconds. He really was big, maybe the biggest one in the barn. She could see the long, lean muscle moving under his skin as he shifted on his feet. A thick, white stripe ran down from his forehead to his snout. Despite his anxious pacing earlier, his eyes looked calm and gentle, surrounded by long, black lashes.

Maybe it was the two beers that made her nod, but anyone in town knew it took more than two measly beers to get Logan doing something stupid. Of course, it only ever took one Cole Tucker.

"Okay, fine," she said before she could take it back. "But I better not fall off this thing."

Cole patted the horse's neck. "Don't worry, Lo. I'd never

let you fall."

LOGAN WAS GETTING the hang of this. Sure, her butt was starting to hurt, and the way she swayed with each step the horse took reminded her of many a drunken walk home after an uproarious college party her freshman year. But it really wasn't so bad.

She was even starting to enjoy herself.

"So how do you know how to do this?" she asked Cole after they'd been riding in silence awhile. With nothing to hold on to, she'd been forced to wrap her arms around Cole's waist. She refused to really hold on to him, so instead her hands were gripping the saddle horn in front of him. Still, this kind of proximity felt strange to her, almost intimate. She'd tried to ignore the way her stomach fluttered nervously—she would be nervous sitting this close to anyone, she told herself—but in the silence, ignoring it had been impossible.

She needed to distract herself. "And how do you know so much about these horses?" she went on.

"It was when I started helping Carithers out around the barn. I'd never been on a horse before, but once I started taking care of them and getting to know them, it was all I wanted to do. Carithers wouldn't let me ride them while I was working, so I started sneaking down here at night."

"How did you learn to ride?"

He shrugged, and she felt her cheek brush the shoulder of his soft T-shirt. "Taught myself. It wasn't too hard. They're well trained and, once I had their trust, it was easy. I snuck out here any chance I had. Gave me some much-needed peace and quiet."

She laughed, trying to picture it. "How did I not know this?"

"There are still some things even you don't know about me, Logan Kase," he said softly. Something about the quiet gentleness of his voice eased the tight knot in her stomach. She took a deep breath, feeling her body relax.

"So, what? You're just going to keep sneaking out here anytime you want like a teenage boy?"

"No. One day I'd like to have some of my own. You know, once I'm done saving up for the big house and all that land."

She pictured it instantly: Cole Tucker in a big ranch-style or farmhouse sitting on several acres of land, his horses running freely in the fields behind it. It was perfect for him. "That sounds nice," she said.

"Yep. Maybe you can come out sometime, and I'll teach you how to handle one of these all by yourself," he teased.

"Yeah, maybe," she muttered, her chest growing heavy. He still didn't know about her inevitable move to California. She wanted to tell him that her time in Willow Creek was temporary, needed to even. They'd been through too much together—not just in the last several weeks but over the past ten years—for her to hide it from him now. "Cole…"

There was a crash of thunder overhead, and the two of them jumped. She hadn't realized her cheek was resting on the back of Cole's shoulder until she felt the cool breeze hit her warm skin. Cole looked up, and Logan followed his gaze, spotting an immense cloud drifting across the starry sky.

"We need to get back before those clouds completely cut out the moonlight." He looked back over his shoulder and grinned. "Hold on tight and try not to scream." Cole kicked his legs.

"Why would I—?" Like the bullet out of the gun, Rocky took off. Logan let out a high-pitched yelp, and she could both feel and hear Cole laughing. She'd abandoned her hold on the saddle horn, instead holding on to Cole for dear life as her thighs squeezed around the horse in a desperate attempt to stay on. She shoved her closed mouth into Cole's shoulder, biting back the scream that tried to escape.

Rocky was a smooth runner, his hooves hammering into the ground at a steady but rapid pace. Fortunately, staying on top of the horse wasn't as difficult as she would have imagined at this speed.

They neared the barn just as another crash of thunder hit overhead. Logan felt drops like fat, cool tears hitting her head and shoulders. Rocky finally slowed as they came around to the front of the barn, and Cole carefully led them into the shelter and out of the rain.

He helped her swing down off the horse before he did so himself. He was grinning broadly, the exhilaration of the ride still shining in his eyes.

She hit him with her shaking hand. "You can't just take off like that without telling me! What if I fell off!"

"Oh, come on. I told you I wouldn't let you fall. And you loved it," he said.

True, she couldn't stop grinning.

In no time, Cole slung the saddle off the horse and set it aside. He removed the saddle pad and reins, replacing the latter with a blue halter before swiftly brushing the horse's neck and back.

He took her hand and placed it on Rocky's halter. "Here, you put him in the stall while I put this away."

She hesitated only a fraction before she guided the half-ton horse back to his door. He went peacefully, no doubt worn out from the mile run he'd just completed. Logan gave him a firm pat on the neck. "Thanks for the ride," she said before turning and closing the stall door.

Then she heard it. It was faint at first, almost blending into the sound of the rain hitting hard on the barn roof. Then it got louder, clearer. The sound of tires racing up the crunchy gravel.

"Cole."

The barn lights went black, and Logan just barely kept herself from screaming. A strong hand grabbed hers. "Come on," he said, pulling her back to the closet he'd been in before, which she was now sure was the tack room.

"Whoever the hell is in there better come out before I start shooting!" Old Man Carithers yelled from the front.

"The window," Cole said, pointing quickly to the small window several feet up in the corner before he locked the tack room door.

Logan sprang into action, using what looked like large barrels of feed to hoist herself up to the window. It was easy enough to push open, and seconds later she wiggled her way through it. She fell hard on the ground, grateful to see that Cole was squeezing his way out right behind her.

"Get up, Moses! You lazy, good for nothin' mutt."

Logan stood, ready to help Cole in his escape, but he shot through that window like he'd done it a hundred times before. He even managed to land somewhat gracefully. He stood, taking her hand in his. "Run!"

The two of them took off for the woods almost a hundred yards away. The rain was hammering down, but Logan didn't care. Her heart was pounding in her throat as she darted as fast as she could up the hill to the tree line ahead of them.

There was a blast—Carithers hadn't been kidding when he said he'd start shooting. She didn't look back, though, couldn't. Not with Cole pulling her along beside him at breakneck speed. Her lungs burned, and her legs begged her to stop.

When they finally made it into the trees, Logan wasn't

sure she could run anymore. Cole didn't force her. Instead, he whipped her around behind a large tree, sandwiching her between it and him as another shot rang out.

She was soaking wet by now. Her flannel shirt stuck to her, her long hair dripping as it clung to her face and neck. The rain was cold, still hitting them beneath the canopy of pine needles. A shiver crept over her skin as goose bumps rose on her flesh.

Cole Tucker was pressed against her, soaked and breathing heavily. She felt his warmth through their wet clothes as both their chests rose and fell in synchronicity. She could feel his erratic heartbeat like it was hammering in her own chest.

Before she could stop it, a memory from a night four years back flooded her senses. Their hearts pounding together to one firm, quick beat. Their breath mingling as their lips found each other over and over. The electrifying feeling of rough hands roaming over naked flesh. Her voice begging him not to stop while her heart silently told him no moment in her life had ever been more perfect.

No. Logan stopped herself there, reality hitting her hard as a sharp pain stabbed within her. She'd learned a long time ago not to think about that night. But as she stood here pressed against him, breathing his breath, she hadn't been strong enough to stop it.

"And if you ever come back, those won't just be warning shots!" Carithers yelled into the black, raining sky.

She felt Cole relax against her. He stayed close, his head

bent down to hers.

"You okay?" he whispered.

She nodded. Neither of them moved or spoke, their eyes searching each other's as their thundering hearts calmed. Finally, when the moment became too much, Logan looked down at his chest where she'd only just realized her hands were clutching his shirt. She let go.

"So much for promising Carly to keep me safe," she choked out, her voice thick and froggy.

He smiled down at her. "For the record, I promised I wouldn't get you arrested. I didn't say anything about getting shot."

"Oh, well then, good job," she said lightly, clapping him on the shoulder while simultaneously pushing him off of her. She needed fresh air and a clear head, neither of which she would get pressed against Cole Tucker.

His eyes followed her as she moved around him, his gaze steady. She waited for him to say something. For the first time, she wasn't sure what she wanted him to say.

Seconds later he gave her a tiny smile. "Come on, let's get you home." He turned and started walking the path back to the Bronco, leaving Logan nothing to do but follow him.

Chapter Twenty-One

LOGAN'S EYES SLOWLY opened as sunlight poured in and pulled her from her sleepy haze. Taking a deep breath, she stretched out her arms and legs. It felt so good, though not as good as the dream she'd just woken from. She grinned, running through it all again.

Lips trailing over her neck and jaw. Powerful hands gripping her waist. Her body coming alive in a way it hadn't for several months now. Crying out his name.

Cole.

Logan's eyes shot wide as that final detail of her dream emerged. *No. No, no, no, no.* This was not happening. She did not just have a sex dream about Cole Tucker.

Except she did.

She sat up, grabbed the pillow behind her, and started punching it hard with her fists. "It's all his fault," she muttered as she hit the pillow again. This would never have happened if he hadn't made her sneak into Carithers's barn last night. All that adrenaline after running to the woods and away from the gunfire and then the two of them pressed together and soaking wet.

Lust. That was all it was. Her body's way of telling her it needed some action and needed it now. It was natural.

That was what she kept telling herself as she crawled out of bed. And when she pulled her hair up on top of her head. And while she brushed her teeth.

"Get it together, Kase," she told her reflection in the mirror after spitting out a mouthful of toothpaste. But even as she did, her mind was flooded with the physical sensations that had felt all too real.

She came down the staircase and into the kitchen, still in her sleep shorts and tank top, and trying not to think about her dream. Maybe Carly's concern for her wasn't completely unfounded.

She'd clearly spent too much time with Cole, and now he was in her head. She was supposed to be figuring out her future with Jacob, but instead, she'd wasted time goofing off and avoiding the future altogether.

She needed to focus so she could finish Cole's stupid game and get back to what really mattered. Then soon she'd be in California with no more Cole to distract her.

"You look glum this morning," her dad said from the breakfast table. He was chowing down on a plate of biscuits and gravy. Breakfast was all set out, but her momma was nowhere to be seen. "You okay, baby girl?"

Logan fell into the chair across from him. "I'm fine, just thinking about something," she said. She certainly wasn't going to explain to her dad that she was having inappropriate dreams about the wrong guy.

"I got an interesting call late last night," he said, eyeing her. "Seems Harrold Carithers found two people sneaking around in his barn when he went to check on his expecting mare. He wasn't able to catch them, but he said it didn't look like they'd managed to take anything either. You wouldn't know anything about that, now would you?"

She forced a laugh, avoiding eye contact. "Daddy, why would I want to go breaking into Old Man Carithers's barn? That doesn't even make sense."

He checked the kitchen door. "I thought maybe it had to do with the bet you and Cole have going," he said, voice low and disapproving.

This time Logan looked him straight in the eyes, glad to be able to tell him the truth for once. "Daddy, I can promise that Cole and I did not sneak into Carithers's barn for our stupid bet."

He gave her a look that said he didn't quite believe her, but then her momma came in and he changed the subject. "One of the guys at the station said Louise Snyder got back in town yesterday."

Logan's head snapped up. "Really?"

Her daddy nodded. "I thought you might like to go pay her a visit today if you aren't already busy. I think she'd really like to see you, catch up."

Logan was already standing. "I'll go right now." Once she got a shower and dressed, of course.

"What about breakfast?" Momma asked, the first thing she'd said to her all morning.

Logan picked up a biscuit and took a big bite. "It's delicious. Thank you," she said through her mouthful of food. She smiled, grabbing another one—because it really *was* good—before she ran out of the room and up the stairs.

⟫⟫⟫⟪⟪⟪

MS. SNYDER WAS sitting in a rocking chair on her front porch when Logan pulled up the drive. She wore her glasses, her black hair almost completely gray now and pulled back into a long braid down her back. Wearing a flowy, flowery dress, she sifted through a large stack of papers.

She looked up and smiled when their eyes met. She was on her feet, papers abandoned on the small table by her chair, and came quickly down the stone path.

"Look at you!" she yelled, her smile wider than Logan remembered ever seeing it.

Logan jumped down out of the truck. "Sorry, I probably should have called first, but I heard you were back in town and came right over."

"Don't you worry about it. You know you're always welcome." She pulled her into a hug. "Come on." She pulled away and led Logan to the porch. "Sit and tell me everything. What have you been doing?"

Logan sat in the second rocking chair. Despite the many

years since they'd last seen each other, it didn't take Logan long at all to catch Ms. Snyder up.

"I'm so proud of you, you know that?" Ms. Snyder was beaming. "I knew you were going to do great things, and now here you are telling me all about them."

"Thanks, Ms. Snyder."

"Oh, stop calling me Ms. You're grown now, honey," she said in her not-quite-Maryland accent. In her years of living in Georgia, she'd picked up a bit of a drawl. "You call me Louise."

"What about you? I heard about your dad. I'm so sorry."

She nodded. "It's all right, sweetie. He was sick for so long, and by the end, I think he was ready."

Still, it must have been hard. If anything happened to her daddy, Logan didn't know if she'd ever be able to cope. "I just wish I'd known. I would have called or done something."

"I know, and I'm sorry. I should have kept in touch better, but it was so chaotic up there."

"It wasn't just you," Logan admitted. "Other than visits from Carly and my parents, I didn't talk to anybody here in town the whole time I was gone. I could have called or e-mailed you." But at that point, she'd been ready to leave it all behind, and that included Ms. Snyder.

She'd had no idea the number of friends and adventures she was saying goodbye to, no idea how much of herself she was losing when she'd left Willow Creek. Given the chance to do it all again, would she have made the same choice, knowing what it had cost her?

"So," Louise said, looking mischievous. "Tell me about this guy. Jacob, you said?" Logan nodded. "How did you meet?"

"Oh, well," Logan said slowly. "He was a doctor in the emergency room in Austin. I met him when I brought my friend in with a twisted ankle." She knew Louise was looking for more details, but Logan didn't really feel like talking about Jacob now.

Her phone had rung earlier that morning, just after she stepped out of the shower, and Logan had been relieved to see that it was him and not Cole with another challenge. She'd lied about her night, of course, telling him she'd spent it at home watching a movie on Netflix. He'd given a noncommittal answer on when they could get together. He tried to talk a little about work, but between her disappointment and annoyance, she hadn't bothered to listen. In only a few minutes, the conversation had died. It was probably the shortest phone call they'd ever shared.

"That's all, really," Logan said, forcing a smile.

Louise nodded. "I see. Well, he sounds nice. I can't wait to meet him. Can I expect an invitation for the big day?"

"Of course." Whenever that would be. Logan twisted the ring on her hand. "We haven't set a date, so everything's still a bit up in the air. But I'll let you know."

She didn't say anything else; her hands were shaking.

She'd heard that it was normal to be this nervous about your wedding day, but she wasn't so sure. Brides were supposed to be ecstatic while their friends secretly wanted to scratch their eyes out just to get them to shut up. Planning a wedding wasn't supposed to be this hard, but for Logan, the mere thought of setting a date left her feeling unsteady.

Louise didn't seem to notice. "So what about after the wedding? You two going to settle nearby or go up to Athens?"

Logan shook her head. "Actually, he applied for a job in San Francisco. As soon as he gets it, which he's confident he will, we're going to get a house or apartment over there."

"That's exciting," Louise said. "How long do you think until that happens?"

"Who knows?" She shrugged. "Could be weeks, could be months. He only just officially put the application in, and I reckon it depends on the doctor he'd replace and when his retirement date is set." Part of her knew that day needed to come soon so she and Jacob could get back to when they were happy and could barely keep their hands off each other. Then, surely, Logan would be able, and even excited, to start planning her wedding and her future with him.

On the other hand, she wasn't sure how she'd be able to leave Willow Creek a second time, even after being back only a few weeks.

Louise nodded, her eyes focused on something far away. "And what are your plans when you get there? Do you have a job lined up for yourself?"

"Nothing now. But I'd like to work in a gallery if I can."

She smiled. "Well, there'll be plenty of galleries there you could apply at."

"Sure." Logan sighed. "But the question is whether or not I can impress someone out there when I'm still fresh out of college and have absolutely no experience to speak for me. I was hoping to find something out here I could do to add to my résumé before I go, but no such luck."

Louise perked up. "Actually, I happen to know a place that could use someone like you."

"Really?"

She picked up the stack of paperwork on the table between them. "I'm just finishing up the planning stages right now. I've decided I'd like to reopen the gallery. The shop is still under my name, and now that everything with my family is calming down I'm realizing just how much I've missed it."

Logan couldn't believe her ears. "And you're saying you want me to help? Why?"

"Who else would I ask? You knew the shop as well as I did, and you've always had a knack for picking out the work of a talented artist. I could use that at the gallery. Not to mention you spent enough time there with me to know how the business works, and I could teach you whatever you don't know."

A smile spread across Logan's face. "You're really doing

this?"

"I've already talked to some of the local artists I used to show. And I've worked up some financial and business plans to get everything started," she said, indicating the stack of papers again. "I can't do it alone. It won't be easy, and the pay will be atrocious. But this could be exactly what you need to stand out in San Francisco. So what do you say? Will you help me? I wouldn't trust anyone else."

Logan felt like she might cry she was so excited. Before she could put too much thought into it, she asked, "When do we start?"

Chapter Twenty-Two

LOGAN DIDN'T THINK she'd ever been so happy in her life. Well, maybe when her momma took her and Carly to see Garth Brooks during his comeback tour, but this was a very close second.

"I'm meeting Ms. Snyder at the shop Monday so we can really visualize everything and get some plans in order," she told both her parents over the celebratory dinner she'd made for them that night.

"And she's already given me a list of local artists to call so we can let them know the gallery's opening back up. And we need to hire someone to get everything ready. She wants to be up and running in a few weeks."

"Weeks, really?" her momma said, grinning at her for the first time since the California bomb had been dropped. "You've really got your work cut out for you. You sure you can handle it?"

"It'll be tough, but this is what I need. I don't know how long it'll be until Jacob and I have to move, and I want to get as much done as possible. I need the experience, not to mention I really don't want to leave Ms. Snyder—I mean,

Louise—in the lurch with everything half finished."

"What about Jacob? What did he say when you told him?"

Logan dropped her fork. In all her excitement, she'd forgotten to call Jacob and tell him the good news. He was going to be so happy for her. He'd said things would work out, and he'd be glad to know he was right. "I haven't even told him yet."

Her momma laughed. "Well, why don't you go do that while your daddy and I clean up here," she said, grabbing the empty plates from the table.

"Are you sure? I made dinner for you guys, I can clean it up."

"Nonsense. You deserve a break after that wonderful meal."

Logan didn't know about wonderful. Her cooking skills were limited, and all she'd really done was throw together some Hamburger Helper and a salad.

"Go on," her mom told her. "I know you're dying to call him. We can handle this."

Logan darted out of the room and up the stairs shouting "Thanks" over her shoulder. She paced in her bedroom as the phone rang in her ear.

"Hello?"

"Hey," she said. "You'll never believe what happened to me today," she squealed.

"Me either. I got the San Francisco spot."

Logan stopped pacing. "What?"

Jacob laughed on the other end. "Isn't it amazing! I got a call from the president of the board of directors. He'll be in Atlanta for a conference this weekend and wants to have dinner in Athens tomorrow night."

She closed her eyes, pinching the bridge of her nose between her fingers. "I didn't realize the president of the board did the hiring."

"He doesn't, but he's taking a special interest in me since he knows my parents, and he's recommending me to the head of emergency."

"But isn't there supposed to be an interview at least? You said they would have you fly out for an interview before any real decision could be made."

"Well, yes, I'll still have to go through the formal interview before they can officially give it to me. But, don't you see, if the president wants to meet with me personally, it's practically a done deal. Everything else is a formality."

Logan shook her head, her stomach heavy. "So how long does that give us? Did he say anything about when the other guy is leaving?"

"Not yet," Jacob said. "But I don't imagine it will be too long. He made it sound like he wanted to get the matter handled rather quickly."

"Oh." Too fast. This was all happening too fast.

"You don't sound very happy for me."

"No, I am," she said. "It's just that I got offered a job

today, too."

"That's great! Now that we've both got jobs lined up, we'll be in San Francisco in no time. This is perfect!"

She sighed. "The job I was offered is here in Willow Creek. I'm going to help a friend of mine with her art gallery in town. She had to close it a while back, but she's ready to get it up and running again, and she wants my help. And it would be good for my résumé."

"That's nice, Logan," he said, audibly frowning. "But I don't know how much good that's going to do you. I imagine they'll want me in San Francisco by the end of the month."

"The end of the month? That's Carly's wedding. You can't expect me to pack up and move the same week as my best friend's wedding. And I told Louise I would help her get the gallery ready. We're talking at least four weeks from now. If not longer."

"I know it's hard, Logan, but the San Francisco deal is already in motion." Jacob's voice was soft. "We'll figure out Carly's wedding, and I'm sure your friend can find someone else to help her with the gallery."

"What if…?" Logan hesitated. She realized how awful it sounded the second it came to mind, but it was the only way they could compromise. "What if you went to California without me?"

"What?" he said flatly.

"Hear me out," she rushed on. "It would only be temporary. You could go to California, get things set up for us. You'll be so busy assimilating to the new job you wouldn't even see me that much anyway. But if I stay here, I could help Louise and get enough time with her to make a difference on my résumé. We'd both win."

Except for the part where they wouldn't get to see each other. But really, how was that any different from their relationship now?

Jacob was quiet a minute. "How long?" he finally asked.

"I don't know. Until our wedding?" she suggested calmly, waiting for the reaction she knew was coming. He didn't disappoint.

"You expect us to live on opposite sides of the country up until the wedding that we haven't even set a date for? How could you possibly think any more distance between us would be a good idea?"

"I know it's not ideal," she said patiently. "But we could make it work. I can stay here with my parents a little longer, spend more time with them. And we could always fly out to each other on weekends. Before we know it, we'll be married and living in California together."

"Does that mean you're ready to set a date then?" he sneered.

"What…right now?"

"Why not? You seem to think it will be so simple for us to be apart and barely ever see each other. I just want to know how long I'd have to wait. Six months? A year?"

"Sweetie…"

"Don't *sweetie* me," he snapped. "Is it too much to ask for you to set a damn date already? Just pick one, pick something, and we can go from there."

Logan's cheeks grew warm, and she felt the same tightness in her stomach she got any time she thought about making it official. "It's not that simple. We don't even know where we want to get married. We have to have a venue, work around other people's schedules. It has to be the right season, the right year—"

"The right year? You don't even know what *year* you want to marry me? Were you even planning on walking down the aisle in the next decade?"

"Of course I want to marry you this decade. Look, I get that you're upset."

"Damn right I'm upset. I'm starting to think you don't want to marry me at all." He huffed before going silent.

"Jacob," she said quietly, her eyes getting cloudy with moisture. Her voice was shaky, as well as her hands. "You know that's not true."

She heard him take a deep breath on the other end of the line. He let it out. "Don't. We'll discuss this in person tomorrow. Be at my place around three."

"Three? Why?"

His voice was cold. "Dinner with the president of the board. I mentioned I was getting married soon, and he insisted you come, too."

"Three is awfully early for dinner."

"Dinner will be at six. I want you here a couple hours early so we can have time to sort everything out, make sure we're on the same page before you meet him."

"Oh," she said, her stomach tightening. She imagined after tonight it was going to be a very strained and awkward afternoon. "Okay, I'll be there. I love you."

The line went dead.

⟫⟫⟫⟪⟪⟪

July—Before Junior Year

COLE'S FINGER TAPPED against the steering wheel. The needle crept higher as he sped down the highway. Once Cole heard Old Man Carithers needed something dropped off at the Kases' house, he couldn't get in his Bronco fast enough.

He probably smelled to high heaven after working in the fields all day, but he didn't care. He'd been working all summer for Old Man Carithers, not to mention helping his dad at the hardware store whenever he could. Now it was the end of summer, and he'd hardly seen Logan aside from church on Sundays. Turned out working all day every day seriously cut into his time for plotting and pulling pranks.

There was technically only one more week before they started their junior year, but he couldn't wait that long. Going all summer barely talking to her, rarely seeing her face, he felt like he was drowning in darkness these last couple months.

Christ, he was a mess. If Cowboy could only hear what went through his head all day, he'd say Cole was whipped.

He turned onto Logan's gravel road, his stomach twisting tighter the closer he got. He could just imagine her playful sneer when she opened the door and realized it was him. It was nearly a hundred degrees outside. Maybe if he was lucky, he'd find her in really short shorts or a bikini or something. Not that it mattered. She could be dressed as an Eskimo and his body would still react to her like it did for no one else.

He was grinning when he pulled up into her driveway. She sat on the porch swing, her legs drawn up, and her arms folded on top of her knees. Her forehead was resting on her arms. The sun already seemed to shine a little brighter.

Cole's boots clunked as he walked up the porch steps.

"Please, don't get up on my account," he teased.

"Go away, Cole," she groaned into her knees.

"No can do, princess. The chief was supposed to come out to Old Man Carithers's farm this morning to grab the tiller, but he never showed. So Carithers asked me to bring it over here for him."

She didn't say anything.

"Hello, Earth to Logan," he said again. Her shoulders shook silently, and his stomach sank.

"Lo," he said, voice softer this time. "You okay?"

She nodded fiercely, and a muffled sob escaped.

His heart nearly stopped. He sat next to her on the

swing. "Hey, what's wrong? Are you hurt?"

She shook her head.

The tension in his chest eased only a fraction. "Tell me what's wrong then," he said, his voice gentler now.

"You'll think it's stupid."

He put his hand on her back and began tracing circles over her tank top. "Try me."

Logan picked her head up and sat cross-legged. "It's Maggie Mae."

"Your dog?"

She nodded. "I came down to feed her this morning," she said between sobs, refusing to look at him. "But when I got down to her she was…she was—"

"Ah, Lo," Cole said. "I'm so sorry."

"Daddy buried her out in the back this morning. That's why he couldn't come get the tiller." She wiped at her eyes and sniffed. "I know she was old. I mean, it's not like we didn't see this coming. But it still hurts so much. I'm never going to see her again!"

Logan cried louder and harder, her last words barely decipherable. The sound was like a pickax stabbing into his chest. He couldn't remember a time he'd ever seen her cry like this, and he would do anything to make it stop.

Still, he hesitated before scooting a few inches nearer and wrapping his arm around her shoulders. He pulled her close, allowing her to cry into his chest.

Despite how desperately she'd pleaded for him to go

away, she relaxed into his arms. He'd never held her like this before, though he'd be lying if he said he hadn't thought about it. It was strange, unlike anything he'd ever felt before, and so much better than he'd imagined. He didn't think he'd ever been so happy and so completely wrenched at the same time.

She nestled deeper into his hold, her body curled up into his side while her cheek rested on his chest. He used his legs to gently swing them back and forth. Could she hear how fast his heart pounded?

"You know," he said, "my aunt says that all the animals we ever had—cats, dogs, hamsters, even fish—every pet is up in heaven waiting for us to come home. So that means Maggie Mae is up there right now, wagging her tail like a little puppy, and looking down on you. She's playing with all the other dogs up there until the day you can go see her."

"That's really sweet." She was silent another minute then took a deep breath. "You're all sweaty," she said before sucking in another breath.

"Yeah, well, what do you expect? I've been working outside all day."

She inhaled deeply one last time before she pulled out of his arms, and he felt the absence like a lost limb. She looked up at him, wiping away the last of her tears. "Why are you being so nice to me?"

Because every one of her tears burned away his confident front like acid rain. "Believe it or not, I can actually be a decent guy when I want to." He leaned back while his legs still rocked them, laid his arm on the back of the swing behind her, and grinned. "You just make it hard sometimes."

Her eyes narrowed, her nose and lips scrunched, and Cole took a mental picture, committing the face to his memory. Christ, she was adorable. "I don't know. I keep waiting for you to give me a noogie or try to shove my face in your smelly armpit or something."

He snorted. "As tempting as that is, I'm not interested in making your day any worse than it already is."

The corners of her mouth fell, a chunk of brown bangs falling over her eye. Without his bidding, his fingers moved to brush it back behind her ear, and Logan's eyes widened just the tiniest bit. He yanked his hand back like the hair stung him. "You going to be okay?"

She nodded.

"Good. I should get back to work then," he said, standing from the swing. He wanted nothing more than to sit back down and pull her into his arms again, but there was no telling what other acts of betrayal his body might commit if he stuck around.

"I'll see you at school, Lo. Tell your dad he can bring the tiller back anytime."

Again she just nodded, her brows drawn together when he turned toward the porch steps. It took everything in his power not to turn back.

Chapter Twenty-Three

LOGAN REMEMBERED THE day Jacob proposed. *Finally*, she'd thought. They'd been dating almost two years, and she'd started to worry the question would never come up. She'd decided long ago this was the guy she was going to marry. He was handsome, smart, responsible. And best of all, he made her feel nothing like the girl she'd been in Willow Creek. She'd be the respectable wife of a doctor, the woman her momma had always wanted to see her become. She'd been so happy.

Now Logan had to wonder if that happiness she'd felt was the realization that she was going to spend the rest of her life with the one man she couldn't live without or if it was the hope that marrying Jacob would be the final step in letting go of the girl she'd been before.

These were the kinds of thoughts one couldn't process while sober. Logan needed something to drown out and dull the overwhelming and confusing feelings before she could step back and properly sort through them. Then and only then would she feel like she could think.

It wasn't a healthy habit, she knew that, but it was one

that had served her well over the years.

As Logan pulled into the parking lot at Wade's, she already felt some of the stress circulating through her veins subside. Yes, this was where she needed to be. She needed a beer, and then maybe another, maybe more. She'd worry about getting home later. Right now she only had one goal.

She took a deep, satisfying breath as she opened the door; the smell of alcohol and fried food was incredibly comforting in her moment of need. She walked over to the nearly empty bar, stopping short when her eyes landed on one man. He sat alone, nursing a beer, his eyes on the Braves game playing on the small TV screen hanging in the corner.

She considered turning around, but the need for alcohol was too strong. She was getting tired of running from Cole Tucker anyway. And besides that, she could always count on getting drunk when he was around.

"Fancy running into you here," she said with evident sarcasm. "Shouldn't you be working or something?"

His eyes, which were hard and focused on the TV, softened when they met hers. He smiled. "Next shift isn't until tomorrow afternoon."

She eyed the stool next to him. "Mind if I sit here?"

"Help yourself." He took a sip of his beer. "I could use the distraction from this lousy game. Braves still haven't gotten a single run in, and it's already the fifth inning. The Nationals are kicking our asses tonight."

She fell into the seat next to him. "So what are you doing

here anyway? Don't you have anything better to do on a Friday night?"

He shrugged. "Cowboy's out with a girl, and I'd rather watch the game here than alone back at our place." He looked back up at the screen. "What about you? No date with the doctor this weekend?"

"He's working," she said flatly. She didn't want to talk to Cole about Jacob. "Can I get a beer, Lilly?" she called.

"Sure thing, doll." She grabbed a bottle of Logan's favorite from behind the counter. Her low-cut, hot pink halter and skinny jeans combo belonged on a twenty-year-old, yet Lilly managed to pull it off effortlessly. "Anything else?"

"Nope. Just keep them coming. Thanks."

Lilly glanced at Cole then frowned at Logan before she nodded.

"Want to talk about it?" Cole asked once Lilly had left to refill a pitcher for another patron.

Logan twisted the top off her beer and took a sip. "Nothing to talk about."

"Really? Then why do you look like you're trying to drown your sorrows?"

She took another sip. "A girl's allowed to drink a little after a rough day."

He laughed. "Sorry, I meant why do you look like you're going to need about twenty more of those to drown said sorrows?"

"Here's an idea," she said, looking pointedly at him.

"Why don't you mind your own business and stop trying to nose your way into mine?"

He held up his hands. "Hey, you came in—looking like hell, I should add—and sat by me. I was just trying to be nice and lend a listening ear since you look like you could use one." He turned back to his drink, taking a long drag from it.

Great, now on top of everything else, she felt bad for yelling at Cole.

She sighed. "Ms. Snyder's opening the gallery. She wants me to help her do it."

He grinned, nudging Logan with his elbow before he turned on his stool to face her. "I told you she'd be the one to talk to." She frowned at him. "That's good news, isn't it? You wanted a job, now you have one. Problem solved."

Yes, one problem solved. And one very big, new problem staring her in the face.

"Yeah, it's great," she said. "At least I thought so. But it turns out I'm not going to be around here long enough to do it."

"What do you mean?"

"Jacob and I...we're moving to San Francisco."

Cole stared at her blankly for a moment then his smile slowly disappeared. "Oh," was all he said before turning back to his drink.

She wasn't sure exactly what kind of reaction she'd been expecting from him when she finally told him about California, but it was more than *Oh*.

"The plan was for us to go once he got the job, but we were supposed to get through Carly's wedding, and even then we thought it would be at least a month before the other doctor retired and Jacob would have to step in. But now we've got dinner with some guy on the board tomorrow night, and Jacob says we'll have to leave in two weeks."

Cole took another pull from his drink, this one twice as long as the last. "Two weeks, huh? That's...soon. How did your parents take it?"

"I only just told them a week ago," she said quietly. "Well, more like Jacob blurted it out at dinner."

Cole gave a forced smile, still not looking at her as he ran his hand through his hair. "You know, I wondered why the chief was in such a foul mood the last few days when I talked to him, but I didn't want to get into his business. Guess now I know."

"Really?" Logan thought her dad had taken the news well. It had been her momma she was most worried about. But maybe Daddy was just better at hiding it from her.

"So what about the gallery?"

"I don't know. I want to help Louise, but two weeks isn't enough time. I even tried to convince Jacob I should stay here while he goes to California without me, but then we got into this huge fight about the distance and the wedding and everything else."

She took another sip of beer. "I'm just not sure what to

do. I don't want to make Jacob mad, but I feel like there's still stuff here I need to take care of. Carly's wedding, the gallery. And I don't want to say goodbye to my parents yet. Or Carly. Or…"

Cole was still staring silently at his drink, his hand rubbing the five o'clock shadow spread across his jaw. She'd miss him. The thought of it physically hurt.

"Lilly, can I get another?" she shouted before downing the rest of her drink.

Cole sat up straight, waving Lilly off just before she grabbed a second bottle. "Don't bother, Lill. She's done."

Logan stared at him. "What are you doing?" All she wanted was a damn beer. Was that too much to ask right now?

"I'm cutting you off," he said, standing from his barstool and indicating she should do the same. "And now I'm going to walk you to your truck and send you home."

"Why?" she asked as she followed him. Unless she wanted to be thrown over his shoulder and carried out, it was all she could do.

He opened the door for her, letting her pass through. "Because I'm desperate to prove that, despite what you seem to think, you and I can actually sit down and kick back just one beer together," he joked. The furrow of deep thought had left his brow, and he was back to teasing her. "And because you're better than this. You said yourself that you're not that girl anymore. I'm just reminding you."

Logan huffed. The last person she'd expected to kick her out of the bar tonight was Cole Tucker. Usually, he was the one filling her shot glass.

"Look," he said as they stopped beside her truck, Logan still in a pout. "You and I have done this enough times to know that drinking doesn't fix the problem. It just allows you to put off worrying about it for another day."

There was concern in his eyes. He'd only ever looked at her like this a few times in their lives. So few, in fact, that she could count them all on one hand. And all this because he thought her biggest worry was whether to stay a few extra weeks in Willow Creek. If only he knew.

A wave of emotion hit her like a sucker punch in the chest. "Cole," she said, her chin trembling. "What am I supposed to do?"

The second the tears started flowing, she was in his arms. "Shh," he murmured. "Don't cry; you'll figure it out. Just do what makes you happy and everything else will sort itself out. You'll see."

She nodded, waiting a few seconds before she pulled away and wiped her tears. She had to hand it to the guy, for being such a jerk most of her life, he had a pretty good track record of making her feel better when she needed it.

"Why are you always so nice to me when I'm sad?" she asked him, forcing a laugh as she wiped her eyes.

He looked pained as he lifted his hand gently to her cheek, wiping a stray tear. "Because seeing you cry damn near kills me," he said softly. Then he pulled his hand away and smiled.

"Now cheer up, go home, and get some sleep," he said, giving her a firm pat on the back. "We've got a challenge tomorrow."

She shook her head. "I can't. I'm supposed to meet Jacob in Athens tomorrow afternoon. And besides, we just had a challenge yesterday."

"Yes, but you may be leaving town soon. And if I remember correctly, you're only one letter away from making me the winner."

Her shoulders slumped. She'd forgotten her woes for a minute. Now their weight felt heavy on her chest.

Cole looked like he was going to walk away but surprised her by taking her face in his hands and leaning in. Her stomach tensed and she forgot to breathe as he looked into her eyes. "If he loves you, he'll want you to be happy," he whispered. "Trust me."

Logan gasped, swallowing hard as he brought his lips to her forehead and placed a gentle kiss there. She swore her heart skipped. And then it was over too soon, and Cole was gone, making his way back to the bar. "I'll call you tomorrow morning with the address for the challenge," he said without looking back.

She stood there staring as Cole walked back into the bar, still trying to process what just happened. As if on autopilot, Logan pulled the keys from her pocket and unlocked the truck door. She put the key in the ignition but didn't turn it.

All she could think of was the way her skin had tingled under the barest touch of his lips, the wave of disappointment when it ended, and how, just now, all she wanted to do was jump out of this truck and run to him.

"Oh no," she whispered, closing her eyes tight and lowering her forehead to rest on the steering wheel as her list of complications grew by one.

Because at that moment what Logan felt for Cole was not hatred, not loathing, and not lust.

What if the real reason she couldn't bring herself to fully commit to marrying Jacob just walked into that bar?

Chapter Twenty-Four

L OGAN WAS ALREADY awake when her phone beeped, one of two messages she'd received in the last ten minutes. With the covers still pulled up over her head, she blindly reached for the cell phone on her nightstand and pulled it back under with her.

The first text was from Jacob. *I'm sorry. See you at 3.* The second was Cole telling her where to meet him in an hour. Logan groaned.

She'd barely slept all night. Instead, she'd stared up at her ceiling: What did this mean? How exactly did she feel about Cole? Was he really the reason she couldn't bring herself to set a wedding date?

But the longer she lay awake thinking about it, the more she rejected the idea.

Sure, maybe there were some romantic feelings for Cole getting mixed in with everything else she already felt about him. She supposed it made sense, after all the time they'd been spending together, and it was probably fueled by the level of excitement she tended to feel around him. Not to mention the fact that he'd been there to comfort her last night.

But she loved Jacob. What she had with her fiancé couldn't possibly compare to these feelings rising for Cole. And whatever caring or affection she harbored for him needed to be buried down deep, ignored until forgotten. She knew with certainty they could be.

Because she'd already done it once four years ago.

The best thing she could do now was put Cole Tucker out of her mind completely. Granted, that would be challenging considering their bet. But Logan had done the math. If she won this challenge today, they'd both be tied with a H-O-R-S. Then the last challenge would be her choice. She just needed to pick something she could easily win, and the whole thing would be hers. Cole would leave her and Jacob alone, and she'd be able to sort out her issues behind why she was struggling to commit to this marriage.

"There is nothing going on between you and Cole," she said. His words from that horrible morning replayed in her head. *It was just sex.* "There's nothing going on between you and Cole. He knows it, and so do you."

Logan threw the covers off before running into her bathroom. All she needed was a quick shower and then she could grab some breakfast and go beat Cole at the game he had planned today. After that, she could put him out of her mind and spend the day getting ready for the big dinner with Jacob.

>>><<<

LOGAN WASN'T AT all surprised to see a trailer hitched to the back of the Bronco and Cole in the process of rolling two dirt bikes down from it.

Everyone in town knew that County Line Road was good for one thing. It was a winding, curvy road about three miles long with nothing but woods and open pastures on each side. It had been a dead end for as long as she could remember, and most people didn't bother coming this way unless they were lost or farmers coming to check on their fields and cows. All of which made it the perfect spot for a race.

The second she read Cole's text to meet him here, she knew that was exactly what this challenge would be.

"Seriously?" she asked. She pulled her thick jacket tightly around her against the strong, cold wind. "You know I suck at this kind of thing."

Cole looked over his shoulder, turning his trademark sexy grin on her. She felt a jolt in her stomach but managed to push away the feelings she'd decided to ignore. "That was kind of my intention. You think I'm going to get this close to winning and let you ruin it?"

She rolled her eyes. Tying up this game was going to be a lot harder than she'd hoped. But considering what all was at stake if she lost, she was going to have to find a way to win.

"Hey, beautiful," a familiar voice called. Logan turned

just in time to see Cowboy coming around the other side of the Bronco. He had a thick jacket over a green John Deere shirt and his UGA cap covering his shaggy blond hair.

Logan smiled. "I didn't expect to see you here. Cole said you had a hot date last night; I thought for sure you'd still be passed out at some girl's place."

He gave her a quick hug. "Oh yeah, she was hot all right. Until I accidentally called her by the wrong name while we were...you know. She kicked me out pretty fast after that," he said with a wicked grin. Cole laughed out loud as he knelt beside one of the bikes and started tinkering with it.

Logan had to smile, too, trying not to think about how the poor girl must have felt. "You are absolutely shameless," she said.

"Yeah, well. What are you gonna do?" he said, shrugging. "So, what's the deal? You ready to win this thing?"

Cole looked up from the bike. "I thought you were on my side."

"I'm on whatever side is willing to feed me after this. And since you already said no"—he turned to Logan, looking hopeful—"what do you say to a victory lunch at Wade's after this?"

"Sure, Cowboy."

He waggled his eyebrows before he grabbed Logan and pulled her into an even tighter hug, planting a huge, playful kiss on her cheek. If he hadn't been like a brother to her, she would have blushed. "That's why I love you. Now let's get this thing started. I'm starving."

Cole stood, brushing his dirty hands on his jeans. "All right, everything looks good. You ready, Lo?"

"How do I know you haven't been tampering with them?" she asked.

"Have a little faith," he said, raising a hand to his heart like the accusation hurt. "I'll even let you pick whichever one you want. Cowboy will start us off," he said, pointing to his best friend. "The first to pass the county sign just before the bridge wins. Simple as that."

She walked over to examine the bikes. They looked virtually the same to her, so she ended up choosing one at random.

"Helmet?" she asked.

Cowboy pulled out two black motorcycle helmets from the passenger side of the Bronco, handing one off to Cole and one to her. Cowboy stood in the middle of the road to mark their starting point.

"This is where it ends, Lo," Cole said as he rolled his bike over to Cowboy's right. "I'm going to win and then we'll know once and for all who the better man is." Though she couldn't see it, she was sure he was grinning.

"Not if I can help it." Logan pulled the bike up next to him on Cowboy's left. She threw her foot down, kick-starting the engine and getting situated in the seat before clicking the bike into first gear. She heard Cole laugh as he did the same.

Once he saw that the two were ready, Cowboy raised both arms out to his sides. "First to reach the bridge wins. Are you ready?"

She nodded. Cowboy's arms dropped. "Go!"

She took off. It had been years since she last rode one of these things, but her body remembered it like it was yesterday. Logan felt a moment of pure joy as the bike sped up, her hands and feet expertly working as she shifted into higher gears. She didn't dare look over her shoulder, but she knew that, despite her quick takeoff, Cole was coming up fast behind her.

Between the roar of the engine and the rush of wind, she couldn't hear anything. Thank God for the thick Carhartt jacket she'd chosen for the unusually chilly day.

She took the first turn in the road carefully. Too carefully. By the time the road straightened out, Cole had cut across and passed her by several feet. She pushed the bike to go faster while trying to avoid the potholes littered on the old, unused road.

The next twist came quickly, and Logan was forced to push the limits of her caution. The engine roared and the bike quivered beneath her as she took the turn sharper than she was used to, managing to lessen the distance between them.

With each new turn, she pushed closer and closer. She knew the end was coming, and Cole was ahead of her by only a few feet now.

She'd driven this street enough times to know that the last and worst curve was coming. Instinct told her to slow down, but if she lost this one, everything she had with Jacob would be at stake. He'd finally see that the version of her he knew was a lie. And then it would be over. Their relationship, their engagement, everything.

She felt the minutest nudge of relief at the thought, but she quickly shoved it away. That was her fear talking.

As the final twist before the county sign came, she knew what she had to do. She had to go all in. No guts, no glory. With a fresh determination, she cut to the inside. Cole hadn't been ready and missed his chance to cut her off. Logan accelerated, steadily creeping past Cole's bike.

The Laurens County sign flashed by her in a blur of green with Logan's bike leading by a good foot or two.

She was laughing in celebration of her victory when the road straightened out and the bridge came in sight. And then she saw it.

Sitting directly in front of the bridge in the middle of the road was a sign declaring the bridge was out. She swerved the bike, just barely missing the sign, only to drive straight into a deep pothole. The next thing she knew, she was rolling across the unforgiving asphalt and over the edge of the steep, rocky slope just in front of the bridge.

Logan's hands scrambled to grab hold of something, and in the chaos, she somehow managed to catch herself on a large, jagged stone. It was steady enough to hold her as she planted her feet on the loose rocks and soil beneath. She lay still as a statue, aside from her frantic breaths, convinced that any sudden movement or shift would send her foothold out from under her. She tried not to look down as she held herself precariously on the edge of the hill, at least a hundred feet above the hard ground and railroad tracks beneath.

"Cole!" she cried, her voice muffled by the large helmet. The sharp rock bit into her palms, but Logan couldn't move to shift them, too scared she might fall. "Cole!"

He didn't answer; an image of his broken, unconscious body flooded her mind and panic clawed its way through her chest. Then she heard feet hitting the ground hard and fast, and she nearly cried.

"Lo!" he yelled, running up to the side of the slope. He knelt down and leaned over the edge. "Here, take my hand."

She looked up to see his hand reaching down for hers. It didn't quite reach, though, so she would have to use her feet to get up to him. All she had to do was let go and push, but she was frozen.

"Look at me, Lo!"

She forced herself to look up, finding his sure and steady gaze. His voice was strong and commanding, but she could see the fear buried deep in his eyes. "Don't worry, okay. I won't let you fall, remember? Just take my hand. Come on."

Logan's eyes returned to his outstretched hand several inches above the stone she clung to. She took a deep breath, drawing on his calm to find her own. She let go of the rock with one hand as she attempted to push up with her legs.

Cole's hand immediately found hers and then he was lifting her with a superhuman strength. "Now let your other hand go," he said. She did as he told her to, her hand flying up to his wrist. He lifted her a foot, then another, and soon his arm was around her, pulling her out into the middle of the road.

Her knees shook as her feet planted on the ground. They started to give, but Cole kept an arm around her, supporting her weight.

He quickly but carefully removed her helmet with one hand and let it clatter to the ground. "Are you okay?" he asked, the panic he'd clearly been suppressing coming out in full force. He let her go and searched nearly every inch of her for anything broken, scratched, or cut.

"I'm fine," she said as she contemplated the pain or even death she'd just narrowly avoided. They were both okay. Her hands trembled and muscles grew heavy as reality settled in.

Cole kept searching as if he hadn't heard her, his hands checking her everywhere. Her clothes were visibly worn and torn from her skid across the road, and she winced when his hand checked her shoulder.

"You're hurt. How bad is it?"

She shook her head. "No, it's fine. Cole." She placed her hands on each side of his face, forcing him to look into her eyes. She smiled. "I'm fine, I promise."

He was breathing heavily, and the harsh lines around his

eyes and forehead softened. "Thank God," he sighed.

She was laughing, giddy, when Cole wrapped his arms around her and pulled her into a somewhat painful hug that she returned.

And then his lips were on hers.

It lasted only for a second and was over before she had a chance to react. Cole pulled away fractionally, and their eyes met.

Their short breaths mingled as they stood completely still, still holding on to each other. "You just kissed me."

His expression didn't waver, but his gaze searched hers frantically. "I did."

"You shouldn't do that," she whispered. Neither of them said anything. Logan knew she should pull away but couldn't figure out how to make her arms work. Her eyes trailed down to his lips.

Without thinking, she threw her hand up to the nape of his neck and drew his mouth back down to hers. He responded instantly, pulling her even tighter into him. One hand traveled down to her waist, the other getting tangled in her long, messy hair as their lips found each other again and again.

Logan felt like the entire world could go up in flames around them and she wouldn't notice. With each press of his lips against hers, she spiraled deeper and deeper into the moment, until she couldn't tell which way was up.

Her heart pounded in her throat, and her tongue took on

a life of its own. It traced a line along his bottom lip. Cole moaned.

"Stop," she said breathlessly. She pulled out of his hold. "I—we can't do this."

"Why?" he pleaded as he took a step closer.

She held up a hand. *Why?* That was a good question. She took a deep breath to try to clear her swimming head. Her hands clenched into fists as she thought, the ring on her left hand pinching her skin.

"I'm engaged," she finally said. "I'm marrying Jacob."

He groaned. "You can't be serious. You're still going to marry this guy?"

"Of course I am," she said. "Why wouldn't I?"

"Because of this," he said, pointing between them. "Because of what just happened."

"You think I'm going to call off my engagement just because you kissed me?" she asked, voice rising. They'd been caught up in the moment, nothing more. Unless, of course, he'd done it on purpose just to mess with her mind.

It was just sex.

"Is that why you did it? Are you that desperate to screw with my life? To win this stupid game?"

"You know that's not what this is about. Stop trying to pretend there's nothing here," he demanded. "We both know this is about a hell of a lot more than a game."

She took a deep breath, ready to give the same argument she'd already given herself several times in the last twelve hours. "What I know is that I love Jacob, and I am a better person when I'm with him. What is so wrong with wanting to be with someone like that?"

"That's not who you are! You are so much more than the person he thinks you are." Cole raked his hands through his hair. "Do you really think he's going to stick around when he finds out it's all been one big lie?"

"He loves me," she said, shaking her head.

"He doesn't even know you!" he yelled. "Not like I do."

"So?" she cried because denying it would be a wasted effort. "So what?"

He tried to take another step closer, and this time she let him. "I know you, and I know you won't be happy pretending to be someone you're not," he said, his voice low and strained.

"Why does it matter to you?" She had to fight the angry tears coming to her eyes. "Why do you even care?"

It was just sex.

"God, you're such an idiot!" he shouted. "How are you so blind that you can't even see that I—" He stopped with a huff, midsentence.

"That you what?" she asked, unable to breathe as she waited for his answer.

He stared into her eyes, hands falling to his sides. "I—" Cole shook his head.

A car horn blasted through the air. The two of them whipped around to see the black Bronco hurling down the narrow road, its trailer no longer in tow.

"A call just came out over the scanner," Cowboy yelled, jumping out of the truck. "There's a fire in town. It sounds bad."

Logan's eyes shot to the sky, and sure enough, there was a dark cloud of smoke billowing nearby. She hadn't noticed it in all the chaos after the accident.

"Where?" Cole asked.

"Wade's."

Her heart plummeted. "You're sure?" Cowboy nodded.

"You guys get the bikes back to Logan's truck and take care of them," Cole told Cowboy quickly before running for the Bronco. "I'll meet you back at the house later."

She shook her head. "I'm going with you." She pulled the keys to her truck from her pocket and tossed them to Cowboy without a second thought.

"No. You need to stay with Cowboy while I go see what I can do to help. There's no point in you coming. You'll either get hurt or be in the way." He ripped the driver's-side door open.

"My dad's there. He has lunch with the mayor every Saturday."

"All the more reason for you to stay away." He was already in the driver's seat, about to slam the door shut when Logan grabbed it.

"He's my dad, Cole," she pleaded. He couldn't possibly expect her to sit around and do nothing while her dad was in danger.

He glowered at her with pursed lips and gritted teeth. "All right, fine." Logan shot to the passenger-side door in a heartbeat, wrenching it open and climbing in. Cole turned the key in the ignition and put the truck in gear.

"Buckle up."

April—Senior Year

THE TREE LEAVES rustled as Cole climbed up another branch to the open window. The lights were off inside, the room lit by moonlight. He peered inside and could just make out a figure lying on the bed.

"Lo," he whispered. "You awake?"

Her head rested at the foot of her bed, her hands folded and lying on her stomach as she stared at the ceiling. She wiped at her face and looked over just as he crawled his way in through the window.

"Go away, Cole. I'm not in the mood."

"I come in peace," he said, his words slurring a little. "I heard the chief was going to be okay, so I thought a celebration was in order."

He'd been drinking with his brothers when they got word that the chief of police had been shot while on duty. He couldn't have explained the sickness he felt shred through his stomach at the news. All he could see was Lo, crying those tears he hated, not knowing if the person she loved most in the world would live until tomorrow. Even after hearing Chief Kase would make a full recovery, all he wanted to do was find Lo and make sure she was okay.

She sat up, took one look at him standing in front of her window, and rolled her eyes. "You're drunk. How did you even get here?"

"I got Cowboy to drive me over. He's outside waiting for us."

"Us?"

He nodded, and the room tilted slightly around him. "Yeah, the three of us are going to go out and celebrate."

"No thanks."

The ache in her voice felt as sharp as a blade. "Don't sound so sad," he pleaded. "The doc said your dad would be fine. You should be happy."

"Right," she said, her voice cracking as she spoke. "I should be so happy after finding out my dad got *shot*."

He sat on the edge of her bed. "He's a cop, Lo. It happens sometimes, part of the job."

"Exactly. Meaning this could happen again."

"I didn't mean it like that," he muttered. "Besides, this is Willow Creek we're talking about. The chances of your dad getting shot again are next to nothing."

"But what if it does happen again?" she cried, wiping her cheeks. "And what if next time he isn't so lucky?"

"Hey," he said softly. He lowered himself down next to

her on the bed and held his arm out in offering. "Come here."

Logan sniffed before rolling over. He put his arm around her, allowing her to rest her heavy head on his shoulder and drape her arm across his chest. This was why he'd come rushing over. To comfort her. Even if, to her, it was nothing more than a friendly gesture.

"Your dad is strong," he said, lifting his hand to run his fingers through her short hair. "You know he won't go down without a fight. And he wouldn't leave you if he could help it. He'll get through this just fine, just like he'll get through anything else that comes at him."

Logan sniffed again. "I just don't understand how he can do it. Go out every day knowing he may not come back. How can he do that, knowing what it would do to me and Momma if he didn't?"

Cole shrugged. "Your dad's a good man. He just wants to help people, protect them."

"Is that why you want to be a firefighter?"

"It's one of the reasons," he admitted before letting out a small laugh. "Not to mention the great pickup lines I'll get to use."

Logan took a deep breath. "I see how Momma is with my dad, all nervous whenever he leaves the house, anxious until he walks through the door in the evening. I just can't imagine loving someone so much and choosing to be with them every day, not knowing if I'll ever see them again." She arched her neck to look up at Cole. "You know that's what you'll be putting your wife through one day when you get married. How could you stand doing that to her?"

"Well," he said slowly. He hadn't really ever thought about it before, getting married, having a wife he adored waiting for him every day when he got home, worrying. Even as he tried to imagine the unknown woman, it didn't feel half as right as the way Logan felt in his arms right now.

"Whoever I do end up marrying, she'll be someone tough. A girl who can handle that kind of uncertainty, because she knows that what I'm doing is important. She won't be selfish; she'll be brave and encouraging, even when the thought of what could happen scares her to death."

She sighed. "You think I'm being selfish."

He closed his eyes, his arms tightening around her. "No. I think you've already lived with it for so long that you know better than anyone just how scary that uncertainty is. And yet, when the time comes for someone you love to put their life on the line like that for someone else, I think you'll let them because you know they're doing the right thing."

They lay there quietly several more minutes. Maybe the alcohol was partly to blame, but Cole had never felt so peaceful in all his life. A guy could get used to this, lying in bed day after day, holding the girl of his dreams.

Not that he'd ever be so lucky. After years of this thing between him and her, he'd gotten used to the idea that nothing would ever happen. No matter what he did, she just didn't see him that way. And with her going off to college in a few months, there wasn't enough time left to convince her. Instead, he'd be happy with small victories like this one.

He was just about to drift into sleep when Logan sat up. He felt her hand settle like a feather on his chest. "Cole?"

He responded by putting his hand over hers. "Hmm."

The bed shifted, and he felt the soft press of her lips on his cheek. He sucked in a breath, and his eyes flew open to meet her gaze. "Thanks for checking on me."

He squeezed her hand on his chest as he stared up at her, and he smiled. "I always will." His chest rose and fell with a new lightness. It was like she was watching him, studying him, with fresh eyes. Maybe he'd given up on her too soon. Maybe he had a little more time. Maybe…

Maybe there was still a chance.

Chapter Twenty-Five

"WHAT'S GOING ON, Lilly?" Cole asked as soon as they reached her. Her face was ashen, and her clothes clung to the sweat on her skin.

Her vacant eyes met his. "Grease fire," she said. Her voice was low, devoid of any feeling. Probably in shock. "I've told Lou so many times to be careful."

"Is everyone okay? Did everybody get out?"

"I think so," she muttered. "I—I don't know."

Logan scanned the parking lot. She saw Mayor Singer trying to calm a woman and her crying child and Big Lou staring dumbfoundedly at the blaze, among others. But she couldn't find the one person she needed to see. "Where's my dad, Lill?"

Lilly managed to focus then. "He wouldn't come out until he got everyone else out." Her head snapped up, looking around. "I haven't seen him. I don't know if he came out."

"No," Logan cried, her eyes shooting to the bar. There was a thick cloud of smoke, flames visible through the windows. She started to run.

Cole grabbed her arm and pulled her back. "You can't go in there, Lo."

"I have to! My dad's still in there," she said, trying to pull out of his grip. "I have to do something."

Cole glanced at the building over her shoulder. "Stay here," he ordered. "Don't move, you understand?"

Her stomach dropped. "What are you doing?"

"I'm going in there to get him."

"You can't!" she yelled. She could just make out the sounds of sirens above the deafening crackle of flames licking over wood. "You could get hurt."

"It's my job. I know what I'm doing." He tried to move past her, but Logan caught his wrist.

"But the firefighters are coming. They've got gear and suits, and you don't." Her voice rose in panic.

He shook his head. "There's no time. Your dad needs me, and the longer I stand here the more danger he's in!"

"But—"

"I have to try, Lo."

She didn't know what to do. She wanted her dad to be safe, needed him to be. And she knew that Cole running in there could be the only way to save him. It should have been easy for her. But the thought of Cole running into a burning building and never coming out—

She could lose both of them.

She let him go, and Cole instantly turned and ran for the bar. He lifted the collar of his long-sleeved T-shirt over his mouth as he ran up the porch steps, through the door, and into the thick cloud of smoke.

The police cars, firetrucks, and an ambulance appeared, honking their horns while people in the crowd moved out of their way. The men scrambled out of the firetruck and set to work readying the hoses. Many of the onlookers in the crowd murmured to each other as they watched, but Logan couldn't take her eyes off the front door of the bar.

They should have been out by now. Logan had to fight the wave of nausea creeping up into her throat.

There was a crack, and everyone in the crowd gasped as a section of the roof collapsed. "Cole!" she cried out. "Daddy!" She felt like a little girl again, crying for her dad when the monsters under her bed tried to get her.

She'd never felt so helpless in her life.

Ten seconds later, she'd yanked her own collar up over her nose and mouth and was calculating how to dodge the officers standing nearby when a figure finally emerged from the smoky doorway. Her knees buckled, and she stumbled forward as Cole escaped the wreckage with a body slung over his shoulder. Two EMTs with a stretcher ran over to Cole and helped him lower her father onto the gurney.

Logan darted toward him, ignoring the officer yelling at her to stay back. Cole was bent over coughing, his skin dark from soot and ash. One of the paramedics placed an oxygen mask over his face as he struggled to breathe, before pulling him over to the ambulance. The other paramedic put a mask on her dad.

"Daddy!" His face was dirtier than Cole's, and a cut on his forehead was bleeding profusely. She touched his arm, but he stayed unresponsive.

"He's alive," the paramedic reassured her as they reached the ambulance. "He's pretty banged up, though. We need to get him to the hospital to check for any internal damage or head trauma."

"I'm coming with him."

The two EMTs worked together to get the stretcher up into the truck. "We don't have room. You'll have to ride behind."

"But—" A warm hand caressed the back of her arm, and Logan turned to see Cole standing behind her.

He lowered the oxygen mask from his face. "They want me to ride in with them to get checked out," he said between coughs. "I'll go with your dad; you take my truck and go get your mom. Explain what happened and meet us at the hospital."

She nodded, and Cole was ushered into the back of the ambulance.

Logan fled to the Bronco still running on the side of the road. She jumped into the driver's side and, with some moderate effort and a few frustrated honks of her horn, she managed to get through the growing crowd in the middle of the street and take off down the main road. She ripped her phone from her coat pocket.

Her mom answered on the third ring. "Hello?"

"Momma, it's me. Listen, I need you to grab your purse and meet me outside the house, okay? I'll be there in just a second."

Her mom was silent for a moment. "What's wrong? Are you okay?"

"I'm fine," she said, making a sharp right onto McGarity. "I'll explain when I get there. Just grab your stuff and meet me out front." Logan hung up. She could just see her momma glaring down at her phone, blood burning hotter than a tin roof on a sunny August day. She threw the phone down in the seat next to her, speeding her way down the two miles to her road.

Just as she'd asked, Logan's mom was standing in front of the house with her bag and a worried frown that deepened when she saw the truck. "Why on earth are you driving Cole Tucker's truck? Have you and that boy gotten into even more trouble?" she asked, the scowl clear on her face as she settled into the passenger seat.

Logan took off again as soon as her momma shut the door. "There was a grease fire at Wade's," she said. "Daddy's okay," she rushed on, "but they're taking him to the hospital. The roof collapsed. Cole was able to get him out."

Tears fell down her momma's cheeks. She wiped them away. "Was anyone else hurt?" Her voice hitched.

Logan shook her head. "I don't know, but Lilly said Daddy was making sure everyone else got out first. So I don't think so."

The nearest hospital was almost thirty minutes out of town, over in Dublin. She tried not to think about her dad or the fear she'd felt waiting for him and Cole to emerge, instead forcing herself to focus on the highway traffic.

They made the trip in eighteen minutes.

THEY'D BEEN SITTING in the waiting room for more than an hour by the time someone came to get them. "Mr. Kase is stable," the doctor told them. She had long, sleek, black hair and umber skin that looked too good to belong to a woman who worked at least seventy hours a week. "There was some smoke inhalation. His right arm is broken along with a few bruised ribs, but there are no signs of serious internal damage. He did suffer a heavy blow to the head, so we'd like to run a few more tests and keep him here for observation. But as long as everything checks out, you should be able to take him home tomorrow morning."

"Can we see him?" Logan asked.

She nodded. "He'll need lots of rest, but I think seeing his family will help ease his mind some. He's been asking about you both," she said with a soft smile. "I'll show you where his room is."

The doctor led them inside, and Logan felt her eyes prickle. Her father was bruised all over, and his forehead was wrapped in a large, white bandage. He lay slumped in the hospital bed, looking defeated and tired and older than he ever had before.

His gaze fell on them as she and her mom walked in. "My favorite girls," he said with a lazy smile, and Logan suspected he was riding a very high dose of morphine. Her eyes watered, and she heard her mother sniffle next to her.

"Don't go getting all weepy on me, now," he told them both. "I'm fine. The doctor's gonna fix me up, and then she says I'll be back home in the morning."

Momma rushed to his side, gently wrapping her arms around him and laying her head on his chest. "I'm just so glad you're okay," she cried as the tears fell freely. "I don't know what I would have done if you weren't."

Logan's throat tightened.

The chief hugged his wife, kissing the top of her head. Logan stood with her arms crossed at the foot of his bed. It was all she could do not to lose it like her mother.

"I heard Cole ran in after me like a dumbass and saved my life," he told her.

"Yep. Dumbass," she repeated. The word described Cole and his act of heroism perfectly.

Daddy nodded. "I'm not surprised. He's a good kid. I owe him my life." Her momma whimpered into his hospital gown.

There was a light knock on the door. Momma sat up and wiped the tears from her eyes. The door cracked open, and the doctor poked her head in. "I'd like the chief to get some rest before we take him in to get the CT. One of you can sit with him, but that's the most I can advise at this time."

Logan nodded, turning back to her parents. "I'll go," she said. She gave Daddy a quick, but heartfelt, hug. "You make sure you do what the doctor says. I'll come pick you both up when you're released."

She kissed his cheek. "I love you, Daddy."

"I love you, too, baby girl."

She stood tall and turned for the door. "Logan," her momma called. "Make sure Cole knows how grateful I am to him."

"I will," she assured her.

Right after she finished kicking his ass.

Chapter Twenty-Six

COWBOY WAS IN the waiting room when Logan walked out.

"Hey," she said. "You looking for Cole? I was just about to track him down."

"He already left. I was actually looking for you." Cowboy pulled Logan's keys from his pocket and placed them in her hand. "It's parked right outside. And don't worry, not a scratch on it," he said with a grin.

She stared at him. "He left?" she practically shouted. "Just like that, without even saying anything?"

Cowboy shrugged. "He was released half an hour ago."

She could punch someone. Of course Cole Tucker would just up and leave without telling anyone he was okay. "Come on," she said through gritted teeth. "I'll give you a ride home."

"That's okay. I have my eye on a sexy nurse whose shift ends in a few minutes." He glanced over at the nurse's station to her left and winked at a redhead in light blue scrubs. "I think Dana will be more than willing to give me a lift."

Logan rolled her eyes. "Shameless," she muttered.

"Hey." Cowboy turned serious as he placed a hand on her shoulder. "I'm glad your dad's okay."

"Thanks. And thanks for bringing me these." She held up the keys in her hand. "I'll see you later. And have fun," she said, nodding toward the nurse's station.

"Oh, I plan to."

⇶⫷

THIRTY MINUTES LATER, Logan pulled into Cole's driveway and parked beside the Bronco. The front door was unlocked, and she didn't hesitate before barging in.

"Cole Tucker, you stupid-ass idiot!" she yelled as she slammed the door behind her. She took a look around, not finding him, and then made a beeline down the hallway to his bedroom. "You really thought that you could not only run into a burning building and almost die but then check yourself out of the hospital without having the decency to tell me you were okay?"

She threw his bedroom door open. Cole stood in the middle of the room, shirtless, wearing a pair of fresh jeans and not so much as flinching when she charged in. He held a white towel in his hands, running it over his wet hair. The towel covered most of his chest and abdomen, but she still had to force herself not to look at the well-defined bits she could see.

"What the hell were you thinking?"

"That I smelled like smoke and needed a shower?" he said with a grin she chose to ignore.

"What if something had happened to you? What if you never came out? What then?"

Cole sighed. "I'm sorry if I scared you. But that's my job, Logan. It's what I was trained for. I go into burning buildings all the time."

"Not without protection you don't. Not when the roof is caving in!"

Cole raised the towel to wipe his neck and shoulders. "I know you're upset—"

"Damn right, I'm upset!" she yelled.

"It was your dad. If I hadn't gone in there, this day would have turned out much worse."

"Don't you think I know that?" Of course she did. She should be happy and grateful right now. And she was. *So* incredibly grateful that both men had come out of that building alive. But she still couldn't shake the feeling that if anything happened to Cole, something inside her would be broken beyond repair. "You just..." Her voice softened. "You can't do that to me again. Promise me you won't do that again."

Cole said nothing, but his look of despair told her exactly what she already knew. That he could never make that kind of promise. He glanced down at the wet towel in his hands, balled it up, and tossed it on the bed behind him. When he turned back, she caught a flash of something black on his side.

"Listen," he said, "about earlier on the bridge—"

"What is that?" She was staring at the spot on the left side of his rib cage. She stepped closer, stopping inches from his bare chest. She couldn't breathe as she slowly raised her hand. Cole's body tensed, his breath hitching as she placed her finger to the elegantly familiar black letters that matched her own.

LBK

Logan Brynn Kase.

"I can explain."

The memory of the night she'd been pushing away for years rushed back to her in a single instant.

"When did you—?" No. She couldn't do this. Not now. She took several steps away from him, unable to meet his gaze. "I can't...I have to go."

Logan turned and ran out the door, making her hurried escape to the front door and ripping it open. In only a second, she was down the steps and sprinting to the truck.

"Lo, let's just talk about this!" Cole raced after her, but she was too fast. She was in the truck with the engine running before he reached the porch steps.

She finally looked at him, her vision blurring.

"Stop, Logan! Don't run away from me again." But she didn't stop. Because apparently running away from Cole Tucker was what she did best.

⫸⫷

August—Night of the Farewell Bonfire

"I CAN'T BELIEVE you talked me into this."

Cole sat in a chair against the wall, arms crossed. "A bet's a bet. You agreed to the terms."

"But this, seriously?" They were in the tattoo parlor in Dublin. Logan sat in the chair, her right arm lying wrist up. "I must be insane."

"I hear they're not so bad if you're not afraid of needles."

Lo bit her lip. Apparently, she wasn't as fearless as she claimed.

A tattoo artist with a shaved head, dark beard, and gauges in his earlobes—Toby, according to the business card he'd given Cole—approached. He put on sterile gloves and opened a new needle. "You ready?" he asked Lo.

She nodded, her bottom lip still caught between her teeth. He grabbed her arm and brought the needle to her skin.

She jumped. "Son of a bitch!" The machine stopped, and Toby pulled it away. She sighed. "Sorry, I just wasn't expecting it to hurt that much."

The machine buzzed to life again, and Lo flinched. A second later, the room went quiet again.

Toby turned to Cole. "Sometimes it helps if the boyfriend holds her hand."

"I'm fine," she assured him. "And besides, he's not my—"

261

Cole's chair scraped as he dragged it across the floor. He took Lo's free hand in his. The buzzing of the needle filled the room once more. She sucked in a breath, her fingers squeezing his tightly as Toby started etching three bold, black letters onto her wrist. Her eyes glistened with moisture.

Cole took the opportunity to study her, the way her lips twitched every few seconds as the needle pricked her skin repeatedly, and his brittle mood softened. He liked seeing her this way, vulnerable. As the chief's daughter, she was always so set on showing the world how tough she was. But, every once in a while, he was lucky enough to slip past her defenses, see her in a way few people ever got to. To be the one to comfort her like he was now.

Not that it meant anything. After tomorrow, she'd be gone, and he'd be lost in a town that didn't make sense without her.

Christ, he was pathetic. And even as she squeezed his hand, she had no idea the kind of effect she had on him just being near him like this. Maybe it was a good thing she was going away. Maybe then he could finally get her out from under his skin.

⟫⟫⟫⟫⟪⟪⟪⟪

LO PICKED AT the bandage on her wrist.

"Knock it off," Cole scolded. "He said to leave it alone for a couple hours."

They were in the Bronco, parked outside the tattoo parlor. He'd completely sobered up more than an hour ago, and as he readied to take her back to the bonfire, that dark disposition settled back over him like a shadow.

"What am I supposed to tell my parents? How am I going to explain this to them?"

"Maybe you should have thought about that before you agreed to the bet," he grumbled.

She glared at him from across the cab. "Why are you in such a shitty mood lately? It's starting to piss me off."

"Doesn't matter." None of it would after tomorrow.

"It matters to me. You've been acting weird all summer. First you were all moody at the bonfire, but just now, inside, you were actually acting like a decent human being. And now you're all grumpy again. Are you mad at me? Did I do something?"

"You didn't do anything."

"Then tell me what's going on."

Cole let out a heavy breath and slumped in the seat. He was so tired of pretending in front of her, of holding everything in. And what good had it done him? She'd be gone soon, and he'd still be in the exact same spot, exhausted and empty.

"I think it's just hitting me."

"What is?"

He looked up to meet her eyes. "You're leaving tomorrow," he whispered.

She stiffened, the harsh set of her lips and jaw melting into a frown. Her forehead crinkled, and she looked down at her lap. "Oh."

"It won't be the same around here," he said, scratching the prickly shadow on his jaw. "Not without you."

Her throat bobbed when she swallowed. "Yeah, but I won't be gone forever, and I'm sure you can find some other girl to torture in the meantime." Logan's fingers toyed with the hem of her Lynyrd Skynyrd tank top. "What about Sarah Newnan? She looked like she wouldn't mind some extra attention from you at the bonfire tonight."

So she had seen that. Was it too much to hope that the bitterness he heard in her voice was real?

"You could tell her the Earth is round and really throw her for a loop," she sneered.

Cole chuckled to himself. "She is a bit of a ditz, isn't she?" He laughed again until it grew so loud that soon Logan joined in. He took in her wrinkled nose and the little lines at the corners of her eyes.

He sighed. "You're so pretty when you laugh." Where the hell had that come from? Maybe he wasn't as sober as he'd thought.

Her eyes doubled in size before she laughed it off. "Okay, maybe I should be the one to drive us back. You've clearly had too much to drink," she echoed his thoughts. Her cheeks were flushed, and she was breathing quickly. Heat spread through his chest at the sight.

Cole turned to face her while he still had the nerve. "I need to tell you something, and I feel like if I don't say all this now, I never will."

"Then say it," she whispered.

Cole scooted closer. They were sitting with their faces mere inches apart. "I don't want you to go. And I don't want to torture some other girl," he told her, blood hammering in his ears. "I only want you."

Logan stared at him silently, and her eyes took on that dark shade he'd loved since that day at the dock in ninth grade. He didn't move or speak, afraid to break whatever spell was cast between them.

He waited, daring her to speak first, but no words came. She glanced down at his lips.

It was all she needed to say. Cole reached forward, placing one hand on her neck before he pulled her toward him. Their lips crashed together, and she gasped.

He'd wondered a million times what it would be like to finally kiss Logan Kase. Dreamed it a million and one. It went beyond anything he'd ever imagined. The raw emotion he'd tried to keep buried these last couple months came bursting at the surface. It burned within him, like the delicious sting of salt in an open wound.

Her fingers crept up to his shirt, crushing the cotton fabric in her hands. And then they were in his hair, pushing their kiss further, until their tongues found each other. She moaned.

He gripped her hips, and he lifted her up to straddle his lap. She obliged, placing her legs on either side of his and slowly settling in. His lips left hers, and he started placing a trail of kisses across her jaw and down her neck, tearing another moan from her. The sound stoked the fire deep in his gut.

Her hands snaked under his shirt, and her fingers traced over the hard muscles of his abdomen.

Logan shifted on Cole's lap, and his entire body tensed. He groaned and drew her lips back to his. His tongue caressed hers before she nipped his bottom lip with her teeth.

His lips curled beneath hers, and he pulled back to look into her eyes. They were bright, like some of his fire had escaped into her. He ran his hand through her short hair. "I *really* don't want you to go now."

She laughed and placed a quick kiss on his jaw. And then another. "It's just a plane ride away. I'll be home for every school break."

Cole wrapped one arm tightly around her waist while the other hand traced lightly over her bare thigh from her knee to the edge of the jean shorts. "It's not enough." He kissed her again, slow and gentle as he savored the moment.

How had things between them changed so drastically in a matter of minutes? One second he'd felt like a man preparing to never see the sun again, and now it was blinding and burning and just within his reach. He'd never felt so light, so free.

Christ, he wanted to feel this way forever. But she was leaving. Was there any chance for a relationship that started with so many miles between them? Was that even what she wanted?

"Hey," she said, her eyebrows drawing together. She placed a hand on his cheek. "What's wrong?"

"Nothing." He brushed his hand through her hair again and placed a featherlight kiss on the tip of her nose. "I should take you back before Carly and Cowboy start worrying."

"Or…"

Cole stilled, and his eyes fluttered when she shifted on his lap. She stared down at him, her eyes dark with need. "Or?" he asked breathlessly.

Her lips parted in a wicked grin. She brought them to his ear. "Or you could take me back to your place."

Chapter Twenty-Seven

LOGAN DROVE AIMLESSLY for hours as if she could outrun the memory of that night four years ago that played over and over in her mind. The smell of bonfire smoke embedded in his cotton shirt, the way Cole had looked at her in the cab of that Bronco—like he was seeing a sunset for the first time. No one had ever looked at her like that. Her walls had crumbled, and the next thing she knew, she was kissing Cole Tucker.

It had been unlike anything she'd felt before, better than what she'd had with Ryan Baker. Better than anything she'd ever imagined. And she'd imagined it more than a few times—not that she ever would have admitted it back then.

She'd been so nervous the next morning. Had last night changed as much for him as it had for her? Was he as impossibly elated as she was? What did it mean for them going forward?

And then he tore apart everything she thought she knew about their night, about him.

It was just sex. The memory still turned her stomach to stone.

Four words completely snuffed out her internal glow. None of it meant anything to him.

She thought of the initials he'd gotten tattooed on his ribs. They weren't there in her memory of that night, which meant he must have gone back to get them sometime after she left. But why?

She was so deep in her own thoughts when she finally pulled up to her parents' house that she didn't even notice the black Lexus parked in the driveway until she was out of the truck. She looked around, her eyes landing on a tall figure pacing across the front porch.

"Jacob?" He went still, and even from this distance, she could see the tension in his shoulders. She stopped in front of the steps. "What are you doing here?"

His forehead creased. "I could ask you the same thing," he said. "Seeing as you were supposed to be at my apartment five hours ago."

Shit. "Oh God. The dinner." She'd completely forgotten. The San Francisco spot, the future they'd planned, it all hinged on that dinner, and she'd missed it. She'd hoped tonight they would be able to get past the issues they'd been having about the wedding, and now she'd just made everything worse.

She stepped closer and squared her shoulders, shoving thoughts of Cole Tucker and that long ago night far away. If she didn't fix this now, she could lose everything she'd spent years working toward. She took his hand in hers. "Jacob, I'm so sorry. Please, just let me explain."

"I've been calling for hours. You, your parents, Carly. Everyone I could think of, but no one would answer. I jumped in the car, thinking you might be hurt or something." He gave her a full once-over. "Clearly, I worried for nothing."

"I had no idea. I never even heard my phone ring." Logan searched her jeans pockets and came up short. She tried to think back to the last time she remembered having it. It was when she'd called her mom as she rushed to the house in the Bronco.

She let out a groan as her head fell back in defeat. "I'm sorry. I must have left it in Cole's truck."

"Cole? That guy from the bar?"

"Yeah, we were over on County Line Road when there was this call on his police scanner—" Jacob was down the steps and in front of her in an instant.

"You mean to tell me that while I've been going crazy thinking you were dead or seriously injured, you were with another guy?"

Logan hesitated. "It wasn't like that."

"Then what was it like?" he asked.

"We were racing dirt bikes."

"Racing? Don't you know how dangerous that is? Not to mention illegal." He was almost fuming now, and she fought to keep her own calm. If she lost her cool at this point, she could kiss it all goodbye: Jacob, the wedding, her new life.

"It's not a big deal," she assured him. "I used to do this kind of thing all the time."

"What's that supposed to mean?"

She shook her head. "Nothing. I didn't mean that. I just—it was all part of this stupid bet. A bunch of challenges and the first one to lose five loses the whole bet." A torrent of words started to rush from her mouth. "There was a poker game, a hungover eating contest, a paintball game. We were just trying to see who was better."

"Trying to see *who was better?*" he asked incredulously. "You realize how juvenile that sounds, don't you? You're a grown woman. You shouldn't be running around with another man racing bikes and playing stupid games."

"It's nothing. We've got this thing from when we were kids and—"

"I asked you that first night how well you knew that guy, and you told me you barely knew him at all."

"Technically, I told you we weren't friends. Which we weren't. I hadn't seen him in years, and we could hardly stand each other half the time growing up. I know the whole thing is stupid, but it's just what Cole and I do. That's all it is. It's just a bet. I shouldn't have even agreed to it in the first place."

"Then why did you?"

"I was drunk. By the time I realized what we'd started we were already onto the next game."

"Since when do you drink!" Jacob shouted, making Logan flinch. He turned on the spot, hands tight at his hips. He took several steps across the yard before coming right back. "How long has this been going on?"

Logan was silent a minute. The look in his eyes told her Jacob was barely keeping his anger at bay, and she didn't know what would set him over the edge. She looked down at the ground, not wanting to see his reaction. "It started the night I moved back home."

"So, you've been lying to me. And not just for the last six weeks when I asked what you'd been doing out here. You've apparently been lying to me throughout our entire relationship."

"It's not—"

Jacob held up a hand.

"You've lied to me, you've put off setting a date for our wedding, and then tonight you made me miss the most important dinner of my life because you were out playing games with another guy."

"That's not why—"

Jacob took a step toward her, bringing his face very close to hers. "These games are going to stop. It's time for you to grow up. I will not have my future wife going around making bets and getting drunk like some wild woman."

"Would you just let me explain?"

Jacob shook his head. "No, I don't want to hear anything from you right now. That's why I am going to leave, and you are going to decide if this relationship is worth anything to you. Because I'm not going to keep wasting my time if it's not."

Without another word, he crossed the lawn and opened the door to the Lexus. Logan stood stunned as he backed quickly out of the driveway and drove off.

Chapter Twenty-Eight

LOGAN SAT ON the porch swing, listening to nothing but the sound of crickets chirping from the bushes. The porch light was on while the rest of the house stood dark and silent. She should go in and get some rest before she went to get her mom and dad from the hospital, but sleep was the last thing on her mind at this point.

How had she managed to make such a mess of her life? She was engaged to one man but realizing she had feelings for another. One made her feel loved and safe, the other lit a fire in her veins at the mere thought of him. One had asked her to spend the rest of her life with him, the other had said it was just sex.

She loved Jacob. She loved who she was with him. And she knew that picking him would be the safest choice. But Cole was such a big part of her. In a way, his presence in her life had become like a piece of herself.

With Jacob, she knew she could be the person he wanted because she'd already been that girl for two years. With Cole, there were too many unknowns. In a way, she knew him better than anyone, but she still didn't know what would happen if they tried to be together.

And then there was the question of who she was around Cole. He'd always brought out the worst in her. Sure, she had fun when she was with him, but how long would these games satisfy them? How long until their antics escalated and someone was seriously hurt? What if Cole got hurt because of her?

Logan pulled her legs in close and wrapped her arms around them, resting her forehead on her knees. She knew what she had to do, knew the choice she had to make. And worst of all, she knew how much it was going to hurt.

Several minutes later she lifted her head as the sound of a familiar truck coming up the gravel road filled the air. She watched as the Bronco pulled into her driveway and parked behind her Chevy.

"I was hoping you'd be here," he said as he came up the porch steps. He stopped in front of her, reaching into his back pocket and pulling out a slim cell phone. "You left this in my truck."

She took the phone from his hand. "Thanks."

"There's a lot of missed calls and texts from Jacob," he said quietly. "I didn't read any of them. But I'm guessing he really wants to talk to you."

She laughed humorlessly. "Yeah, he was actually here when I got home. Said what he needed to say and left."

"I take it he wasn't happy you missed dinner."

That was an understatement. She put her hands through

her hair slowly. "I completely forgot about it until I came home and found him. And even then he had to remind me."

"He can't blame you for that. I'm sure he understood once you explained the situation."

Yes, she imagined he would have understood if he'd ever given her the chance to tell him.

Cole shifted on his feet. They were silent for a while before he sat on the swing next to her. She had to fight the urge to curl up in his side and let him hold her.

"Do you want to talk about the tattoo?"

Not really, but she was tired of running. "Okay."

He leaned forward, resting his elbows on his knees, and rubbed his hands together. "How much do you remember about that night?"

"All of it. The tattoo parlor, the truck, your place. I remember waking up and you coming in and telling me it was just sex to you."

"I shouldn't have said that."

"Then why did you? Why tell me that what happened between us that night didn't mean anything when clearly it did?"

"I was scared. After all those years, I finally told you how I felt, and you seemed to feel the same way. I can't even put into words how it felt waking up next to you that morning. How right it was. I thought I finally had you, that it was the start of the rest of our lives," he said, his voice rough, as if the words were razor blades in his throat.

"But then I heard you on the phone with Carly, and you sounded so upset. You begged her to come get you, told her you'd made a huge mistake. I couldn't risk hearing you say that you didn't mean any of it."

"So instead you said it to me," she said softly.

"After you ran out, I was miserable for weeks. I'd finally gotten the girl of my dreams, only to lose her within a few hours." He scratched the nape of his neck. "I felt so lost. I think I just wanted some piece of you to keep with me, so I got the tattoo. I told myself it would be a reminder of how it felt to get rejected, that it would help me get over you. And after a while I thought I had. But the second I saw you at Wade's, I knew you were still as much a part of me as ever."

"You could have talked to me. You could have called or something."

"And have you laugh in my face? For all I knew, none of it had been real and you were only with me that night because you were drunker than I thought. I couldn't stand to hear you call me a mistake again."

"You weren't the mistake." She sighed, hugging her knees closer. "When I woke up that morning, I realized I had only an hour before I was supposed to leave for the airport. I asked Carly to bring me my truck so I could go home without my parents knowing where I'd been all night. It had nothing to do with you."

There was a flicker of something in Cole's eyes, and his shoulders lifted as he took a deep breath. He took her hand in his, running his thumb gently over the road rash on her palm. "So it was all real?"

Hope, Logan realized. And she'd seen it in his eyes before, though she hadn't recognized it until today. It was the same look she saw when he first kissed her that night. If tearing her own heart out meant she could spare his, she'd do it in an instant because she knew what she had to do next.

She had to extinguish it.

Again.

She couldn't keep doing this to him. She couldn't keep stringing him along. And as long as there remained any hope for the two of them, Cole would not be able to let go. He wouldn't be able to settle down and start the family he wanted with the big house and the picket fence.

She strained to keep her voice calm and even. "I don't know," she said, praying he couldn't hear the lie in it. "Maybe, but it was so long ago. And things are different now."

"Why?" he pleaded. "Why can't we just give this a shot and see where it goes?"

She shook her head, fighting the tears that wanted to come. "I'm marrying Jacob," she said for the last time. "I made him a promise, and I can't back down from that. I won't."

"You haven't promised him anything until you've said *I do*."

"I'm sorry," Logan said, closing her eyes. "I don't want

to hurt you." *But I know I have to.*

Cole sucked in a long breath beside her. "Hey." He placed his hand on her chin and used it to gently turn her face toward his. When she opened her eyes, she was met with a kind smile. "All that matters is that you're happy. And if you really think he's the one who'll do that, then I won't try to stand in the way."

"Thank you," she barely whispered. Her lungs felt frozen, aching as he placed his lips on her forehead for the second time in as many days. It took everything she had to not melt into his touch.

He stood from the swing. "I'll see you around, Lo. Try to stay out of trouble in California, okay?"

She nodded, watching as he crossed the porch and walked to his truck. "What about the bet?" she called out. She'd won the dirt bike race that morning, which meant they were tied. "There's still one more challenge left."

Not that it mattered much now. Jacob knew about her reckless past, and she was sure Cole would keep the secret about the night she got the tattoo. But still, in the ten years since they'd started their games, they'd never left one unfinished.

"Consider this my forfeit," he said with one last glance over his shoulder. "Bye, Lo."

Logan forced herself to take long, slow breaths and willed the tears not to come until the red of his taillights disappeared.

August—Five Days After the Bonfire

COLE SAT ON the sofa in the living room, his right hand wrapped in puffy white bandages while the other held a beer he'd just taken from the stash Keith replenished for him the day before. His eyes were trained on the Braves game playing out on the TV screen in front of him, but his mind was fixated on a memory of angry blue eyes.

He took a long drag from his bottle. It would be another four drinks until those eyes started blur, at least seven before he could erase them completely.

Cowboy came around the corner of the sofa, his hair still damp from his shower. He'd put on a nice shirt and dark jeans in preparation for a night with yet another random girl.

"I'm heading out," he said. He stared at Cole, eyes scanning over his sweatpants and stained shirt. They landed on his bandaged hand. "Why don't you come with us? I'm sure Nina can find a friend. We could all hang out, the four of us."

"Nah, I'm good right here." He patted the couch cushion. He'd barely left it the last few days other than to use the bathroom and grab another beer. He hadn't even managed to take a shower, much to Cowboy's dismay, he was sure. "You two have a good time."

Cowboy took a step closer. "Look, I don't know what happened the other night, but if this has something to do with Lo leaving—"

"I said have a good time, Cowboy. I'll see you in the morning."

He nodded before backing off. "Sure. See ya."

Cole drained the rest of his bottle as the front door closed. He ran his injured hand over the thick scruff on his jaw then lowered his head into his palm.

Five days. Five days since she'd stormed out that same door. Since he'd let her storm out. He should have stopped her. He should have told her the truth. He'd been afraid of the rejection, of that pitying look in her eye that told him it was all one-sided. But there was no way it could have been any worse than the way he felt now. Like his heart, lungs, and throat had been ripped out of his chest.

He hated this feeling. Had been trying to drown it every night since she left, only to wake feeling sick the next morning when it all came back. Only this time with the added bonus of a killer hangover.

Seven years. Seven years of history between them, and he'd watched it all blow up in his face after a single night. She was gone, a thousand miles away. She'd literally never been further out of his reach.

What the hell was he supposed to do now? Keep going as if he hadn't just ruined the best thing in his life? Like he hadn't just lost the one person he'd ever truly cared about? He had no idea when or if he'd ever see her again, and he was supposed to do what? Move on? It didn't even feel possible.

Meanwhile, she'd go off to school, party, meet a bunch of guys. Or worse, she'd meet the one guy who would make Cole and everything they'd shared over the years nothing more than a distant memory.

Cowboy would tell him there were plenty of other girls out there. His brothers would tell him to suck it up and grow a pair. Maybe they were all right. Lo was gone and clearly not interested in him after the way she'd run out like the devil himself was on her tail. There was nothing he could do about her feelings. It was out of his control.

The only thing he could control was himself. And one thing he knew for sure—he didn't want to feel this gaping black hole where his heart should be. He set his beer bottle aside, sniffed, and sat up straight on the couch.

Starting tomorrow, he was putting Logan Kase and her grip on his soul behind him. He'd let her go, move on the way he should have years ago. And when she finally came back into town, he'd pretend none of it had ever happened.

But first, he needed closure, something to remember all the hell she'd put him through over the years. A reminder to never lose himself to one person so completely. He couldn't risk feeling this way over anyone ever again.

Cole shot up from the couch and darted to his bedroom, rifling through piles of dirty clothes until he found the pair of blue jeans that still smelled like smoke. He pulled the small business card from his pocket and punched the number into his phone.

He answered on the third ring. "Hello?"

"Hey, Toby? I don't know if you remember me. I came in with a girl a few nights ago, and she got three letters tattooed on her wrist."

"Yeah, I remember."

He took a deep breath. "Any chance you've got an opening tonight?"

Chapter Twenty-Nine

J UDGING BY THE height of the sun the next morning when Logan woke, it was already late. A quick glance at the clock beside her bed only confirmed it. She rubbed her swollen, sensitive eyes.

Last night had probably been the worst she'd slept since her first night in her dorm freshman year. Just like then, she'd gone to bed an emotional wreck, unable to control the immense waves that tried to drown her. Anytime she'd closed her eyes, all she could see were Cole's as that glimmer of hope died over and over again.

She knew it was for the best, but that didn't make it hurt any less. She spent hours remembering the good—and not so good—times they'd shared, especially in the last several weeks. She began to notice how each memory carried a certain fondness in her heart. And with each passing day, with each new challenge, that fondness had only increased. How had she not realized the way she felt about Cole until it was too late?

Logan rubbed her eyes again before she climbed out of bed and over to her bathroom. She turned the cold water on and splashed some over her face. With luck, it would help with the redness and the swelling before she went downstairs. When her eyes finally looked satisfactory, She ran a brush through her tangled hair and threw on some clothes.

Down the stairs, she could hear her parents talking in the kitchen, which wasn't terribly surprising since her daddy had never known the meaning of the word *rest*.

"Hey, baby girl. I was wondering when we'd see that beautiful face again." He was sipping his coffee and reading the paper, a big smile spreading across his face. She wasn't sure the last time she'd seen him in such a good mood. Was it the euphoria of surviving a near-death experience or just the painkillers? "You know it's almost eleven already, don't you?"

Momma brought over a plate of pancakes and eggs and set it in front of her. "How did you sleep?"

"Fine," she lied.

The chief's eyes were fixed on the newspaper in his one good hand. "Would ya look at that. Apparently, the fire at Wade's is front-page news around here."

Momma laughed. "I don't think it's the fire so much as the two heroes who risked their lives to try to get everybody out."

Logan's head snapped up. "What?"

The chief turned the paper over to show Logan. Three different pictures were printed under the bold headline: a charred and dilapidated bar, her daddy in his police uniform, and Cole Tucker. The sight of him grinning at her both set her insides ablaze and punched a hole in her gut.

Logan looked away. She used her fork to cut a big piece of pancake and shoved it in her mouth without really tasting it.

"You feelin' okay?"

She forced a smile before she looked at him. "I'm fine, Daddy. But more importantly, how are you feeling?"

"I'm okay. Still a little sore, but that's to be expected. I should be up and going in a few days." He shifted his arm in the sling and winced.

Momma frowned. "We're supposed to go to the hospital later today to get the cast put on now that the swelling's gone down. And I imagine we'll get a few visitors from the church this afternoon coming to check up on us once the service is over this morning."

"What about your plans today? Made it sound like you've got a lot of work to start on for the gallery."

Her stomach twisted. In all the chaos, she still had yet to tell her parents about her argument with Jacob over California. "Mom, Dad. There's something I need to tell you about the gallery. I don't think—"

A hard knock from the front of the house cut her off. "Well, who would that be? Church hasn't even let out yet," Momma said, walking out of the kitchen. Logan focused on her plate. How was she supposed to tell them their only daughter was about to leave them again so soon?

A minute later her mother returned. "Lo, someone's here to see you."

She looked up from her plate, her eyes widening ever so slightly.

"Jacob?"

"Hey." He looked almost as awful as she felt. He had on a T-shirt and sweatpants, a combination she rarely ever saw him in. His usually well-kempt, light hair hung over his dark-circled eyes. "Can we talk for a minute?"

She rose from her seat. Her momma frowned as Logan led him out of the kitchen and up the stairs to her room where she knew there was less chance of being overheard.

She shut the door and turned to Jacob. He was standing at her window, looking out through the branches of the tall tree. She waited for him to start, but he said nothing.

"Jacob?"

He continued to stare out the window. "I read about what happened to your dad. The fire and all. It was in the paper this morning."

"Oh." She didn't know what else to say.

"You tried to tell me, and I wouldn't listen."

Logan's shoulders eased. She sat on the end of the bed, her back turned to her fiancé. "It's okay, you were upset. I missed your dinner and never answered my phone when you called, and then after you drove all the way out here to check on me it looked like I'd just forgotten about it...which I had, but only because my dad was in the hospital."

"I understand. And I'm glad your dad is okay."

She shook her head. "I'm sorry. I should have thought to call or something. I shouldn't have worried you like that."

"*I'm* sorry," he said. "I should have given you the chance to explain. I shouldn't have blown up at you like that. It was unfair of me, and I promise I won't let it happen again."

"So…so we're good now? You and me?" She took a deep breath. "You were right. I have been struggling to set a date. Not because I don't love you and want to marry you; I do. It's just hard for me. I know that once we do, the move to California will be real and I'll be closing the book on this huge chapter of my life. And that scared me.

"But I'm ready now. I'm ready to set a date and move to California with you. I'm going to go see Ms. Snyder today and tell her that I can't help her with the gallery. If you're going to be in San Francisco, that's where I need to be, too."

Logan turned to watch Jacob carefully. She'd expected him to turn around and throw his arms out wide at her declaration. Or at the very least smile at her. But he didn't.

"I'm glad to hear that," he said, letting out a heavy breath with it. "I can't tell you how awful I felt when I read about what happened. I wanted to punch myself for how I treated you. I grabbed my keys and was ready to jump in the car, come out here and apologize, beg you to forgive me."

"You were?" Logan smiled, feeling that heavy weight in her chest ease some.

"I was." He paused stoically. Where was all that emotion

now? "I was so relieved that it was all just one big misunderstanding. I even read the article again, I was so happy. But then I saw something I hadn't before."

"What?"

"I promised I would always give you a chance to explain, and I'm going to start right now." He finally turned around, the shadows under his eyes looking even darker than they had minutes ago. He crossed his arms over his chest, eyes on Logan.

She wrinkled her forehead. "Explain what?"

"Explain to me why you have Cole's initials tattooed on your wrist."

Chapter Thirty

"WHY, I—" SHE could hardly breathe, a wave of dizziness coming over her. "How did you know?"

Jacob started pacing the floor in front of her bed.

"Cole Elijah Tucker," he said quickly. "That was how they addressed him in the paper. CET." He stopped, his gaze accusing. "There was never any Caroline, was there? You've been lying to me about that, too."

Logan closed her eyes. It wasn't supposed to happen this way. She was supposed to have won the bet and Jacob was supposed to have never known what the tattoo really meant.

Jacob continued to pace the floor, going on about trust and how making up a dead aunt was hardly a good sign for the future of their relationship.

"You're right," she said, interrupting his rant. He stopped again in front of her. "There is no Caroline Teague. I made her up as soon as I moved to Austin."

"Why?"

"Because I didn't want to have to explain how I really got it."

"Why not?"

"Because it was part of a bet."

"A bet?" Jacob asked. "You're serious? You got something permanently etched into your skin over a bet. Who would be reckless enough to do something like that?"

"I would. Before I met you, that was the kind of girl I was. Reckless. Especially when it came to Cole. And I guess I still am."

"So you two were a thing."

"It wasn't like that between us." At least, not before the bonfire. "Look, he and I just have a really complicated past."

"Then uncomplicate it for me." Jacob's eyes were pleading. "I can't come to grips with all of this or get past it until I know what it is I'm trying to get past. Please just tell me the truth. How can we have a real relationship if you aren't honest with me?"

She curled her legs up underneath her. This could take a while. She forced down the panic that tried to claw its way out of her stomach.

"Ever since we were kids, Cole and I have had a very strange relationship. It started as pranks and games. He told everyone in our class I stuffed my bra; I replaced his breath spray with jalapeño juice. Cole made me ride my new bike into the creek; I poured itching powder into his pants. On and on, just like that. Sometimes we'd make bets so that the loser had to do something embarrassing, and sometimes we just bet money."

"So you really weren't friends?"

Logan laughed. "Definitely not at first. I could barely stand him. But after a while, it was almost like we were better than friends. We respected each other. We picked on each other all the time, but we always had each other's backs. In a way, we knew each other better than almost anyone else. I don't know what to call that."

Jacob leaned back against her white dresser, watching her carefully.

"We got older, but the games never got old. And I think I liked knowing that there was someone as crazy and reckless as me."

"Did you have feelings for him?"

She could deny it, say it had never been like that between her and Cole. It would be so easy, especially when the truth meant admitting to feelings she's been denying for months. But after everything she'd put Jacob through, all the lies she'd told him, she owed it to him to be honest now.

"Not at first," she finally said. "I'm not sure when it happened exactly. They must have built up over time, and I just kept ignoring them, like all those feelings were stuck behind this dam. And then the night before I was supposed to leave for Austin, he kissed me, and it was like the dam broke. I realized that I did care about him, more than I'd ever cared about another person before. That I had for a while."

"Did you love him?" He didn't sound angry or sad, just curious.

"I think so, yes," she whispered.

"Were you in love with him when we started dating?"

"No," Logan said, already sure of this one. "I hadn't seen him in two years. How can you love someone you haven't seen or talked to for that long? We didn't even know each other anymore, not really."

"You're sure?"

She smiled softly. "I can honestly say that the only guy I had feelings for, the only guy I thought about, and the only guy I was in love with was you."

"What about now?" he asked, his Adam's apple bobbing as he swallowed. "Can you still say that?"

Her smile faltered, and Jacob's shoulders fell. "I didn't think so."

"I'm sorry." Her voice trembled as the words tumbled out. "I didn't mean for it to happen. I didn't even know it was happening until it was too late. I'm so sorry, Jacob." The tears spilled out over her cheeks.

"Hey, don't cry," he said softly. He sat next to her on the bed, wrapping his arms around her. "This isn't your fault. He's your first love. I understand that."

"You do?"

He nodded. "Everything will be fine as soon as we get out of this town. You can stay in Athens with me until the spot in San Francisco is settled. And then, after Carly's wedding, we can go for good and start planning our own wedding."

"Our wedding?" Logan pulled back. "You mean you still want to marry me?"

He offered her a gentle smile. "Of course I do."

"But I just told you I have feelings for another man." How could he be so calm and understanding about this?

"You love me, right?"

"You know I do," she said instantly.

He smiled. "And I still love you, despite everything."

"But I lied to you about my past. About who I was."

Jacob's smile grew bigger. "So you used to pull pranks and get drunken tattoos. You really thought I'd be upset over something like that?" He rolled his eyes. "Okay, I'm still not thrilled about the tattoo, but we can fix that."

"No, Jacob. It's not just pranks and a tattoo. I drink...*a lot*. I do stupid shit that could get me killed. I race dirt bikes off bridges, and I get shot at for trespassing on people's property—"

"Someone shot you?" Jacob asked loudly, eyes wide.

"Shot *at*," she corrected. "I go to the bar almost every night. And I've ridden in the back of at least half of the squad cars down at the police station. You really want to marry that?"

"That's who you used to be, not who you are now."

"It's exactly who I am now." Logan jumped up from her spot on the bed and spun around to face him. "I changed who I was to impress you because I knew that was the kind of girl you wanted. And after two years, I really thought I was that girl."

"Because you are."

"Then why did it only take one night for the old me to come back? One night and that person I'd been pretending to be was gone."

"It's just this place, being back here and around him. When we leave, we can go back to the way things were between us. You can be that girl. You changed yourself once; you can change again."

Logan was silent. She could change again. She'd done it before, and she'd been happy to do it just to be with him.

But in the last several weeks, she'd felt more alive than she could ever remember feeling in the last two years. Yes, she could be that girl again, but that girl would be a lie. Jacob deserved better than that.

"Oh." Logan clutched her hand to her chest and felt like the wind was being knocked out of her. All this time, she'd been constantly reassuring herself that Jacob would make her truly happy. But not once had she wondered if she could possibly make him happy.

"This isn't going to work," she said quietly, turning back to him sitting on the edge of the bed, watching her.

"What isn't?"

"This...us." She looked down at the sparkling ring on her left hand. "Jacob, I'm *so* sorry."

He stared at her, but no words came out.

"I've been so selfish. All this time I've been clinging to

you, to this relationship, because I knew that you were the best thing for me. But I never stopped to think about what was best for you."

"What are you talking about?" He stood slowly. "Why does this sound like you're breaking up with me?"

"You're asking me to change for you, and I did once before. But you shouldn't settle for someone like me, someone who has to pretend to be the perfect girl for you. You deserve someone who doesn't need to change to be perfect. You deserve the real thing."

Slowly, she pulled the ring off her finger. She took his hand in hers before she placed the ring in his palm. She looked into his eyes. "I love you, Jacob. But I'm not what's best for you."

"Don't do this," he whispered.

She bit her lip as she looked into his pleading eyes. She was hurting him, and she, too, ached as she let go of the best thing she'd had in the last four years and the future she'd thought she was supposed to have. But along with that ache came a strange sense of calm and relief.

This was right. She knew it, and deep down he had to know it, too. "Your perfect girl is out there still waiting for you. It's not fair of me to hold on to what's hers."

Jacob was still as she wrapped her arms around him. His shoulders tensed at first, but they slowly relaxed as he let out a heavy breath. He embraced her, burying his face in her neck. His breath tickled her flesh. "I wish I could convince you you're wrong, but I don't think I can."

They stood, unmoving, holding each other, and Logan waited for the tears to come. Only this time, there were no tears. Surely, it made her an awful person, but standing here in his familiar hold as she said goodbye, she felt oddly at peace.

Logan pulled out of his arms and kissed his cheek softly. "I'll miss you," she said.

"I'll miss you, too." His arms fell away from her. He shoved the ring he held deep into his pocket and grabbed the doorknob, glancing at her over his shoulder. "Goodbye, Logan." Then he walked out, closing the door gently behind him.

"Goodbye."

Chapter Thirty-One

L OUISE STEPPED BACK and examined the wall in front of her. "I think we should do another coat of paint after it dries, just to be safe."

Logan set her roller down in the paint pan and wiped the sweat from her forehead. They'd been in the gallery all week, slowly but surely getting it back to its former glory and hopefully even better once they finished. Together they'd cleaned every inch of the place and, aside from updating the electrical system, the whole process had been almost painless.

In just one week since they'd started, they'd completely transformed the place.

Logan wiped her paint-speckled hands off on her old, faded jeans, adding to the collection of light blue smears on her thighs. "This color definitely opens the place up. And it's a perfect contrast to the exposed brick on the back wall. It was a good choice."

Louise nodded her agreement. "So, when are you going to start telling people that you and Jacob broke up?"

Logan sighed, turning to face her. "How did you know?" So far, the only people she'd told about their breakup two weeks ago were her mom, dad, and Carly, and she'd made them swear not to spread the word until she was ready.

"Well, for starters you haven't been wearing your ring. And then there's the way your eyes dart around the room whenever anyone mentions him. That's a long time not to tell anyone your engagement is over. So, spill."

She shrugged. "I don't want to ruin Carly's wedding."

"And?"

"And what?"

Louise put a hand on Logan's shoulder. "And maybe because of Cole?"

"I just…it doesn't seem right. After all we've been through, he deserves to hear it from me first, doesn't he? I don't want someone else to get the word to him before I can." Not that it would fix this new rift between them. Despite how kind and understanding he'd been when she chose Jacob, she didn't think he could ever forgive her for how she'd treated him. Could she even blame him?

"Sounds reasonable to me. So, what's your plan now? Still going to look for gallery jobs in San Francisco?"

"Probably not," Logan said. "San Francisco was Jacob's dream, and I always just planned to go wherever he went. I'm not sure where that leaves me now."

"Well, you've got a job here as long as you want it. And there's nothing wrong with sticking around town for a while. Especially if there's someone here worth sticking around for." She nudged Logan's side.

Logan shook her head. "Whatever Cole and I had, it's over. I told him as much before he took off."

In their small town, it hadn't taken long for news to spread that Cole was taking some time off work after the fire and staying out of town for a while.

Logan knew the real reason, of course.

"Do you really believe that? That it's over?"

He told her he just wanted to see her happy. *And if you really think he's the one who'll do that, I won't try to stand in the way.* And then, for the first time in their lives, he'd forfeited their bet. If that wasn't a sign he was done, she didn't know what was. "He knows it's over, too. And I think the fact that he skipped town is proof of that."

She expected Louise to understand, offer words of comfort and assurance. Instead, the gallery owner let out a long sigh.

"That's got to be the dumbest thing I've ever heard. I'm sorry. It's just, we all know you and that boy were made for each other. The sooner you admit that the sooner you two can go on with your happy lives together."

"Not you, too." Louise was starting to sound a lot like Carly.

"I can't help it. I went to Wade's just like everyone else. I heard all about the games, and I can't say it surprises me. I saw something between you two a long time ago, and I've been rooting for him ever since."

Logan's eyes rolled. "How? You barely even know him."

"Do you remember that day he followed you in here? It was only a few months after you'd first wandered in here yourself."

Of course she remembered. Logan remembered everything when it came to Cole Tucker. He'd sauntered in, pretending to look at some art when really he'd just wanted to annoy her in what had started to feel like a safe haven. Even as a sixth grader, he'd won Louise over quickly with his smile and charm.

Louise smiled. "That was when I knew."

"Knew what?"

"That he was crazy about you. Maybe not the kind of love he feels now—who truly understands love that young? But I could see just how much he cared about you."

"How? All he did was look around at the paintings and call me weird."

"That's what you saw," she chuckled. "I saw a kid who genuinely wanted to know more about you and what you like. I saw how mesmerized he was when you started talking about that sunflower painting, the way his face lit up whenever yours did. That boy's heart was a goner long before he ever stepped foot in here."

Logan stared down at her paint-smeared shoes. "You saw what you wanted to see. There is no way he already had feelings back then."

Louise crossed her arms over her chest. "You know, he came back to see me again the next day."

"He did?"

She nodded. "The next afternoon, he came in, said he was thinking about getting one of the pieces for his mom since Mother's Day was coming up. I told him to look around awhile and see what caught his eye, but he shook his head. He knew exactly which one he wanted."

"The sunflower painting," Logan muttered quietly. How had she not guessed it? She'd seen her favorite painting on the wall of his mother's house, and she'd never made the connection to the time she told Cole it was her favorite.

"I teased him a little, asked how he knew his mom would like it since he admitted he wasn't the artsy type." Louise smiled at the memory. "And you know what he told me?"

Logan shook her head.

"He told me that if you liked it, it was perfect. So I rung it up, and he paid me with cash right there. He didn't care how much it cost. I think he was just happy to have something you cared so much about."

"Why didn't you say anything?"

"He asked me not to. I think even back then he was afraid you'd find out how he felt."

She rolled her eyes. "Unbelievable. So just like everyone else in this town, you knew how he felt but never told me."

Louise's head tilted to the side, a sharp edge in her tone. "Is that what they taught you at that school of yours in Texas? To blame everyone else for your problems? 'Cause the Logan I know would never play the victim like this."

Logan's face grew warm. She'd valued Ms. Snyder's opinion since middle school, and to hear the disappointment in her voice now was like taking a scolding from her own mother. Maybe even worse.

"You're right. I'm sorry," she told Louise. "I've been putting this on other people, but really it's my own fault. My fault for not seeing what was right in front of me the whole time. My fault for running out instead of just talking to Cole that morning before I left. If I hadn't done all that, maybe…"

"Things would be different," Louise finished for her. "Is that what you want? For things to be different?"

"Yeah, I guess."

"Then make it different. You can't change what happened, but that doesn't mean you can't fix the mess you're in now."

"It's not that easy. Cole and I already missed our chance."

"I don't believe that. Nothing in this life happens that isn't supposed to. If you two are truly meant to be, then you haven't missed anything."

Louise grabbed her right hand and squeezed it. Logan's eyes fell to the black letters on her wrist. Not once had she looked at them without thinking of the man they belonged to, but it wasn't until now that she realized how perfectly they represented the impact he'd had on her all these years. Bold, permanent, a reminder that he would always be there, that he would always be a part of her.

If she meant even half as much to him, maybe there was still hope for them.

"You and Cole haven't missed your chance," Louise went on. "If anything, your chance is still coming."

Chapter Thirty-Two

LOGAN WAS EXHAUSTED. She didn't think she'd sat down once since the start of the ceremony, spending almost the entire reception running around grabbing this and that for Carly or whoever. She'd spent a good hour cleaning up the bridal suite of the church and another half hour with the groom's brother and best man, decorating the car the newlyweds had just driven off in.

Not that she minded. She slowly made her way back to the church's reception hall behind the other select guests who'd come out to see Carly and Darren off. She wiped at her eyes, removing the tears of joy and sadness she hadn't been able to fight.

Logan stopped at the door to the reception hall and took a deep, sobering breath. Inside, a blast of music and cheering hit her at full force. The crowd had dwindled down some now that the happy couple was gone. Many stood around chatting and laughing, and a small mixture of kids, teens, and likely very drunk adults were cheering each other on while jerking and grinding away on the dance floor to the end of an old Nelly song she remembered from middle school.

Logan caught a glimpse of her parents in one corner of the room, and her painful four-inch heels clicked against the hardwood floor as she made her way to them.

"There you are, wild girl. I feel like I've hardly seen you all day." Her mom raised a hand to Logan's dark hair, trying to smooth a spot in her tight, complicated updo. The chief went back to his beer.

"I wanted to find you and tell you that your daddy and I are going to leave. He wants to go back to the house to get out of his monkey suit, and then the two of us are going to drive over to Dublin to catch a movie and maybe get some drinks somewhere."

Logan checked her watch. "Seriously? It's almost nine o'clock at night."

"Don't sound so surprised," Daddy said, snaking his casted arm around her momma's waist. "Your mother and I have been known to have a good time out every now and then. We aren't geriatric just yet. And besides, where do you think that wild side of yours comes from anyway?" He nuzzled her ear playfully.

"Ew, get out of here before you two make me sick," Logan half teased.

"Love you, wild girl," her momma said, pulling her into a hug. "We'll see you later tonight." She turned, and the chief practically chased his wife out of the hall and to the car.

Logan hadn't stood there more than two seconds before

Leon, Darren's cousin and one of the groomsmen, sauntered over to her with two beers in hand and a sleazy grin on his face. "There you are, pretty lady. I've been looking all over for you." He offered her one of the bottles.

"No thanks, I still have to drive home after this."

"Not necessarily. You could be coming home with me."

She cringed as his gaze roamed over her strapless, burgundy bridesmaid's dress. "Still, it's probably best I don't."

"So where have you been?" he asked, leaning closer.

Logan's eyes wandered around the room, hoping to find someone she could use as an excuse to get away. "Oh, you know, helping with a few odds and ends."

"Well, I hope you're done because I've been waiting to dance with you all day."

Dammit. The DJ was slowly winding the party down, which meant music was on the slower side right now. The last thing she wanted to do was stand pressed against him while his hands tried to roam to intimate and inappropriate places. And she suspected from the alcohol on his breath that he wouldn't be so easy to shut down.

"I would, but..." She struggled, trying to come up with something, some excuse to let him down gently.

"There you are." Logan jumped when a muscular arm came from behind to rest around her waist. She turned, and her heart thumped up in her throat as she was greeted by the familiar sight and smell of Cole Tucker. His smile was carefree and easy, nothing like the last time she'd seen him on her front porch. It was accompanied by a clean-shaven face and neatly combed dark hair.

He wore a dark suit and tie over a light blue shirt, something she had never in her life seen him wear. And the way he looked in it tonight, it was a damn shame it had taken this long.

Cole pulled her into his side. "Nice to see you again, Leon."

Leon nodded with a tight smile. "Tucker."

"I don't mean to interrupt, but didn't you promise me a dance?" Cole asked her.

She was so overwhelmed by his closeness and the wave of heat radiating from where his hand gripped her hip that it took her a minute to understand what he was saying.

"Sure did. I was just about to tell Leon here that, while I would love to dance with him, I've already committed myself." She turned to Darren's cousin, trying to look apologetic. "Sorry."

"No worries. I'll just have to get the next one."

She blanched at the threat as Cole led her out to the dance floor and took her hand in his. He kept his eyes on Leon while he pulled her close and placed his hand on the curve of her lower back.

She'd had no idea how much she'd missed being this close to him. Her skin tingled all over. Still, she could feel the tightness in his arms and shoulder where she'd placed her hand, and it was clear now that his easy smile had been forced.

Neither of them spoke or looked at each other, and the tingle quickly turned to an uncomfortable itch to say something to ease the tension.

"Thanks, by the way."

Cole tore himself from whatever thought was occupying his mind and met her eyes. "For what?"

"For saving me back there," she said, nodding her head at the redhead watching them on the edge of the dance floor. "You're getting really good at this whole rescue thing. I guess that comes with being the town hero."

"You know, they're talking about giving me an award for running into that bar. How crazy is that?" His eyes lit up. Thank God she could still put a real smile on that face.

"I don't think it's crazy at all. You saved the chief of police's life. Daddy's even asking if he can be the one to give it to you."

"I didn't do anything any of the other guys wouldn't have done."

"That's not the point. What matters is that you were there, and you risked your life for his. And you'll never know how grateful my family and I are for that. Thank you."

Cole's smile fell a bit. "You know I'd do it again in a heartbeat. I couldn't live with myself if I ever let anything hurt you like that."

Logan looked away and tried to focus on something else before the tears could surface. They danced quietly again for a minute, and Logan only spoke once she'd regained her composure.

"When did you get back?"

"This morning."

"I didn't know if you'd make it in time for the wedding." She stared at his perfectly knotted blue tie, unable to bring herself to look up at him. "You left so suddenly, and none of us knew when you were coming home."

"I had a lot of thinking to do," he said soberly. "Honestly, I thought I'd be gone a lot longer. But I couldn't let myself miss Carly and Darren's big day. Plus, I sort of promised Tater I'd be her date, and I was never going to hear the end of it if I didn't make it. Especially after leaving town and missing her first prom."

"That's right. How did it go?"

"She and her friends had a blast. My mom made sure to show me lots of pictures. You and Carly did real good picking out that dress."

"Yeah? She looked good?"

"She looked gorgeous," he said with a shake of his head. "And way too mature to be my innocent baby sister."

"So, where is she? I haven't seen her here anywhere."

"She left just as Carly and Darren were heading out. She's got some plans with her friends. Figures, she makes me come and then ditches me. And then Cowboy and Harper left me."

"Cowboy and who?"

"You know Harper. Quiet blonde, glasses, valedictorian of our class."

"Wait, seriously? Cowboy is on a date with Harper Maddox?" She could not have come up with two people more completely opposite if she tried. "When did this happen?"

"He ran into her the day after the fire at Wade's, and apparently they've been hanging out. But he swears tonight wasn't a date and that they're just friends. Anyway, they left maybe ten minutes ago. Something about a dare, maybe? I don't know."

He shrugged. "I was about to head out, too, but then I saw you floundering over there." He looked her up and down, a grin spreading across his face. "And seeing you in this dress, I'm very glad I didn't."

"Shut up," she muttered.

He laughed. "No really, you look incredible. Our friends should get married more often if this is how you dress."

Logan ignored his comment, but she was incapable of ignoring the way his words made her heart race. She felt herself relax into Cole as they continued to step with the music.

"Carly did a great job with this thing. I think the whole town will be talking about it for a while. And don't even get me started on the cake Byrdie made. I'm half tempted to steal what's left and take it home with me."

"I've been so busy I never even got to try it," she mused.

"You really missed out then. But I guess you'll have your

own cake soon enough."

She blinked. "Huh?"

"Have you and Jacob set a date yet?"

In all the chaos of fixing up the gallery and last-minute wedding preparations, Logan had completely forgotten that, as far as Cole and the rest of the town knew, she was still engaged.

"Oh, um…actually, the wedding's not happening. Jacob and I aren't together anymore."

Cole stopped midstep. "What? When?"

Logan's face grew warm under the sudden intensity of his gaze. "The morning after the fire."

"I had no idea. Cowboy and Tater didn't say anything."

"Up until now the only people who knew were my parents and Carly. I didn't think it was fair for everyone to find out before you got back into town. I wanted you to hear it from me."

He nodded silently while he seemed to process it all. Logan didn't know when they'd started dancing again, but sure enough, they were swaying to the music.

"Can I…do you mind if I ask who ended it?"

"It was a mutual decision. I realized you were right. I wasn't going to be happy pretending to be someone I wasn't. And, honestly, I didn't want to pretend anymore. It's exhausting, and neither of us would have lasted long in that relationship if I wasn't honest. I told Jacob it wasn't fair to him." Just like it wasn't fair to marry him when she had feelings for someone else.

"Sounds more like your decision than a mutual one."

"Yeah, well, he didn't try very hard to stop me, so I figure he knew I was right and that there was no point in fighting it."

"Then he's an even bigger dumbass than I thought. What's next for you then? Some fancy gallery job in New York? LA?"

"Actually, I was thinking about staying around town for a while. I told Louise I'd help her with the gallery, and I plan on sticking to that promise. Besides, my parents are here, and Carly. I'm not quite ready to leave yet."

"Well, that's good to hear. Willow Creek just isn't the same without the infamous Logan Kase."

The song they'd been dancing to ended, soon replaced by an even slower one. Logan watched as the few couples still on the dance floor leaned into each other intimately.

Cole stopped. "Well, I believe I told Leon it was one dance. I should probably let you get back to whatever you were doing."

He started to pull his hands away, but Logan held on. "Cole, wait. Can we just...?" It was too much to ask of him, but she didn't want it to end yet. After weeks without seeing or talking to him, one song just wasn't enough.

"Just one more song, please?"

Cole looked uncertain at first. But something in her face seemed to decide it for him. Instead of turning away, he slowly pulled her closer, until any space between them disappeared. Cole's hand was low on her back again.

She felt his cheek brush hers as his deep voice whispered in her ear, "This okay?"

Threads of electric energy spread through her body. "Mm-hmm." Eyes closed, she rested her head on his shoulder and allowed herself to forget everything that had happened between them in the last couple weeks. They moved together with the soft music.

Logan took a deep breath, filling her lungs with the familiar scent of Cole. She didn't think she'd ever smelled anything so warm and comforting in all her life.

She took another deep breath and sighed, the pressure in her chest easing. No matter how long they held each other dancing, it just wouldn't be enough. His hold on her tightened, and Logan tried not to think about how much less vibrant her world would be if, at the end of this song, he walked away for good.

Instead, she started thinking about all the wonderful and beautiful things that were waiting for Cole. The Sunday lunches with family at his parents' house. Acres of land with the big house and horses and the white picket fence he always wanted. Even the nights out at the bar with Cowboy and the guys from the station.

And then it happened.

She had no idea when, but at some point in her mental wandering, Logan became part of the vision.

Sitting with Cole and Tater in one of the front pews at church. Laughing and joking with the Tucker family while they exchanged stories from Cole's childhood. Clinging to Cole and grinning wildly as he took her for a middle-of-the-night horseback ride.

It was all there, and as she watched each scene play out before her as if through her own eyes she felt happier than she could ever remember.

Walking hand-in-hand with a beaming Cole Tucker. Dancing in an elegant, slim, white dress with Cole just like this, while all of Willow Creek stood back and watched. Standing in front of the house he'd just bought her, crying happy tears as Cole lovingly stroked the small bump of her growing belly and kissed her over and over.

For the first time in her life, she saw her future. The details shifted and changed each time she pictured it, but the one constant in each of them was him.

Logan's eyes snapped open, and she tore her head from his shoulder. His eyebrows drew together, but they softened as moisture crept into her eyes.

"You okay?"

She wanted to tell him so badly, needed to tell him that her future, the one she'd never been able to see with Jacob in all the time they were together, was now looking directly at her. Logan opened her mouth to let the words spill out, but one sobering thought stopped her.

What if it didn't last? What if she finally got everything

she didn't know she wanted until now, the kind of happiness she didn't even know existed, and she lost it all? She couldn't bear even the thought of it.

"I have to go." Her voice broke on the words, and her hand flew to wipe away the single tear that had slipped out. She gently placed the other on his smooth jaw, memorizing the feel of him one last time.

Logan brought her lips to his cheek. "Thanks again for saving my dad."

"Lo?"

"Goodnight, Cole." Before she could stop herself, she pulled out of Cole's arms and nearly ran to the door.

Chapter Thirty-Three

LOGAN STOOD AT the kitchen counter in a pair of sweatpants and the oversized camo shirt she'd worn playing paintball that was more comfortable than anything she owned—and still kind of smelled like him—scooping out mint chocolate chip ice cream when her parents finally came downstairs, ready to leave for the movies.

The chief's arm was around Momma's waist, and the two were beaming at each other, laughing while they debated which candy-popcorn collaboration was best.

They'd been together for almost twenty-five years now and they still looked just as happy and in love as they had in all the wedding pictures Logan used to look at when she was a kid.

"You guys look great." Logan felt a small pang in her chest.

Mom's smile turned into a soft frown. "You okay, wild girl?"

Logan stood taller. "I'm fine, Momma. You two have fun at your movie tonight."

Momma watched her for a moment, glancing to the frozen carton on the island counter. "Marshall, why don't you go warm up the truck. I'll be out in just a second."

"Sure thing, baby." He kissed her gently on the cheek before exiting.

Her mom reached for Logan's hand across the counter. "What's going on, honey?"

"Nothing, I just like seeing you and Daddy so happy together. I hope I get to find that someday."

"You will. I wouldn't doubt that for a second." Momma squeezed her hand once before letting go. "So, what are your big plans for tonight? Nothing too dangerous, I hope."

"Don't worry. Your wild girl is taking the night off." She laughed, indicating the bowl in front of her. "I won't be disgracing the family name tonight."

The room was quiet while Logan scooped out another spoonful.

"I'm so sorry, sweetheart."

Logan froze. Her momma's eyes were glistening. "What? Why should you be sorry?"

"For trying to make you someone you're not. You've always been so brave, so independent, and so alive. You learned to run practically before you could walk. You jumped without knowing where you'd land.

"I thought that if you could just grow out of that reckless phase and finally settle down...but it wasn't a phase. It's who you are, and I've been lying to myself all these years. I'm so, so sorry."

Logan wrapped her arms around her. "It's okay, Momma."

"No, it's not. If I hadn't been pushing you so hard then you wouldn't have felt like you needed to be with Jacob in order to be someone else. And now you've been walking around like a zombie the last couple weeks—"

"It's not about Jacob."

"It's not?" Logan shook her head. "Then what's wrong?"

Logan took a deep breath and swallowed, readying herself for that look of disapproval in her mom's eyes. "The night before Jacob and I called off the wedding, Cole told me he had feelings for me."

"Why didn't you tell me?" her momma cried.

"Well, you've made it abundantly clear that you hate Cole Tucker."

"It's true, he's never been one of my favorite people. You're reckless when you're around him. But after what he did for your daddy...I think you'd be hard-pressed to find a better man in this town. Even if he is wilder than you are."

Seriously? Years of hating Cole, and suddenly Logan would be lucky to get a guy like him? "So you're not disappointed?"

"Of course not. You're old enough to know what you want, and I just want you to be happy. But, Lo, what I think shouldn't matter if you really care about him. Go tell him how you feel."

She stared down at her fingers. "It's not that simple."

"Why not?"

"I've said no to him so many times. And every time things got real between us I ran away. What if I go to him and he's the one who says no now?"

"I love you, baby, but sometimes you can be really slow." Momma grabbed her phone from its dock, her voice rising. "Now it's time for some tough love. You can sit here eating your half-melted ice cream, feeling sorry for yourself, and give him time to get over you for real"—she took Logan's hand and placed the phone in it—"or you can give him a call right now, giving yourself the chance to be the happiest you've ever been. It's entirely up to you."

➤➤➤◄◄◄

LOGAN WATCHED FROM the window as her parents pulled out of the driveway, the phone still gripped tightly in her hand.

Her mom was right. What good had running from Cole Tucker done her so far? She needed to face this head-on or else she'd end up losing the one man who'd loved her exactly as she was. The one person who'd made her proud to be that girl.

Before she could change her mind, Logan pulled up the too-long sleeves of her shirt and started dialing the number she knew by heart. She held it up to her ear, her heart racing.

Ring.

She couldn't tell him all she needed to say over the phone. Maybe she'd ask to meet him at his place.

Ring.

Then again, Cowboy might be there with Harper right now, so that probably wasn't the best idea.

Ring.

She could invite Cole to her place. But it seemed wrong to ask him to come all the way out here, especially after the way she'd treated him.

Ring.

Maybe somewhere neutral would be best. But where?

Ring.

She'd figure it out as soon as he picked up the phone.

Ring.

If he ever picked up the damn phone.

This is Cole Tucker. Leave a message.

Logan hung up. Was Cole so busy that he missed her call, or was he avoiding her on purpose? The way she'd stormed out of the wedding reception without an explanation, she wouldn't blame him.

She hit redial, waiting out the rings anxiously until she was sent to voice mail again. Instead of hanging up, she took a breath.

"Hey, it's Lo. I, uh...sorry for running out like I did. It was kinda spazzy of me." Oh God, what was she saying? "Listen, I need to talk to you about something important. Um, the sooner the better. So just call me back whenever you get this…unless you're just ignoring my calls. But please don't. So, yeah. Bye."

She'd done what she could. Now all that was left was to wait until he called her back. The ice cream in her bowl now resembled more of a green soup than anything. Didn't matter. Her craving was gone. She placed the bowl in the sink and put the carton back in the freezer.

She was walking to the living room when someone knocked at the door. Cole! It didn't seem likely since she'd only just left him a message, but who else would be knocking on her door this late at night? She felt her stomach start to go all fluttery as she raced for the door.

She wrenched it open, and sure enough, Cole stood there in the same suit and light blue shirt he'd been wearing earlier, only now the jacket and tie were gone and his sleeves were rolled up a few inches. Impossibly, he looked even better than before.

"That was fast."

"What was fast?"

"I left you a voice mail not even five minutes ago."

"You did?" He reached into his pocket with his right hand, his left holding something covered in aluminum foil. "Oh yeah. I forgot it was still on silent."

He hadn't been avoiding her call after all. That alone was enough to make what she had to say easier. "Do you want to come in and sit down?"

"Yeah." Yet despite two brown leather sofas and her

dad's favorite recliner, they both remained standing.

"Here," Cole said, setting the foil-wrapped thing in his hand down on the coffee table beside them. "I grabbed a piece of cake for you since you said you didn't get one."

"Oh, thanks. That's really sweet, but you didn't have to come all this way just for that." Logan started fidgeting with the hem of her shirt—*his* shirt—that fell to her midthigh. If she'd known he was coming over, she would have put on something much less frumpy.

"Actually, I didn't." Cole slowly walked around the room, scanning various pictures of Logan and her parents. As long as they'd known each other, and as many times as he'd come by the house, she didn't think he'd ever actually been anywhere other than the porch or her bedroom. "I also wanted to ask you a question. Something I didn't get to ask before."

"Oh, okay."

He stopped by the fireplace and turned to her. "You said you broke it off with Jacob because it wasn't fair to him. Was that the only reason?"

This was it. The chance to tell him everything that was staring her right in the face. All she had to do was be honest with him and hope for the best.

"No."

Cole's tense shoulders fell.

"I also broke it off because, no matter how hard I tried, I couldn't picture my future with him. But then tonight…"

"Tonight what?"

Her voice shook. "While we were dancing, I saw it all. The life I'd never been able to picture when I was with Jacob. I saw a wedding and a house and kids. But it wasn't Jacob standing there with me through all of it. It was you."

Her lips twitched, her stomach fluttering at the possibility of the life and future those images represented. Of love and joy and laughter and excitement.

The corners of Cole's mouth started to curve upward, but the smile fell short. "Then why did you run away tonight?"

"The same reason I ran away four years ago. The same reason I told you I was still going to marry Jacob even after everything. I was scared. Just like I was scared when I woke up that morning after the bonfire. Because I realized that you, being with you, makes me happier than anything else ever has."

Cole took several steps toward her. "Why the hell would that scare you?"

"Maybe because you told me that it didn't mean anything." The words came out harsher than she'd intended.

"That's because you called it a mistake. I was sure that what we did that night was the worst possible thing you could imagine." He sounded defensive, his voice rising.

"Well, if you had been honest with me, we could have talked it out!"

"Maybe we would have if you hadn't run away! And

sure, I lied about how I felt. But that excuse only works for the first time. What about all the other times? What were you so scared of then?"

"Of you. Of getting hurt. What if we do this, put ourselves all in, and one of us backs out? How do we know if this is really going to work?"

"We can't know that. No one knows for sure if it's going to last."

"And that doesn't terrify you?"

"Honestly, no. Not near as much as a life without you in it. Nothing I've ever faced scares me as much as that. I can't make you promises that everything will be easy and perfect. But I will tell you that I've wanted this since the sixth grade. And I can promise that I'm going to hold on to you with everything I've got because I love you! And there is nothing you could ever say that's going to change that."

Her breath caught, heart hammering in her chest as her lips curled. *I love you.* Those three words fluttered under her skin. "I love you, too."

Every muscle in his face and shoulders relaxed, his anger washed away like pollen after a heavy storm. His breath hitched. "What did you say?" he asked, his dark eyes unnaturally bright.

"I said, I love y—" Cole closed the distance between them, gripping her arms and pulling her closer until his lips found hers. They were firm and unyielding before the kiss gave way to several quick ones. She returned them with her own passionate fervor, rejoicing in the feel of his lips but still needing more.

He pushed forward, guiding her backward blindly until her back hit the wall. Her legs felt shaky beneath her, and she wasn't sure if she was currently managing to hold herself up or if he was doing it for her.

His hands cradled her jaw delicately, but then took on a life of their own, tangling into her hair and sending deliciously intoxicating electric currents from the top of her head to the soles of her feet and back up again. She welcomed his tongue caressing hers desperately, and her body began to fill with a growing need she hadn't felt this strongly in an excruciatingly long time.

Her hands moved slowly over his shoulders and back, taking the time to feel every muscle beneath his blue dress shirt. Once they reached the curve of his lower back, they traced their way around to his abdomen and gradually snaked up over the buttons of his shirt. They slipped between two of the middle buttons and gripped the sides before she yanked the dress shirt open and exposed the white cotton T-shirt underneath.

She squealed as some of the buttons went flying. Then they were both laughing.

"I've always wanted to do that," she whispered between gasping breaths.

She worked to untuck the dress shirt, then Cole helped by removing the whole thing and tossing it to the floor.

When he'd finished, she took his face in her hands and pulled his lips back down to her starving ones.

His hands worked their way under her T-shirt. Logan pulled her mouth from his. "I wasn't supposed to be wearing this when we talked, you know. Not that I knew this was going to happen, but still. I was not supposed to look this tragic."

"You look incredible."

She laughed. "Smart answer."

"I'm serious. You have no idea how amazing you look in my shirt. It took everything I had not to kiss you during that paintball game."

"Good thing you got a second chance."

"Where are your parents?" His hands were under her long shirt, teasing the sensitive skin on her belly and hips. God, she didn't think anyone's touch had ever felt so good.

"Out. Won't be back for hours."

He leaned into her harder, his body putting just the right amount of pressure in all the good places, simultaneously pulling a low, primal moan from somewhere deep inside her. "Not nearly long enough for what all I want to do to you right now."

"We should get started then," she said. She could feel his lips curve against hers. "I'll show you the way to my room."

"I think I can find it." Without another word, he lifted her into his arms.

Chapter Thirty-Four

"HOLY SHIT." COLE fell onto the bed beside her, his chest rising and falling in rhythm with hers. "I don't mean to be crass, but that was even better than I remembered."

"Definitely." Logan couldn't remember a time that came close. But then again, she was having trouble remembering anything before the last half hour.

"No, seriously. You have a gift or something, 'cause that was...wow."

She attempted to move the hair sticking to her damp neck and chest. "Thank you," she said proudly, glancing across the bed at him. She loved the euphoric grin on his face and the fact that she was responsible for it even more. "For the compliment, and especially for...you know."

Cole leaned over her, one eyebrow raised. "Which time?"

"Don't even," she said through her laughter. To make it worse, he started tickling her side under the green sheets.

"No, really. I think I lost count somewhere in there."

"Shut up!" Logan shoved his chest to push him off her, and he fell back while managing to pull her with him. He kissed her lips once, then twice, before he let her settle on top of his chest.

Logan relished the feel of his body beneath hers, solid and alive, and all hers, at least for this moment. She found the elegant black scrawl of initials on his rib cage and traced them with a tender touch while her other hand rested over his calming heart. She kissed the black letters once.

"I need to tell you something," she said, placing another kiss on the smooth, tan skin of his chest.

With a gentle smile, he ran his fingers through her hair and then settled his palm on her cheek, where she leaned into it. "Okay."

"I love you, Cole Tucker. I think I have for a long time."

His face lit up with an incandescent grin, and her heart was going to burst. "God, I love it when you say that." He pulled her face to his one more time, placing a soft, lingering kiss on her lips.

"So, what now?" he asked once he let her go.

She took his hand in hers, interlocking their fingers. "Well, I believe you and I still have a bet to settle."

"Seriously? I thought I told you the bet was off. I forfeited, remember?"

"Oh, I remember. But after over ten years, I've decided I have the right not to accept it. Which means we're in desperate need of a tiebreaker."

Cole laughed. "Fine. Any suggestions?"

"Just one," she said. "I say we try this thing. You and me.

We go out on dates, do the boyfriend and girlfriend thing. Get in fights, have great makeup sex, the whole relationship package."

"I like where this is going," he said, kissing her again.

"The first one to call it quits, to give up and pull out because things get a little difficult, loses." Logan had to admit, this was easily her best idea yet.

"I'm game if you are."

"Great, then let's talk about stakes. Jacob already figured out about the tattoo—and he wasn't thrilled, I should add."

"We can come up with something. I just want you to be sure this is what you want. If we're going to do this, you have to really be in it with me. There will be days when I make you want to rip your hair out and you make me want to stuff that beautiful mouth of yours with a towel just to shut you up. It'll probably be the hardest challenge we've ever faced."

Logan squeezed his hand in hers, the paralyzing fear nowhere to be found. "Well," she said smiling, "it's a good thing I love a challenge."

Epilogue

Two Years Later

LOGAN WAS IN the back room of the gallery sorting through receipts when the bells on the front door rang through the room. She checked the clock on the wall; it was only ten minutes until closing.

"Logan, could you come help me for a minute?" Louise called from the main room. "There's a customer here in need of your keen eye."

Logan cursed under her breath. She was going to lose her place and have to start all over again. She set the receipts down on the counter and made her way slowly out to the open gallery.

Standing by the door in jeans and a T-shirt was a beaming Cole. But his attention wasn't on Logan—it was focused on the adorable one-year-old he was carrying. The toddler was grinning up a storm beneath his reddish-blond hair, mesmerized as Cole made silly faces for him.

"If it isn't two of my favorite boys." Logan raced across the room to kiss the bundle of childish giggles on the cheek, immediately followed by kissing Cole's lips. "What are you guys doing here? I thought I was meeting you at the house."

"Well, Carter was getting a little cranky at home, so we decided to get out for some fresh air."

The toddler reached out for Logan. She scooped him up in her arms, more than willing to snuggle this sweet, dimpled boy she loved so much. "You just wanted some time with me, didn't you?" She planted quick, sneak-attack kisses all over his cheeks and neck, at which Carter giggled profusely.

She laughed, too, hitching him on her hip and tickling him while she adjusted his bunched-up shirt. She stopped.

"What is this?" she asked, pointing to the one-year-old's green "She Thinks My Tractor's Sexy" shirt.

Cole shrugged. "What's what?"

"Carly's going to kill you. You know how she feels about you putting her son in suggestive shirts like this."

"Well, at least it's not the matching 'Save a Horse, Ride a Cowboy' shirts Cowboy bought them last weekend," he said defensively. "And besides, if Carly's got a problem with how I dress him, she can stop asking me to babysit every day I have off."

"You volunteer." Logan was still amazed at how quickly he'd taken to Carly and Darren's first, and so far only, child. He absolutely lived for the days he got to keep baby Carter while they were at work. It was the same love he felt for each of his brothers' kids.

Logan shook her head. "Just know that, when we have kids, you will not be the one dressing them."

Cole watched her as she bounced the baby on her hip, then surprised her by pulling her into a deep kiss. "What was that for?" she asked breathlessly when he let her go.

"For reminding me what a lucky man I am. I love you, Mrs. Tucker."

"I love you, too." She leaned forward, placing a shorter but just as sweet kiss on his lips. It was still strange to hear him call her his wife or refer to her as Mrs. Tucker, but it was the good kind of strange that made her skin tingle. They had officially tied the knot almost a month ago and had only just gotten back from their honeymoon in Aruba earlier in the week.

"Somebody missed Aunt Lo and Uncle Cole, didn't he?" she said to the toddler on her hip.

The bell jingled as the front door flew open.

The next thing Logan knew, Carter was being pulled out of her arms. "Cowboy! What are you doing? I was giving him some much-needed Aunt Lo love."

"You can do that later," he said in a rush. He was already pulling the diaper bag from Cole's shoulder. "I'm a man on a mission."

"A mission that involves kidnapping a one-year-old against his will?" Cole laughed.

"Carter here is my bro, my wingman. And wingmen have each other's backs no matter what."

Logan cringed. "So, who's the unlucky victim of your charms today?"

"Lisa VanCamp, over at the ice cream shop," he said proudly. "She loves when I bring Carter in with me. Not to mention she gives us a free scoop whenever we want."

"Do you have any shame?" she asked. Lisa had only just barely graduated high school last year, and what she lacked in smarts she more than made up for with tight clothes and unabashed flirting.

Cowboy thought for a minute. "Nope. Not when it comes to women and certainly not when it comes to free ice cream. Don't worry. I'll bring him over to Carly when we're done. Wish me luck!"

"Good luck," Cole called out to Cowboy's back as he raced out the door and down the sidewalk, tickling and talking to Carter as he went. Despite the way he used him, Cowboy's attachment to the child was just as strong as Cole's. If nothing else, Carter Whitehead was easily one of the most loved babies in all of Willow Creek.

"Hey, what are you doing right now?" Cole asked quietly, pulling Logan into him.

"Finishing up the books, closing down the shop. Why?"

"I've got something I want to show you. A surprise."

"Ooh, I love surprises," she said, feeding off his excitement. "Give me just a few minutes, and then I'm all yours."

"I've got it under control," Louise called from the back room. Logan didn't know when she'd gone back there, but she'd clearly heard every word. "You two kids get out of here."

"Are you sure?"

Louise came out of the back room, papers and receipts in hand. "Of course I'm sure. Now go before I have to kick you out myself."

Logan absolutely adored this woman. "Thanks, Louise. I'll see you in the morning."

"You're the best!" Cole shouted while Logan grabbed her bag from behind the register.

"Have fun, you two," she called just as Cole was pulling Logan out the door.

He led her to the Bronco a short distance down the sidewalk, then instructed her to get in without so much as a hint as to where they were going.

Logan might have tried to ask where he was taking her, but she'd learned long ago that, when it came to surprises, Cole's lips were tighter than Lisa VanCamp's skinny jeans. They drove for several minutes in complete silence. But after a few miles and familiar turns, Logan started to get an idea of where they were going. They were off the beaten path and a good mile from the nearest house when Cole finally pulled off on the side of the gravel road.

"You know where we are?" he asked after he turned the Bronco off.

"Of course I do." Did he even feel the need to ask? "This is where we used to meet for the bonfires. But why are we here?"

"Come on." Cole opened the driver's-side door and

stepped out. He rounded the truck, took her hand, and leaned back against the warm metal, pulling her against his chest and wrapping his arms around her.

He sighed. "You have no idea how happy you make me."

"And yet it's nothing to how I feel when I'm with you." Logan kissed him, placing her hand on his rib cage.

"Ow," Cole hissed through his teeth, pulling back.

Logan instinctively lifted her hand. "Sorry, I keep forgetting."

"It's not that bad really. Just surprised me more than anything. See…" Cole lifted his T-shirt, exposing the slightly red skin over his rib. "It's already starting to heal."

Logan examined the three black letters first, exactly as she'd memorized them. Then she paid extra special attention to the fourth one. Cole had insisted on adding the *T* on the end the second they'd gotten back from their honeymoon. That one was already her favorite.

She kissed the skin next to the healing tattoo ever so gently before allowing Cole to pull his shirt back down.

"So," she said, turning around in his arms to face the field in front of them, "why are we here?"

"I haven't told you this yet, but a little over a month ago, I got a visit from Old Man Carithers."

"Really? What about?"

"He asked how you were and what my plans were. Then he mentioned how old he was getting, that he couldn't really keep up with all his property like he used to. Said he's looking to sell some of it, maybe look into retiring."

"Wow." Logan never thought she'd see the day Carithers was ready to sell his land and retire. When you put all his properties together, the man owned at least half of Willow Creek. "So why was he telling you?"

"He said that, despite all the trouble I'd been in over the years, he knew I was a good kid and a hard worker. Said he liked me, and he wanted to see me do right by my family. Then he told me to take my pick of any of his properties, and he'd sell it to me for a good price. A wedding present from him to us."

Logan turned to face Cole head-on. "You're kidding." He shook his head. "What did you say?"

"I told him it was a generous offer, but I'd need some time to look into land quality and pricing and talk to the bank. Not to mention discussing it with my wife. And Carithers told me to take my time.

"Well, you can probably guess why this was the first place I thought of. I had Keith come out and check on the lot size, the quality, and Carithers's suggested price. I talked to the bank, and they cleared us for the loan in case we want to move forward. So now all that's left is you."

"Me?"

He nodded. "You say the word and I'll do it. I'll tell Carithers we have a deal and start getting all the paperwork squared away. Or, if you decide you don't want it, we'll start looking at some of the other lots he's offering. It's completely up to you."

Cole placed his hands on her shoulders, turning her back around to look out over the several acres of land that stretched before them. It was hard to believe that this was where it all started. If it hadn't been for this field, for the events of the farewell bonfire, nothing in Logan's life would have been the same. She owed every ounce of happiness she had to this field.

"So, what do you think?"

Logan pushed away the memory of a cool summer night and a roaring fire, of a life-changing bet and the smell of smoke on Cole's skin. Instead, she thought of the house with the picket fence and the barn next to acres of horse pastures, standing on the porch while little kids ran screaming with joy in the front yard.

"It's perfect."

"I WAS WONDERING when I'd see the two lovebirds again!"

Within seconds, Lilly was around the bar and headed their way. She threw her arms out to Logan first, wrapping her in a quick hug before she did the same to Cole. "You guys have been back for three days, and you only just now come to see me?"

"I'm sorry, Lilly. Things have been a little crazy since we got back."

"That's all right, doll. I'm just glad to see you two. Come on over and I'll get you two a drink, on the house." Lilly led them from the door to the rebuilt bar, announcing their presence to everyone within earshot.

Wade's was busy tonight. Country music blared over the speakers, and quite a few couples were dancing in the middle of the floor, while a group of guys started arguing over a game of pool that didn't seem to be going their way.

Lilly put two beer bottles on the bar for them.

Cole took a long sip of his. "Lilly, my love, you always know just how to please a man."

She leaned her elbows on the counter. "The two of us could always get out of here and really have a good time," she teased.

"Oh, Lill." He laughed, throwing his arm around Logan's waist. "If I weren't already a happily married man, I would definitely take you up on that."

"Well, if you change your mind, you know where to find me." Lilly winked playfully before moving on to another customer.

Logan and Cole proceeded to drink their beers, attempting to talk, but being interrupted as each and every one of the bar patrons took a second to greet them. Some were good with a simple *welcome home* or a wave. Others, like Big Lou, felt the need to hug them and tell them everything they'd missed.

"So now that you guys have tied the knot, are we ever

going to get a winner?" Lou asked. He pointed at the wall behind the bar. There, framed in dark, charred wood and hanging for all the world to see, was the original section of chalkboard they'd been using as the scoreboard in their bet, one of the few things that had been salvaged after the fire. In neon green chalk, patrons could still find Cole and Logan's names, each with the letters H-O-R-S underneath. No one in town knew what the last challenge of the bet was, only that they were still tied two years later.

Logan felt the warmth in her chest she got every time she saw the old scoreboard. "I wouldn't bet on it, Lou."

"As stubborn as this one is," Cole told the listening crowd around them before smiling at her, "I plan on being tied with this woman for a very, very long time."

The End

If you enjoyed this book, please leave a review at your favorite online retailer!
Even if it's just a sentence or two it makes all the difference.

Thanks for reading *Keeping Score* by Shannon Stults!

Discover your next romance at TulePublishing.com.

TULE
PUBLISHING

If you enjoyed *Keeping Score,* you'll love the next book in....

The Willow Creek series

Book 1: *Keeping Score*

Book 2: *Daring to Fall*
Coming September 2019!

Book 3: *Coming soon!*

Available now at your favorite online retailer!

If you enjoyed *Keeping Score*, you'll love these other Tule books!

Punk Rock Cowgirl
by Kasey Lane

Forever, Alabama
by Susan Sands

Her Sweetheart Brand
by Paula Altenburg

Available now at your favorite online retailer!

About the Author

A small-town Georgia girl, Shannon finds no greater joy than stepping into the lives and worlds created by the written word. Despite a severe aversion to reading as a child, Shannon has since found a passion for literature that she's nurtured with incessant reading and a Bachelor's degree in English. It's this passion that lets her bring her own imagination to life. Living in Athens, Ga with her sister and their four-legged furry friends, she is almost always in the middle of a book, working on her own stories, or traveling to seek inspiration in the world around her.

Thank you for reading

Keeping Score

If you enjoyed this book, you can find more from all our great authors at TulePublishing.com, or from your favorite online retailer.

TULE
PUBLISHING

Made in the USA
Columbia, SC
27 November 2019

83975739R00212